Mesaerion
The Best Science Fiction Stories
1800-1849

Andrew Barger

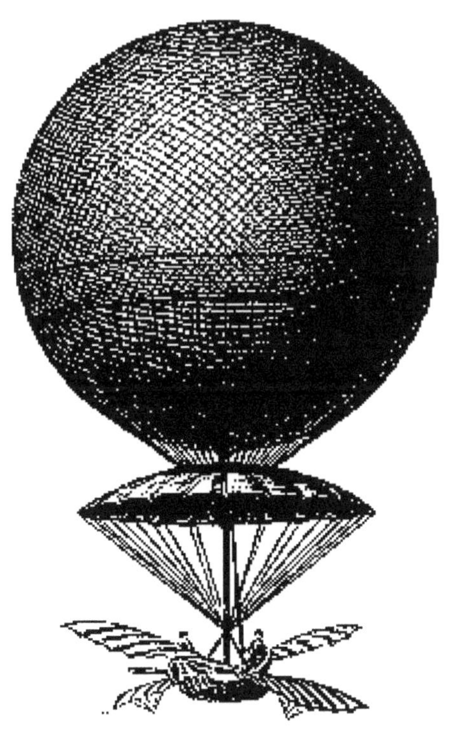

Blanchard's Balloon
1818

**Once again for Sage,
my little mad pianist and scientist.**

Our Own Country
(Knickerbocker, or, New York Monthly Magazine)
May 1835

So mechanical has the age become, that men seriously talk of flying machines, to go by steam, not your air-balloons, but real Daedalian wings, made of wood and joints, nailed to your shoulder,--not wings of feathers and wax like the wings of Icarus, who fell into the Cretan sea, but real, solid, substantial, rock-maple wings with wrought-iron hinges, and huge concavities, to propel us through the air.

Contents

We Are Modernists, Dern It!

Automata. Aeroplanes. Galvanism. Phrenology. Magnetism. Electricity. Aeronauts. Mesmerism. Androids. Perpetual Motion. Velocipedes. Diving bells. Parachutes. Automatrons.

These were bandied about terms among the denizens of the first half of the 19th century. They coined them; many of which we still use today. By air, land, sea, space, and even the mind, scientific means of exploration grew exponentially during this crucial period for science. It truly was the age of technological enlightenment, though we Modernists tend to think otherwise.

Our modern world is jam packed with electronic gizmos of every sort. They have become part of us. We move around with them as if external vital organs, rarely noticing those around us. They enable us to have the world's information in our pockets and, ironically, a means to electronically communicate with those very same people we fail to notice in public. Our children best respond to text not talk. Beyond it all we somehow feel closer to our relatives than ever before. We receive their status updates and doctored photos and feel *connected*.

We are Modernists, dern it! We live in a technological world far removed from those simpletons who came 200 years before us. Today's technology has adopted us, not the other way around. The ring of a cellphone or blip of a text message quickens our pulse and sometimes makes us perspire like the Pavlov dogs of science that we are. Today's technology has become biological and universal as we begin to use 3-D printers to make functioning body parts. We have our robotic drones shooting missiles from the sky.

Many who are considered poor in the industrialized world have smart phones. They have better technology in their pockets than that of the wealthiest person who lived in the twentieth century. What simpletons we all were two decades ago, let alone those of 200 years prior. The gentlepeople living in the first half of the 19th century knew very little of technology—we wrongly believe.

Great authors like Edgar Allan Poe and Nathaniel Hawthorne in America, and Mary Shelley in England, were true Modernists in a literary sense. They seized on the mechanical age of scientific enlightenment and exploited it to the fullest.

In doing so, they invented the science fiction story and readers have rejoiced ever since. The venerable German musicologist and author, Ernst Theodor Hoffmann, preceded them all in penning short horror, ghost and science fiction stories. His "Der Automate," published in 1814, is likely the first robot short story. His short horror tale, "The Deserted House," rose to such a level that it was included in *6a66le: The Best Horror Short Stories 1800-1849*. Unfortunately, the scope of Hoffmann's short sci-fi tales reached no further than automata, and even then were lacking in technical scope. This includes his 1816 story "The Sand-Man," which was included a year later in his German collection of stories: *The Night-pieces*. As a result, none of his stories are included here.

Nathaniel Hawthorne went further in the sci-fi genre by using biology ("Rappaccini's Daughter"), chemistry ("The Birthmark"), futuristic machines ("The Hall of Fantasy") and insect automata ("The Artist of the Beautiful") to create graceful science fiction stories that were character driven. Hawthorne was truly a pioneer in the sci-fi genre.

Then there's another American man of letters named Edgar Allan Poe, who gave us over 15 fictional short stories with scientific elements. Just as with the horror and detective short story genres, Poe dominated the science fiction genre for the period under review. He quickly realized that adding *science* to fiction would make it believable. This "verisimilitude" to real life events, walking on the sturdy legs of scientific description, opened the door to some of his best literary hoaxes: "[The Balloon Hoax]" and "The Facts in the Case of M. Valdemar" and "The Unparalleled Adventure of One Hans Pfaall." His science fiction stories are too numerous to list in this foreword, but can be found at the end of this anthology. The trouble with Poe is not figuring out which of his sci-fi tales rise to the level of this anthology, but rather which to exclude. At the risk of sounding like a TV commercial, Edgar Allan Poe didn't invent the science fiction story, he perfected it.

Mary Shelley, on the other hand, is an oddity in the science fiction genre. In *Frankenstein, or, The Modern Prometheus* (1818) and *The Last Man* (1826) she gave us two wonderful novels with science fiction elements, which appear to be the first sci-fi novels by a woman. Yet, none of her short stories contained science or scientific principles to any degree worth noting. This includes "Roger Dodsworth: The Reanimated Englishman" that she submitted as a hoax in 1826. The article was rejected for publication; perhaps for the complete lack of actual *science* in the story. For these reasons nothing Mary Shelley penned is included here.

But let's not stop at Shelley. America's Washington Irving wrote a novel in 1809 called: *A History of New York from the Beginning of the World to the End of the Dutch Dynasty*. In it he tells of Lunarians that transport themselves to earth on hippogriffs while clothed in impenetrable armor and carrying concentrated sunbeams for weapons. It was a political simile on how outmatched American Indians were when European settlers landed on our shores. Similar to Shelley, Irving failed to give us one science fiction short story after penning a groundbreaking novel in the genre. There are some who claim "Rip Van Winkle" is a sci-fi tale, but where is the *science*?

As mentioned, at the end of this anthology is a list of the short science fiction stories considered. Note that fantasy stories where magic happens with no scientific explanation have been excluded. This explains why such tales as Honoré de Balzac's "The Exlir of Life" and Mary Shelley's "The Mortal Immortal" and Nathaniel Hawthorne's "Dr. Heidegger's Experiment" were left off the list.

Another near miss is "The Thunder-Struck and the Boxer" by Dr. Samuel Warren, published in 1832. It foretells the destruction of earth by a comet and predates Poe's apocalyptic sci-fi tale "The Coversation of Eiros and Charmion" by seven years. Although "The Thunder-Struck and the Boxer" contains bizarre medical terminology of the day (leeches and blisters and bloodletting, oh my!), there is no futuristic technology on its pages and as a result it failed to make the cut. It too was included in *6a66le: The Best Horror Short Stories 1800-1849*.

There is little question that the short story science fiction genre was invented in the first half of the 19th century when, for the first time in literature, science was used in fiction to add a touch of realism; to prop up the story on the study legs of scientific evidence; to give it Poe's "verisimilitude;" to make the futuristic believable.

Other fiction sub-genres were created, too. Clockmech (pronounced clock-meck) is a tale where a tower's mechanical clock plays a central role in the storyline. It is, almost, a character unto itself. Eighteen thirty-eight's "A Predicament" by Poe is perhaps the first Clockmech short story. It was preceded by Victor Hugo's novel *Notre-Dame de Paris* (*The Hunchback of Notre-Dame,* as it is commonly referred to in English) in 1831. In 1843 Charles Dickens gave us *A Christmas Carol* where the striking of the clock foretells the next spirit to visit Ebenezer Scrooge. A modern example is *The Invention of Hugo Cabret* by Brian Selznick.

Detective, science fiction, Steampunk, and Clockmech stories, along with other sub-genres of short stories were created after the turn of the 19th century. We should pay reverence. We should care a great deal. After all,

we are Modernists, dern it!

Andrew Barger
March 4, 2013

EDGAR ALLAN POE
(1809-1849)

Introduction
The Facts in the Case of M. Valdemar

It is fitting that Edgar Allan Poe is the first author in this anthology of the finest science fiction short stories for the first half of the 19th century because his collective body of work in the genre surpasses other writers in character generation, storylines and the interweaving of technology into those storylines. He also surpasses them in sheer volume, having penned the most science fiction short stories for this period.

Similar to his horror and detective short stories, Poe did not invent the science fiction genre, but he took it to heights unimagined and unequalled by his literary contemporaries. Countless authors have drawn on the writings of Poe to develop their own stories. T.S. Eliot in his 1949 essay "From Poe to Valery," pointed out that "one cannot be sure that one's own writing has *not* been influenced by Poe." It would be easier to separate salt from the seas than the impact of Edgar Allan Poe's writings on our literature.

"The Facts in the Case of M. Valdemar" is a story about flirting with death and who better to pen it than Poe? At the time it was written the medical community was experimenting with putting patients under "magnetic sleep" so they would not feel pain during surgery. Rumors of this mesmeric treatment, a precursor to hypnosis, were spreading across New England. Poe, being a literary practical joker at heart, was quick to play on the misguided beliefs of the medical community and society at large.

When "The Facts in the Case of M. Valdemar" was published in 1845, it garnered much attention from practicing mesmerists, who so badly wanted the story to be true. One of the most prominent, Robert Collyer, queried Poe from Boston on December 16, 1845: "Your account of M. Valdemar's case has been universally copied in this city, and has created a very great sensation." He then asked Poe to confirm the story was true "to put at rest the growing impression that your account is merely a splendid creation of your own brain, not having any truth in fact."

Poe responded by placing Collyer's letter in the Decmeber 27, 1845 issue of the *Broadway Journal* of which Poe was part owner. "We have no doubt that Mr. Collyer is perfectly correct in all that he says – and all that he desires us to say – but the truth is, there was a very small modicum of truth in the case of M. Valdemar – which, in consequence, may be called a hard case – very hard for M. Valdemar, for Mr. Collyer, and ourselves."

"The Facts in the Case of M. Valdemar" was popular in both the United States and in Europe. It was reprinted seven times in December of 1845. The following year it was reprinted another three times and on August 4th Philip Pendleton Cooke, Poe's friend, read the story while hunting and remarked: "The 'Valdemar Case' I read in a number of your Broadway Journal last winter – as I lay in a Turkey blind, muffled to the eyes in overcoats, &c., and pronounce it without hesitation the most damnable, vraisemblable, horrible, hair-lifting, shocking, ingenious chapter of fiction that any brain ever conceived, or hands traced. That gelatinous, viscous sound of man's voice! there never was such an idea before. That story scared me in broad day, armed with a double-barrel Tryon Turkey gun. What would it have done at midnight in some old ghostly countryhouse? I have always found some one remarkable thing in your stories to haunt me long after reading them." In December of 1846 Poe warned, "Some few persons believe it–but I do not–and don't you."

To add to the story's "verisimilitude," Poe used the letter P for the narrator's surname just as he did in his "Mesmeric Revelation" published the year before.

The Facts in the Case of M. Valdemar (1845)

OF COURSE I shall not pretend to consider it any matter for wonder, that the extraordinary case of M. Valdemar has excited discussion. It would have been a miracle had it not-especially under the circumstances. Through the desire of all parties concerned, to keep the affair from the public, at least for the present, or until we had farther opportunities for investigation – through our endeavors to effect this – a garbled or exaggerated account made its way into society, and became the source of many unpleasant misrepresentations, and, very naturally, of a great deal of disbelief.

It is now rendered necessary that I give the *facts* – as far as I comprehend them myself. They are, succinctly, these:

My attention, for the last three years, had been repeatedly drawn to the subject of Mesmerism;[1] and, about nine months ago it occurred to me, quite suddenly, that in the series of experiments made hitherto, there had been a very remarkable and most unaccountable omission: – no person had as yet been mesmerized *in articulo mortis*.[2] It remained to be seen, first, whether, in such condition, there existed in the patient any susceptibility to the magnetic influence; secondly, whether, if any existed, it was impaired or increased by the condition; thirdly, to what extent, or for how long a period, the encroachments of Death

---

[1] Hypnotic trance brought on by the use of hypnosis and/or the application of magnets

[2] Near death and without the use of joints and muscles

might be arrested by the process. There were other points to be ascertained, but these most excited my curiosity – the last in especial, from the immensely important character of its consequences.

In looking around me for some subject by whose means I might test these particulars, I was brought to think of my friend, M. Ernest Valdemar, the well-known compiler of the "Bibliotheca Forensica,"[3] and author (under the *nom de plume* of Issachar Marx) of the Polish versions of "Wallenstein"[4] and "Gargantua."[5] M. Valdemar, who has resided principally at Harlaem, N.Y., since the year 1839, is (or was) particularly noticeable for the extreme spareness of his person – his lower limbs much resembling those of John Randolph;[6] and, also, for the whiteness of his whiskers, in violent contrast to the blackness of his hair – the latter, in consequence, being very generally mistaken for a wig. His temperament was markedly nervous, and rendered him a good subject for mesmeric experiment. On two or three occasions I had put him to sleep with little difficulty, but was disappointed in other results which his peculiar constitution had naturally led me to anticipate. His will was at no period positively, or thoroughly, under my control, and in regard to *clairvoyance*,[7] I could accomplish with him nothing to be relied upon. I always attributed my failure at these points to the disordered state of his health. For some months previous to my becoming acquainted with him, his physicians had declared him in a confirmed phthisis.[8]

---

[3] Bible of Forensics, fictional book

[4] Play written in 1800 by Johann Christoph Friedrich von Schiller (1759-1805), German poet and historian

[5] Comic novel (*Gargantua and Pantagruel*) by Francois Rabelais (1449-1553) that tells the story of the giant Gargantua and his son Pantagruel

[6] John Randolph (1773-1833) was a Virginia congressman who was bedridden off and on through years of living with tuberculosis

[7] In this case, trying to obtain information about the subject in question beyond the normal senses known to science

[8] Tuberculosis of the lungs

It was his custom, indeed, to speak calmly of his approaching dissolution, as of a matter neither to be avoided nor regretted.

When the ideas to which I have alluded first occurred to me, it was of course very natural that I should think of M. Valdemar. I knew the steady philosophy of the man too well to apprehend any scruples from *him*; and he had no relatives in America who would be likely to interfere. I spoke to him frankly upon the subject; and, to my surprise, his interest seemed vividly excited. I say to my surprise, for, although he had always yielded his person freely to my experiments, he had never before given me any tokens of sympathy with what I did. His disease was if that character which would admit of exact calculation in respect to the epoch of its termination in death; and it was finally arranged between us that he would send for me about twenty-four hours before the period announced by his physicians as that of his decease.

It is now rather more than seven months since I received, from M. Valdemar himself, the subjoined note:

MY DEAR P–,
You may as well come *now*. D– and F– are agreed that I cannot hold out beyond to-morrow midnight; and I think they have hit the time very nearly.
VALDEMAR

I received this note within half an hour after it was written, and in fifteen minutes more I was in the dying man's chamber. I had not seen him for ten days, and was appalled by the fearful alteration which the brief interval had wrought in him. His face wore a leaden hue; the eyes were utterly lustreless; and the emaciation was so extreme that the skin had been broken through by the cheek-bones. His expectoration[9] was excessive. The pulse was barely perceptible. He

---

[9] Spitting up

retained, nevertheless, in a very remarkable manner, both his mental power and a certain degree of physical strength. He spoke with distinctness – took some palliative medicines[10] without aid – and, when I entered the room, was occupied in penciling memoranda in a pocket-book. He was propped up in the bed by pillows. Doctors D– and F– were in attendance.

After pressing Valdemar's hand, I took these gentlemen aside, and obtained from them a minute account of the patient's condition. The left lung had been for eighteen months in a semi-osseous or cartilaginous state,[11] and was, of course, entirely useless for all purposes of vitality. The right, in its upper portion, was also partially, if not thoroughly, ossified, while the lower region was merely a mass of purulent tubercles,[12] running one into another. Several extensive perforations existed; and, at one point, permanent adhesion to the ribs had taken place. These appearances in the right lobe were of comparatively recent date. The ossification had proceeded with very unusual rapidity; no sign of it had discovered a month before, and the adhesion had only been observed during the three previous days. Independently of the phthisis, the patient was suspected of aneurism of the aorta;[13] but on this point the osseous symptoms rendered an exact diagnosis impossible. It was the opinion of both physicians that M. Valdemar would die about midnight on the morrow (Sunday). It was then seven o'clock on Saturday evening.

On quitting the invalid's bed-side to hold conversation with myself, Doctors D– and F– had bidden him a final farewell. It had not been their

---

[10] Medicines that do not cure, but relieve the pain and symptoms of the patient

[11] Resembling bone or cartilage

[12] Infected pus

[13] Expansion of the great artery to all parts of the body

intention to return; but, at my request, they agreed to look in upon the patient about ten the next night.

When they had gone, I spoke freely with M. Valdemar on the subject of his approaching dissolution, as well as, more particularly, of the experiment proposed. He still professed himself quite willing and even anxious to have it made, and urged me to commence it at once. A male and a female nurse were in attendance; but I did not feel myself altogether at liberty to engage in a task of this character with no more reliable witnesses than these people, in case of sudden accident, might prove. I therefore postponed operations until about eight the next night, when the arrival of a medical student with whom I had some acquaintance, (Mr. Theodore L–l,) relieved me from farther embarrassment. It had been my design, originally, to wait for the physicians; but I was induced to proceed, first, by the urgent entreaties of M. Valdemar, and secondly, by my conviction that I had not a moment to lose, as he was evidently sinking fast.

Mr. L–l was so kind as to accede to my desire that he would take notes of all that occurred, and it is from his memoranda that what I now have to relate is, for the most part, either condensed or copied *verbatim*.

It wanted about five minutes of eight when, taking the patient's hand, I begged him to state, as distinctly as he could, to Mr. L–l, whether he (M. Valdemar) was entirely willing that I should make the experiment of mesmerizing him in his then condition.

He replied feebly, yet quite audibly, "Yes, I wish to be mesmerized" –adding immediately afterwards: "I fear you have deferred it too long."

While he spoke thus, I commenced the passes which I had already found most effectual in subduing him. He was evidently influenced with the first lateral stroke of my hand across his forehead; but although I exerted all my powers, no farther perceptible effect was induced until some minutes after ten o'clock, when Doctors D–and F–called, according to appointment. I explained to them, in a few words, what I designed, and as they opposed no objection, saying that the patient was already in the death agony, I proceeded without hesitation – exchanging, however, the lateral passes for downward ones, and directing my gaze entirely into the right eye of the sufferer.

By this time his pulse was imperceptible and his breathing was stertorous,[14] and at intervals of half a minute.

This condition was nearly unaltered for a quarter of an hour. At the expiration of this period, however, a natural although a very deep sigh escaped the bosom of the dying man, and the stertorous breathing ceased – that is to say, its stertorousness was no longer apparent; the intervals were undiminished. The patient's extremities were of an icy coldness.

At five minutes before eleven I perceived unequivocal signs of the mesmeric influence. The glassy roll of the eye was changed for that expression of uneasy *inward* examination which is never seen except in cases of sleep-waking, and which it is quite impossible to mistake. With a few rapid lateral passes I made the lids quiver, as in incipient sleep,[15] and with a few more I closed them altogether. I was not satisfied, however, with this, but continued the manipulations vigorously, and with the fullest exertion of the will, until I had completely stiffened the limbs of the slumberer, after placing them in a seemingly easy position. The legs were at full length; the arms were nearly so, and reposed on the bed at a moderate distance from the loin. The head was very slightly elevated.

When I had accomplished this, it was fully midnight, and I requested the gentlemen present to examine M. Valdemar's condition. After a few experiments, they admitted him to be an unusually perfect state of mesmeric trance. The curiosity of both the physicians was greatly excited. Dr. D– resolved at once to remain

---

[14] Heavy

[15] Beginning stage of sleep

with the patient all night, while Dr. F– took leave with a promise to return at daybreak. Mr. L–l and the nurses remained.

We left M. Valdemar entirely undisturbed until about three o'clock in the morning, when I approached him and found him in precisely the same condition as when Dr. F– went away – that is to say, he lay in the same position; the pulse was imperceptible; the breathing was gentle (scarcely noticeable, unless through the application of a mirror to the lips); the eyes were closed naturally; and the limbs were as rigid and as cold as marble. Still, the general appearance was certainly not that of death.

As I approached M. Valdemar I made a kind of half effort to influence his right arm into pursuit of my own, as I passed the latter gently to and fro above his person. In such experiments with this patient had never perfectly succeeded before, and assuredly I had little thought of succeeding now; but to my astonishment, his arm very readily, although feebly, followed every direction I assigned it with mine. I determined to hazard a few words of conversation.

"M. Valdemar," I said, "are you asleep?" He made no answer, but I perceived a tremor about the lips, and was thus induced to repeat the question, again and again. At its third repetition, his whole frame was agitated by a very slight shivering; the eyelids unclosed themselves so far as to display a white line of the ball; the lips moved sluggishly, and from between them, in a barely audible whisper, issued the words:

"Yes; – asleep now. Do not wake me! – let me die so!"

I here felt the limbs and found them as rigid as ever. The right arm, as before, obeyed the direction of my hand. I questioned the sleep-waker again:

"Do you still feel pain in the breast, M. Valdemar?"

The answer now was immediate, but even less audible than before: "No pain – I am dying."

I did not think it advisable to disturb him farther just then, and nothing more was said or done until the arrival of Dr. F – , who came a little before sunrise, and expressed unbounded astonishment at finding the patient still alive. After feeling the pulse and applying a mirror to the lips, he requested me to speak to the sleep-waker again. I did so, saying:

"M. Valdemar, do you still sleep?"

As before, some minutes elapsed ere a reply was made; and during the interval the dying man seemed to be collecting his energies to speak. At my fourth repetition of the question, he said very faintly, almost inaudibly:

"Yes; still asleep – dying."

It was now the opinion, or rather the wish, of the physicians, that M. Valdemar should be suffered to remain undisturbed in his present apparently tranquil condition, until death should supervene – and this, it was generally agreed, must now take place within a few minutes. I concluded, however, to speak to him once more, and merely repeated my previous question.

While I spoke, there came a marked change over the countenance of the sleep-waker. The eyes rolled themselves slowly open, the pupils disappearing upwardly; the skin generally assumed a cadaverous hue, resembling not so much parchment as white paper; and the circular hectic spots which, hitherto, had been strongly defined in the centre of each cheek, *went out* at once. I use this expression, because the suddenness of their departure put me in mind of nothing so much as the extinguishment of a candle by a puff of the breath. The upper lip, at the same time, writhed itself away from the teeth, which it had previously covered completely; while the lower jaw fell with an audible jerk, leaving the mouth widely extended, and disclosing in full view the swollen and blackened tongue. I presume that no member of the party then present had been unaccustomed to death-bed horrors; but so hideous beyond conception was the appearance of M. Valdemar at this moment, that there was a general shrinking back from the region of the bed.

I now feel that I have reached a point of this narrative at which every reader will be startled into positive disbelief. It is my business, however, simply to proceed.

There was no longer the faintest sign of vitality in M. Valdemar; and concluding him to be dead, we were consigning him to the charge of the nurses, when a strong vibratory motion was observable in the tongue. This continued for perhaps a minute. At the expiration of this period, there issued from the distended and motionless jaws a voice – such as it would be madness in me to attempt describing. There are, indeed, two or three epithets which might be considered as applicable to it in part; I might say, for example, that the sound was harsh, and broken and hollow; but the hideous whole is indescribable, for the simple reason that no similar sounds have ever jarred upon the ear of humanity. There were two particulars, nevertheless, which I thought then, and still think, might fairly be stated as characteristic of the intonation – as well adapted to convey some idea of its unearthly peculiarity. In the first place, the voice seemed to reach our ears – at least mine – from a vast distance, or from some deep cavern within the earth. In the second place, it impressed me (I fear, indeed, that it will be impossible to make myself comprehended) as gelatinous or glutinous matters impress the sense of touch.

I have spoken both of "sound" and of "voice." I mean to say that the sound was one of distinct – of even wonderfully, thrillingly distinct – syllabification. M. Valdemar *spoke* – obviously in reply to the question I had propounded to him a few minutes before. I had asked him, it will be remembered, if he still slept. He now said:

"Yes; – no; – I *have been* sleeping – and now – now – *I am dead.*

No person present even affected to deny, or attempted to repress, the unutterable, shuddering horror which these few words, thus uttered, were so well calculated to convey. Mr. L – l (the student) swooned. The nurses immediately left the chamber, and could not be induced to return. My own impressions I would not pretend to render intelligible to the reader. For nearly an hour, we busied ourselves, silently – without the utterance of a word – in endeavors to revive Mr. L – l. When he came to himself, we addressed ourselves again to an investigation of M. Valdemar's condition.

It remained in all respects as I have last described it, with the exception that the mirror no longer afforded evidence of respiration. An attempt to draw blood from the arm failed. I should mention, too, that this limb was no farther subject to my will. I endeavored in vain to make it follow the direction of my hand. The only real indication, indeed, of the mesmeric influence, was now found in the vibratory movement of the tongue, whenever I addressed M. Valdemar a question. He seemed to be making an effort to reply, but had no longer sufficient volition. To queries put to him by any other person than myself he seemed utterly insensible – although I endeavored to place each member of the company in mesmeric *rapport* with him. I believe that I have now related all that is necessary to an understanding of the sleep-waker's state at this epoch. Other nurses were procured; and at ten o'clock I left the house in company with the two physicians and Mr. L – l.

In the afternoon we all called again to see the patient. His condition remained precisely the same. We had now some discussion as to the propriety and feasibility of awakening him; but we had little difficulty in agreeing that no good purpose would be served by so doing. It was evident that, so far, death (or what is usually termed death) had been arrested by the mesmeric process. It seemed clear to us all that to awaken M. Valdemar would be merely to insure his instant, or at least his speedy dissolution.

From this period until the close of last week – *an interval of nearly seven months* – we continued to make daily calls at M. Valdemar's house, accompanied, now and then, by medical and other friends. All this time the sleeper-waker remained *exactly* as I have last described him. The nurses' attentions were continual.

It was on Friday last that we finally resolved to make the experiment of awakening or attempting to awaken him; and it is the (perhaps) unfortunate result of this latter experiment which has given rise to so much discussion in private circles – to so much of what I cannot help thinking unwarranted popular feeling.

For the purpose of relieving M. Valdemar from the mesmeric trance, I made use of the customary passes. These, for a time, were unsuccessful. The first indication of revival was afforded by a partial descent of the iris. It was observed, as especially remarkable, that this lowering of the pupil was accompanied by the profuse out-flowing of a yellowish ichor[16] (from beneath the lids) of a pungent and highly offensive odor.

It was now suggested that I should attempt to influence the patient's arm, as heretofore. I made the attempt and failed. Dr. F– then intimated a desire to have me put a question. I did so, as follows:

"M. Valdemar, can you explain to us what are your feelings or wishes now?"

There was an instant return of the hectic circles on the cheeks; the tongue quivered, or rather rolled violently in the mouth (although the jaws and lips remained rigid as before;) and at length the same hideous voice which I have already described, broke forth:

---

[16] Acrid discharge

"For God's sake! – quick! – quick! – put me to sleep – or, quick! – waken me! – quick! – *I say to you that I am dead!*"

I was thoroughly unnerved, and for an instant remained undecided what to do. At first I made an endeavor to re-compose the patient; but, failing in this through total abeyance of the will, I retraced my steps and as earnestly struggled to awaken him. In this attempt I soon saw that I should be successful – or at least I soon fancied that my success would be complete – and I am sure that all in the room were prepared to see the patient awaken.

For what really occurred, however, it is quite impossible that any human being could have been prepared.

As I rapidly made the mesmeric passes, amid ejaculations of "dead! dead!" absolutely *bursting* from the tongue and not from the lips of the sufferer, his whole frame at once – within the space of a single minute, or even less, shrunk – crumbled – absolutely *rotted* away beneath my hands. Upon the bed, before that whole company, there lay a nearly liquid mass of loathsome – of detestable putridity.

PERCIVAL LEIGH
(1813-1889)

Introduction
The Aerial Burglar

The writer of this story was listed as "The author of the *Comic Latin and Comic English Grammars*," which poked fun at "ye Englyshe" and the idiosyncrasies of their language. The *Grammars* were published under the name Paul Prendergast, a thinly-veiled pseudonym of Percival Leigh. The illustration above is from the frontispiece of *The Comic Latin Grammar* published in 1840.

Leigh was a Scottish surgeon turned comic author who continued to practice medicine in London "for friends" as provided by the 1881 English census. Because of his scientific background, Leigh was asked by Charles Dickens to adapt a series of lectures by Michael Faraday that appeared in Dickens's magazine, *Household Words* during 1850. Leigh became associated with *Punch* magazine in London and was a frequent contributor. *Punch* was the *Mad* magazine of England.

"The Aerial Burglar" appeared in *The Comic Album: A Book for Every Table* of 1844. The story is a tale supposedly written during "the process of being Mesmerised" and despite the tongue-in-cheek background of this story it is groundbreaking in the science fiction genre. It contains the first aerial chase by people on individual flying machines in literature. The first "electrical" weapon is also on display, which shoots lightning.

With its steam-powered flying apparatus and brass instruments and clocks striking midnight and unique Victorian clothing, "The Aerial Burglar" is also perhaps the first Steampunk short story. It is provided for the first time since its original publication in 1844.

The Aerial Burglar
(1844)

WE LATELY SUBMITTED to the process of being Mesmerised;[1] and during the magnetic state, which was that of the highest degree of *clairvoyance,*[2] were favoured with a peep into futurity. We recollect nothing, whatever, of all that we saw; but we are told that we wrote part of it down at the time, our eyes then being fast closed, and we sitting in a Windsor-chair[3] upon the points of twelve tenpenny nails,[4] which, for our own accommodation, and for the satisfaction of the company present, that we were in a state of physical insensibility, had been driven up through the bottom of it.

The ensuing narrative is compiled from the account, which, as we are informed, we indited upon that occasion.

We *found* ourselves, all at once (where many Mesmerists, as well as their patients—also sundry metaphysicians, theologians, and moralists—very often *lose* themselves), in the clouds.

Over the broad fields of air were spread innumerable islands of immense magnitude, of a circular form, and flattened above and below, so—to compare great things with small—as to resemble Cheshire cheeses.[5] These we at first thought were planets, but we presently came to find that they were

---

[1] Hypnotic trance brought on by hypnosis and/or the use of magnets

[2] Extra-sensory perception beyond the senses known to science

[3] Wooden chair with rounded back formed by spindles

[4] Nails three inches long

[5] Round, flattened shape of this popular cheese from the Cheshire county of England

structures of human invention, composed as follows:—
over a case, forming an enormous air-cushion, was
disposed a sort of wood-pavement, made of cork,
which had been subjected to a process securing it
from decomposition. Upon this was placed an artificial
soil of earth, where grew herbage and trees of various
kinds; and on which, dwelling-places, made of light yet
warm materials, had been erected. The interiors of
these artificial islands were filled with the Mesmeric
fluid[6] itself,—a gas many millions of times lighter than
the most rarefied hydrogen; enabling them,
notwithstanding the weight of their solid parts, to
remain suspended in the air. Each of them was
furnished with a stop-cock,[7] whereby the gas might be
let out at pleasure, and upon them all there was kept a
large number of cats, from which creatures it had
been discovered that the Mesmerogen, as the gas was
termed, was procurable. These islands were tenanted
by men, women, children, cattle, and other animals.
When the aerial islanders wanted to descend, they let
a quantity of the fluid out; when they wished to rise,
they forced some of it in; displacing, of course, by so
doing, the atmospheric air. This was Dean Swift's[8]
idea of a flying island realised, without the aid of
magic!

The epoch in which we were existing, was the year
2000,—to such a pitch had science by that time
attained! But, alas! morality had not made a
corresponding advancement; and it was with pain that
we contemplated an aerial police, patrolling on flying
machines, which were like huge turbots[9] with wings,
between the isles in mid-air. There was no mistaking
them; the dark blue of their attire was relieved upon

---

[6] Anton Mesmer (1734-1815) believed that the nervous system of the human body contained the energy of life that he called "mesmeric fluid"

[7] Valve used to restrict the flow of gas through a conduit

[8] Jonathan "Dean" Swift (1667-1745) who portrayed the floating island of Laputa in his novel, *Gulliver's Travels*

[9] European flatfish

the lighter azure, their collars were lettered and numbered, and they wore list around their cuffs, which shewed that they were upon duty.

Yes; crime, without leaving the earth, had soared into the sky; and theft and robbery contaminated the air.

Dodging among the clouds, and evidently desirous of avoiding observation, we remarked an individual on a machine that seemed like a flying narwhal, or unicorn fish, the snout being furnished with a long and formidable spike resembling that creature's horn. As he threaded his way through the darker masses of vapours, he threw around him into every nook and corner the rays of a dark lantern, which lighted up their gloomy recesses and kindled their lurid promontories with a red glare. As night came on these appearances were the more observable, and the policemen, now indistinguishable in the darkness, save by the lanterns which they also carried, seemed like portentous meteors flashing athwart the sky.

Our consciousness, now, for a moment, became suspended. When it returned, we found ourselves in a bedchamber of a small cottage, which stood upon the verge of one of these islands. It was still night. The moon was shining through the open casement, in whose front, overshadowing the right angle, hung a graceful cluster of ivy, through which the night-breeze was sighing at intervals. Lights, now rendered less conspicuous by the moonshine, were still gliding about at a distance, and leisurely emerging from, and then disappearing amidst the clouds.

Whilst we were enjoying this singular and wonderful spectacle, a light footstep approached; the chamber door opened, and a young and lovely girl, whose age might have been about twenty, entered with a rushlight[10] in her hand. She was attired with a mixture of elegance and simplicity, in virgin-white muslin, with a black ribbon round the waist; a dress which became

---

[10] Candle made by dipping a rush or reed in tallow

a cheek fair, but slightly pale, sparkling grey eyes, raven tresses, and a snowy brow, exceedingly. In a corner, on a chair, hung a richer garment of similar hue, but of satin, with appropriate accompaniments; ready to all appearance for the morrow, and being, unequivocally, a wedding costume. Placing her candle on the toilette-table, whereupon were arranged a variety of articles of feminine elegance, she approached the window, and pensively reclined with her cheek upon her hand, and her elbow on the sill.

Presently a voice was heard below, singing to the accompaniment of an ophicleide.[11]

> "Louisa, sleep till morning's sun
> Shall gild thy cloud-built home;
> And rise to see us two made one,
> In yonder sacred dome.
> La, la, la, lira la!
> Until the holy rite be done,
> Ah! whither shall I roam?
> Lira la!"

"'Tis Edward!" exclaimed the maiden. "Oh, Edward, go to bed; thou wilt catch cold in the night air."

"Not a bit of it," answered the lover, with the accents of youth. "I can't go to bed. I am all impatience for the happy hour that shall unite me for ever with thee. Meanwhile I shall be unable to close these eyes. But I will not disturb thy slumbers, Louisa. First let me charm thee, with the magic power of melody, to repose; and then, whirled about on my trusty Pegasus,[12] I go to wander till morn in the moonlit air."

At these words the maiden threw herself listlessly on her couch; and the lover commenced a slow and soothing lullaby on his deep-toned instrument. In a few moments she slept, and the musician, striking into a lively air, which seemed very much like "The girls we

---

[11] Large brass instrument with keys and a precursor to the tuba
[12] Winged horse

leave behind us," mounted his machine, and, the tune dying away as he ascended, was soon out of sight.

Louisa still slept, and the chamber, save with her musical breathing, was hushed. The rushlight was burning low, and the room consequently darkened, when suddenly a flash of light illuminated its interior, as some aerial navigator glided by. Presently this phenomenon was repeated; the person, whoever he was, having again crossed the window, and, during his course, having evidently taken a glance at the apartment.

In a few moments there was a noise outside, as of somebody alighting; and suddenly the apparition of a man presented itself at the window, leaning with folded arms upon the sill, and gazing full into the room. The countenance was singularly forbidding; the eyes were deeply set in the head, the nose snubbed, the lips thick, and the whole expression sullen and scowling. There was a short pipe in the mouth, and a thick bludgeon,[13] crossing the chest diagonally, rose over the left shoulder. The individual wore a white hat, much battered, with a piece of black crape round it, and by this circumstance we identified him with the person we had seen lurking among the clouds.

After standing in this position for a second or two, he looked cautiously around, first on the right and then on the left, as if to see whether any one was watching him. He then noiselessly lifted one leg up through the casement into the room, displaying the lower part of a nether garment of soiled drab, a not very clean white stocking, and a boot, laced in front, which came a little above the ankle. He then introduced the other leg; and next resting himself on the palm of either hand, let himself down into the room. He looked a tall powerful man, and was dressed in a velveteen shooting jacket, and a waistcoat of faded black. A figured cotton neckcloth, twisted like a rope, was tied around his throat in a knot, and from the pocket of his coat there

---

[13] Rod for use as a weapon

stuck out the stock of a pistol. It was plain that he was a burglar.

He now, with the pace of one who is treading upon eggs, a precaution which his hob-nailed boots rendered very necessary, approached the fair sleeper. He bent over her, and threw the light of his lantern full in her face. She moved not—with a gesture expressive of satisfaction he put his finger to the side of his nose; and then, after fumbling a little in his pocket, drew forth a large clasp knife. Raising the implement of destruction, he was about to plunge it in her breast, when a sudden cry of "Past twelve o'clock," outside the window, arrested his uplifted arm, and baulked his sanguinary purpose; he slunk hastily behind the bed. The whizzing sound of the watchman's flying machine died away in the distance; the coast was now clear again, and the housebreaker, emerging from his place of concealment, proceeded to make the most of his time, by transferring to his pockets as many moveables as he could find. A brooch, a vinaigrette,[14] a gold clasp, a tortoiseshell-comb, a white cambric handkerchief, and the miniature of a young gentleman, had been thus feloniously appropriated, when the ruffian proceeded to lay his profane hands on the satin wedding-dress, which, as before stated, was hanging on a chair in a corner. The rustling of the material awoke the sleeper, who instantly started up from the bed, and, perceiving a man in the room, gave utterance to a loud scream.

The robber for a moment stood aghast; during which interval the courageous girl, with an unavailing instinct of self-defence, discharged one of her tiny slippers at the villain's head. Ducking, he avoided the harmless missile; and his next act was to rush upon the shrieking victim; and, while with one hand he stopped her mouth, fumbled in his waistcoat pocket for his knife with the other. She, in the meanwhile, perceiving the pistol projecting from beneath the

---

[14] Decorative bottle that typically held smelling salts

lappet of his coat, with wonderful presence of mind snatched it out, and discharged it full in his face. The ball infringed upon the skull; but instead of penetrating the brain, and thus terminating at once his career of guilt, it glanced, as often happens, and making the circuit of the head beneath the scalp, came out by the hole by which it went in; to the imminent peril of the young lady, one of whose curls it grazed in its backward passage, and then lodged in the bed-post.

Half stunned, the housebreaker staggered back for an instant; and then collecting himself, and brandishing his knife, prepared, with clenched teeth and flashing eyes, to spring, tiger-like, on his prey, when a violent hammering at the door convinced him that the family was alarmed. He rushed, therefore, to the window, but as he was getting out the undaunted Louisa clung to the skirts of his coat. Not a moment was to be lost!—suddenly seizing her in his arms, he disappeared through the casement; and, quick as thought, mounting his aerostatic[15] vehicle, flew off like a sparrow-hawk with a chicken.

At this moment the unhappy Edward arrived from his midnight ramble, just in time to behold all that he held dear upon earth, apparently on her way to the moon. Sounding a fearful blast of alarm upon his ophicleide, he instantly touched a spring in his own conveyance, which let on the steam that it was moved by, and started after the villain in full chase; the whole aerial police, whom the summons had called to his aid, joining in the hue and cry.

It was a grand sight to behold myriads of oxy-hydrogen lights, far and wide over the islets, blazing with an instantaneous splendour, and darting their noon-day radiance deep into the bosom of night. It appeared that every dwelling in the regions of air was furnished with these precautionary appliances, which

---

[15] Gas that is static or not moving

were capable of being put in action at a moment's notice.

The chase, of which a complete view was thus afforded, was animated beyond description. The burglar kept for some time considerably in advance of his pursuers, who however, at last, rapidly gained upon him. He then sought to baffle them by turning and winding, after the manner of a fox, in and out of the clouds. Now he plunged, with Edward, closely followed by the police, each on his several machine directly upon his track, into a dense body of vapour; now he appeared rounding the illuminated outline of one of its bold capes; the hunters instantly succeeding him. Then he dived with incredible velocity beneath an island, and anon soared aloft again, till both he and they looked like small specks among the stars.

The different flying machines of the police force, also, formed a singular display. Some were in the form of birds or of fishes, others resembled dragons, griffins, and other fabulous animals; and the noise which they made in their progress, with the steam by which they were moved, was terrific.

At length the housebreaker was seen descending, with the officers of justice hard upon him. He now made a desperate effort and stood at bay, darting, with infuriated despair into the midst of the throng, and running, with the spike with which his car was armed, full tilt against his foes, whose dexterity in avoiding him was admirable. At last, one of the policemen knocked off that dangerous weapon with his truncheon.[16]

The miscreant, upon this, perceived that his only safety lay in flight; and, with a cruelty and cowardice that must be considered unparalleled, by a sudden jerk disengaged himself from the burden of his prey. Horrible sight for a lover! Louisa fell screaming, with a velocity increasing with the square of the distance, earthward; but the wings of love are fleeter than the

---

[16] Rod uses as a weapon

force of gravitation, and, ere she had fallen half a mile, Edward, descending with the rapidity of a sunbeam, had caught her in his arms. He conveyed her instantly to her parental home. She had fainted, and was apparently dead; but a dose of *elixir vitae* having been promptly administered to her, she speedily returned to life and love. Lovers only can understand the transports which were then the lot of herself and her Edward.

In the meantime the burglar, surrounded by his pursuers, used every effort to escape. At last, finding all other resources fail him, he drew his remaining pistol; and balancing his car, stood in act to fire. His aim was known to be unerring, and it was clear that he could only be taken alive at the expense of the life of some one of those around him.

Accordingly C. 24, drawing an electrical blunderbuss[17] from a case which hung at his girdle, discharged a flash of lightning at his guilty head. The blow was sure and fatal. His hat, singed and blazing, flew to the winds, and his blackened and shattered form fell, with innumerable gyrations to earth; nor rested till it stuck upon some area railings.

The next morning Edward and Louisa were married, with every prospect of a life of perpetual bliss, enhanced by a recollection of the peril which attended its commencement.

---

[17] Short barreled gun with flared muzzle

Captain Frederick Marryat
(1792-1848)

Introduction
A Visit to the Lunar Sphere

Was Captain Frederick Marryat the anonymous author of the groundbreaking sci-fi story "A Visit to the Lunar Sphere?" The evidence around its publication seems to point to him.

In 1819 Marryat wed Catherine Shairp, the daughter of the Scot, Stephen Shairp. It was then he formed ties with the editors of *Blackwood's Edinburgh Magazine*, especially John Wilson (also known by the pseudonym Christopher North). In June of 1820 Marryat was appointed captain of his first ship, the *Beacon*. He left Scotland and sailed for most of the following year. Still, he was in contact with his family and friends, any of which could have delivered "A Visit to the Lunar Sphere" to be published anonymously by *Blackwood's Edinburgh Magazine* in November of 1820.

The story closes with the valuable discoveries made by Professor Heidelberg slated to be laid before the Royal Society of Edinburgh. The year prior, in 1819, Marryat was elected as a member of the Royal

Society for Scientific Knowledge. In the introduction to *Peter Simple* of 1907 the editor tells us that since 1815 Marryat had "occupied himself in acquiring a perfect knowledge of such branches of science as might prove useful should the Lords of the Admiralty think fit to employ him in a voyage of discovery or survery." In addition, the author of this story addresses many scientific principles and was schooled in advanced scientific of the day.

When it was recommended that Marryat be elected to the newly established Astronomical Society, he replied: "I beg you will inscribe Capt. Marryat, R.N., F.R.S., F.L.S., F.G.S., F.W.S. . . .. They will think me some new comet by the length of my tail." In "A Visit to the Lunar Sphere" Professor Heidelberg logs information from a comet with a long tail. The story further contains Marryat's trademark blend of humor and adventure.

Marryat was a proponent of supernatural stories as evidenced by his serialized novel that he began publishing in 1837 titled *The Phantom Ship*. In it he explores the tradition of the Flying Dutchman doomed to sail the seas, and even an episode about a female werewolf that was included in *Shifters: The Best Werewolf Short Stories 1800-1849*. He was also the editor of the *Metropolitan Magazine* during 1835 when Sir Thomas Morgan's "Glimpses of Other Worlds" was published, which is the next story in this anthology.

In the P.S.S. of "A Visit to the Lunar Sphere" the author assures: "Depend on hearing from me again before next month." That apparently did not happen until four months later when "A Letter from the Man in the Moon" was published in *Blackwood's Edinburgh Magazine*. In the second paragraph it references "Dr Heidelberg's upward voyage" while stating that his (i.e., the author's) moon is "of the common people . . .." Marryat worked his way up from a common midshipman to captain. He was an opponent of the impressment navel system that required common young men to serve in the navy given its brutal assignments at sea.

The letter begins with an epigram from *A Midsummer Night's Dream*: "A Calendar, a Calendar! Look in the Almanack; find out Moonshine—find out Moonshine!" In Marryat's comedic play, *Ill Will: An Acting Charade* of 1837, Act III, there is the following dialogue:

Jel. No more than the man in moon, my dear sir.

Gum. Man in the moon!—odd comparison that from a woman!—very odd! Hope my choice won't prove all moonshine!

A year earlier, in 1836, Marryat published a novella titled "Moonshine."

The strongest evidentiary link to Captain Frederick Marryat and his penning of "A Visit to the Lunar Sphere" is from the signature block, which reads: A MIDSHIPMAN. His first two novels, *The Naval Officer; or, Scenes in the Life and Adventures of Frank Mildmay* (1829) and *The King's Own* (1830) were also published anonymously. In 1820, the year "A Visit to the Lunar Sphere" was published, Marryat created a series of illustrations that focused on his life as a midshipman. They were titled "The Progress of a Midshipman." Marryat would go on to publish the novel *Mr. Midshipman Easy* in 1836 and in 1838 *Peter Simple; or, the Adventures of a Midshipman*.

This story offers many firsts in science fiction literature, keeping in mind that in 1752 Voltaire gave the world what is likely the first sci-fi short story concerning a space alien. "Micromégas" was the name of the story that told of an extraterrestrial from a plant that orbits Sirius. In it the 20,000 foot tall Micromégas visits earth to impart knowledge to Earthlings.

The first trip to the moon and the first lunar alien in a short story (keeping in mind that Washington Irving included Lunarians in his 1809 novel *A History of New York from the Beginning of the World to the End of the*

Dutch Dynasty), however, are found in "A Visit to the Lunar Sphere." Without giving away too much, the trip is by balloon, which is also a first in short sci-fi literature. In it perpetual motion is applied to "timekeepers" and there is a foray into calculus. Zuloc, the Lunarian, hands the protagonist a prism from the ceiling, which casts light into bottles, creating a darkness machine. This is another case of first impression in science fiction literature.

This vitally important short story to the science fiction genre is published here for the first time since its original publication in 1820. It is, perhaps, the first short story penned by Captain Frederick Marryat.

A Visit to the Lunar Sphere
(1820)

ON MY PASSING through the Hague, in the autumn of last year, I took occasion to pay a visit to the famous Professor Heidelbergus,[1] in order to present him with an account of the observations made in the late voyage to the Arctic Regions. I found him mighty busily employed in his study, arranging a huge pile of papers, maps, and instruments, from which he seemed very unwilling to be disturbed. "Pretty discoveries, indeed," said the Doctor, "for an inhabitant of this globe; but had they possessed the advantage of a lunar view of these continents, we should see a very different account of them."

I scarcely knew which way to look, at this observation, when the Doctor, perceiving my confusion, desired me to listen to him without skepticism, and he would communicate a portion of the wonders which he had seen in that delightful planet; with a full relation of which he proposed shortly to favour the world.

In his last aeronautic excursion,[2] he inadvertently set off with too much inflammable air, and was carried to a prodigious height, before he could possibly throw a single Number of your Magazine out; where, meeting with a vacuum, occasioned by the tail of an Aurora Borealis,[3] and a pressure from the surrounding element, the Doctor was whisked completely out of the atmosphere. Here he was taken in the eddy of a furious vortex, and whirled with inconceivable

---

[1] Fictional person

[2] In this instance, a trip by air balloon

[3] Light display in the sky

swiftness, in a spiral direction, towards the lunar regions. He laments extremely, that from the informal manner in which he was tossed about, being sometimes himself uppermost, and sometimes his balloon, he was precluded from making any observations in his flight; but he consoles himself by supposing that, as the moon was then at the full, these atoms were proceeding outwards to form some new planet, which he will have the satisfaction to give the first notice of.

Here I requested to know how he came to sustain respiration in such dreary parts, which we are taught to believe are quite a void. Heidelberg said that, so far from there being a void outside our atmosphere, he was almost choked with the pressure and commotion of the circumambient[4] element; but he begged me not to interrupt his relation any more, where) the accidents seemed to me unaccountable, as he would explain them in such a manner, in his publication, as should satisfy skepticism itself.

When he had arrived at that point, where the attractions of the moon and of our orb balance each other, his balloon was a considerable time in doubt what course to pursue; and would certainly have remained there in jeopardy to all eternity, had not a lucky impulse from one of the before mentioned eddies, inclined it some fractions of an inch (the exact quantity he intends computing) towards the former of these globes. It now assumed a rapid movement onwards, when the Doctor suddenly experienced a violent concussion on the head, which rendered him senseless. This was no other than a shower of meteoric stones, that was proceeding on a visit to our earth, and was attracted, by a sympathy or particles, to that uncivil invasion of the Doctor's person.

When Heidelberg recovered, he found himself landed near a large pit, that appears from our globe like a dimple on the moon's chin; and his balloon, at a

---

[4] Surrounding

little distance, entangled amongst the bushes. Nothing could be more enchanting than the surrounding scenery. Rows of poplars and of elms here presented a grateful shelter from the solar beams, and there the majestic oak and cedar a secure refuge to the eagle and the vulture. Fields of waving corn and of smiling meadows occupied the plains, bounded by groves of evergreens, where the birds, in ceaseless carols, filled the air with their melody. Here and there, too, on the plain, was seen a flock of sheep, and several grotesque figures, that looked like the Sylvan deities[5] of the Planet. There wanted only the meanderings of some rivulet, or the plashing of a waterfall, to constitute the place romantic ground.

Without in the least minding this charming prospect, Heidelberg had no sooner shook his limbs, and found them not materially bruised, than he set himself to measure a degree of the meridian[6] with the utmost alacrity. For this purpose he seized the branch of a tree, and was proceeding to the measurement of a base line, when he recollected that he must have some standard length to measure with. Why, take a foot, to be sure, thought he—But how much is a foot?—Twelve inches certainly—And how much is an inch?—The twelfth part of a foot. With that ready ingenuity which adapts itself to every emergency, the Doctor took up a large round stone, and, drawing several threads out of his handkerchief, which he fastened to each other, and round the stone, he suspended the apparatus to the branch of a tree, which projected laterally.

Then looking around, and making an allowance for the buoyancy and temperature of the atmosphere, as well as for the attraction of a mountain, which he observed peeping above the horizon, he took out his watch, and set his pendulum a swinging, to find what length would vibrate seconds at that latitude. After swinging it with great patience for two hours, the thread gave way, owing to the Doctor's jerking it rather

---

[5] Creatures of the forest
[6] Circle of longitude passing through a point on a planet's surface

too suddenly; but this he quickly replaced, and continued the experiment, computing the movements lost from the doctrine of chances; as he considered that, in observations of such delicacy, the seldomer they were repeated the better. Then shifting his point of vibration for a centre of suspension, he set the other end of his pendulum in motion, to verify the experiment.

After watching the thread, shaking about in the wind, for a time corresponding to the first, he took the means of all the observations; and having now obtained a determinate measure, he took down the apparatus. But he was again at a stand for want of something to compute angles with. While in this perplexity he perceived a strange figure, mounted upon an animal, somewhat resembling the fabled being of a griffin,[7] emerge from the woods, and advance swiftly towards him, with a kind of movement between bounding and flying. He was above the size of a man, but resembled him in other respects, except that his feet were parted, like a goat's. A single garment was passed with numerous folds around his body, and came upon his shoulder in a knot, that added a dignity to his benign aspect and silvery locks. The only notice that Heidelberg took of this grotesque apparition, was that of making him a sign of what he wanted.

The Lunarian pulled out a small theodolite,[8] which he offered to our philosopher, who immediately flung the instrument, with all his might, into the moon's dimple, and asked him, in a passion, if he did not know that the three angles of a triangle, had been discovered to be greater than two right angles?[9] The Lunarian, smiling, asked him in Latin, whether, since the moon was in motion through absolute space, at the same rate, and in precisely the contrary direction

---

[7] Mythological creature having the body of a lion and head/wings of an eagle

[8] A telescopic instrument for measuring angles

[9] Ninety degree angles

to that in which he had projected the instrument, it could be positively said to have moved or not?

Certainly, said the doctor, it has never stirred, but the moon ran against it; likewise, he observed, the gravity of the machine is increased, since it has approached the centre of the planet. Well then, returned the Lunarian, whose name was Zuloc, since my theodolite has not stirred from this, I will thank you to hand it me, as it was the best I had. But come, added he, do not trouble yourself any farther about this matter, for we have already ascertained the exact degree of curvature to every point, not only on our planet, but on yours also, even to the ten millionth part of an inch. If you will mount behind me, I will take you to my observatory, and also show you a few other things worthy of your notice.

They accordingly journeyed onwards; and in the way the Doctor obtained much curious information: but it is much to be regretted that his intelligence is very scanty, except in what relates to his favourite pursuits. Zuloc had heard nothing either of the knight Astolpho,[10] or of Father Kircher;[11] but the three ancient philosophers who were transported to the Lunar Regions to examine their natural productions, and who squandered their time in singing and dancing, left behind them some Latin manuscripts, which enabled the learned men to acquire that language. The inhabitants are divided into two classes; the Satyrs or learned men, and the Shepherds; and they reside almost wholly upon this side of the moon; the other being considered, from the absence of the Earth's light, as a kind of purgatory. They do not exceed nine or ten thousand altogether; but they live to a very advanced age, sometimes five hundred years. The shepherds live in the most charming state of primeval simplicity, tending their flocks, and dancing

---

[10] A fictional, heroic knight in French legend that uses magic to defeat his enemies

[11] Father Athanasius Kircher (1602-1680) was a scholar and leader in the fields of science and geology

to the melody of lutes[12] and Pans-pipes.[13] Almost all the philosophers have observatories and apparatus of their own; which they have brought to such perfection as to have made the most surprising discoveries. Their telescopes bring the sight within a very few miles of the terrestrial globe, so that they easily distinguish our towns and rivers, fleets and armies.

Heidelberg has procured the most accurate maps of the regions within our polar circles, together with tables of the curvature of the earth, to the hundredth part of an inch; from which there appears to be a difference of some inches between our two hemispheres, that will occasion an alteration of our geological systems. But their most profound discovery is that of perpetual motion, which they have applied to almost every subject; and which has enabled them to erect works in a very short space of time, which it would cost us ages to finish. By this they have constructed timekeepers, which will shew the longitude to the thousandth part of a second, for such as have occasion to visit the nether side of the Lunar Sphere, where they have not the advantage of observing this great dial of the Earth.

As our travellers were passing a pool of water, the first which Heidelberg had seen in the moon, he was astonished to observe it boiling and bubbling up, as if it had been in a cauldron. Zuloc acquainted him that this was occasioned by the extreme levity of the Lunar atmosphere; and were it not for the pneumatic apparatus for condensing fluids, which the philosophers have placed over certain wells, and which are kept constantly going, by their admirable invention of perpetual motion, all the waters of the moon would soon evaporate.

But the philosophers themselves will seldom be at the trouble of resorting to these wells; for, by the mixture of several kinds of air in a glass, and the mere

---

[12] String instrument with a long neck

[13] Also called a pan flute, short wind instrument similar to modern recorder

compression of a fillip,[14] they can obtain as much water as they please. Indeed, this is one of the means they have in contemplation for replenishing the ocean, which, in the infancy of the moon, was very considerable, but which has gradually vanished from the preceding cause. To illustrate this great tendency of the air to ignition, our Lunarian gently struck one of the trees with his cudgel[15], and immediately the whole forest was in flames. Zuloc has computed the Lunar atmosphere to be seven furlongs, two metres, and one inch, in height;[16] its weight, one million and six tons, three ounces, and two grains, troy; and that it would fill a globe, of the density of our earth, of one mile, nine inches, and three tenths, in diameter. These results Heidelberg has rendered according to the English method of computation; as all measures and weights, periods and quantities whatever, whether natural or artificial, are subdivided into decimal parts, for the convenience of mathematicians.

This conversation brought them to the observatory of Zuloc, which is situated in the principal town, near the left corner of the moon's mouth. It consisted of an immense concave of entire glass, with numerous doors and skylights, which could be opened or closed at pleasure, by mechanical appendages. The first objects that struck Heidelberg were a number of prodigious prisms, suspended to the ceiling. These were for separating and conducting the rays of the sun into different places.

Zuloc placed the Doctor beneath one of them, and decoyed the several rays of light into different bottles, so that Heidelberg was left perfectly in the dark, notwithstanding that the sun appeared to be shining full upon him; but he still experienced the influence of its heat. Our Lunarian now attracted away the heating beam, and Heidelberg was obliged speedily to decamp, or he would soon have been frozen to death.

---

[14] Stimulus
[15] Club
[16] Nearly one mile

The first of these phenomena is employed for producing artificial night,[17] when the astronomers wish to sleep; since the natural nights and days are too long for the common purposes of life; and the second is made use of in the torture of criminals.

This experiment convinced Heidelberg of the fantastic existence of colours; and he now thinks that the dispute concerning the nature of substances is for ever laid at rest. Zuloc proved to him, that neither colours nor bodies had any existence but in the imagination. He defines the last to be nothing but shape and extension; and accounts the resistance we meet with from solids, to be merely a quality, or affection, and not a real essence; just as melting is a faculty of lead, or heat an affection of fire. Tastes, smells, sounds, and shadows, he has also added to our list of substances. Heidelberg was rather startled at the admission of this last; but Zuloc assured him, that if he would only divest himself of the prejudice which the sound occasioned, he would perceive that it had a better title to that rank than many phantasms of the brain which are admitted, since it possessed the various properties of extension, motion, and figure.

The Doctor saw here barometers, which were supplied with that delightful metal oxygen, which has so lately been discovered on the earth, and has such levity as to swim on the water:[18] indeed no other substance would have been sensitive enough to be affected by the impressions of so volatile an atmosphere.

Here were substances, lying upon one another, whose parts had such an aversion, that though the undermost were pressed by the whole weight of the upper, yet their surfaces continued half an inch apart; and other bodies, so partial to each other, that their parts mutually overtopped nearly an inch.

---

[17] A darkness machine

[18] Metal oxides such as alkali metals Li, Na and K have a density less than water and float on its surface

Here were a variety of pendulums, vibrating, in all directions, without ceasing, by the application of that delightful invention of perpetual motion; and all the mathematic figures in nature, physically expressed, in the most beautiful manner, with silver wires—the spiral of Archimedes,[19] the cissoid,[20] the conchoid,[21] the caustic[22] and catenary[23] curves, and those two lines which are said continually to be approaching, yet never to meet.[24] These, indeed, seemed to incline to each other so much, near one of the doors of the observatory, that the Doctor slyly opened it, to see whether they met outside, but was delighted to find that they proceeded as far as the eye could reach without touching.

Lines, points, and circles, were flowing about in every direction, by the contrivance of perpetual motion; and forming pyramids and cylinders, by means of which, the most abstruse operations were performed from simple mechanism. In all these experiments, lunar children, from forty to fifty years of age, attended, to learn how to deduce ultimate causes from their physical effects. The Doctor, at this scene, rubbed his hands with delight—but, at the same time, received a knock on the head from a huge pendulum, and set his nails on fire with the friction of his hands. Zuloc cautioned him against making too sudden motions in an atmosphere so subject to combustion.

At one end of this delightful repository of the sciences, was another party of little Lunarians, from twenty to thirty years old, amusing themselves at a

---

[19] Archimedes (287-212 B.C.) Greek mathematician who first graphed a spiral that corresponds to the location of a point over time

[20] A unique curve derived from two curves and the intersection of single point

[21] A curve defined by another curve, a fixed point, and a set length

[22] A curve where the ray of light as reflected or refracted by a curve, are tangents

[23] A curve that a physical object makes when strung between two points due to the effects of gravity

[24] A hyperbola curve and a straight line asymptote can continuously approach each other but never meet

curious kind of play, called the Games of Ideas, to render them familiar with the operations of the understanding, in comparing and producing images.

There was a large dark chamber, which excluded every admission, but from two small windows; the one of glass, for exhibiting Ideas to the spectators outside; the other open, for receiving Images, but provided with a shutter inside. A Lunar child was turned into this room by itself, while one party outside was continually employed in throwing into the open window a quantity of toys and images, the symbols of ideas; and another at the glass window, demanding the exhibition of whatever they pleased, whether simple or compound words, sentences, or even orations; all of which were to be physically expressed by producing images in succession at the window. When the child was more than ten minutes searching for an idea, which, from the vast heap of objects, was often no easy task to find, it was considered as very stupid, and turned out.

When it wished to abstract, it shut both windows, and employed itself considering a subject without any extraneous appendages; but the sportsmen outside would seldom permit this indulgence long, as the inmate often made it a pretence for gaining time to arrange its ideas, and sometimes was even accused of going to sleep. Sometimes the same set of images had been so often called for, that the child had strung them together in an association; so that it often happened, that when a single object was demanded, it was so careless as to produce the whole string.

Some children were considered very witty for taking a handful of ideas, at half-hazard, and displaying them at the window.

As Heidelberg was endeavouring to look inside, the little Lunarian within held up an astronomer, a butterfly, and a thief, with several other objects, all in a string.

When our philosopher had sufficiently amused himself with admiring these wonderful objects, Zuloc pressed him to partake of a Lunar repast; but he felt himself so much affected by the fineness of the air, that he was obliged, however unwillingly, to express his intention of departing from this delightful planet. Zuloc accordingly repaired his balloon, and provided him with an aereal dipping needle,[25] for pointing out the several objects he should pass in his flight; and an instrument for ascertaining the position, and measuring the distances, between bodies not in view.

The only phenomenon which Heidelberg observed in his passage, was a view of the upper region of the terrestrial atmosphere, oscillating to and fro, like the pendulum of a clock, from the joint influence of the sun and moon.

Among the valuable discoveries Professor Heidelberg has brought with him, is an account of a comet that will fall into the sun in the year 2715, which by that time will stand in great need of such a reinforcement, and which will cause a great disturbance in our system, by altering the centres of gyration and gravity, and occasioning an anomaly in our tables of equation and the tides. From this comet Zuloc intends sequestrating a part of the tail, in its passage, to densify the Lunar atmosphere withal; also a table of the specific gravities-of Lunar bodies, and a method of determining the most difficult problems from impossible premises; all of which will, together with the before-mentioned improvements in natural knowledge, be laid in due time before the Royal Society of Edinburgh![26] A MIDSHIPMAN.

P. S.—I forgot to say that Professor Heidelberg's great work is to be dedicated to Lord----------.

Depend upon hearing from me again before next month.

---

[25] An instrument used to show the angle between the horizon and a planet's magnetic field

[26] Scotland's Royal Society of Edinburgh founded in 1783

Sir Thomas Charles Morgan
(1783-1843)

Introduction
Glimpses of Other Worlds

The year 1835 ushered in a host of balloon hoax science fictions stories. This was largely due to the public's fascination with the possibility of balloon trips across the Atlantic that would take a fraction of the two weeks required by ship. Daring explorers were no longer those of the sea, but of the air. "Aeronauts" became the coined term.

January kicked off the balloon story barrage with the science fiction story "Leaves from an Aeronaut," published in *The Knickerbocker; or, New York Monthly Magazine*. Penned by Willis Gaylord Clark, it tells of a man's five-mile journey into the atmosphere after having constructed his own balloon.

Edgar Allan Poe was next. His first manuscript of "The Unparalleled Adventure of One Hans Pfaall" dates to April or May and was first published during June in the *Southern Literary Messenger*. Where the protagonist in "Leaves from an Aeronaut" only travels five miles into the air, Hans Pfaall journeys to the moon; though 15 years after Professor Heidelbergus did it in "A Visit to the Lunar Sphere."

Yet the public had not had their fill of sci-fi balloon tales during 1835. In late August and early September, Richard Adams Locke published "Great Astronomical Discoveries Lately Made by Sir John Herschel, L.L.D. F.R.S. &C. at the Cape of Good Hope" in *The Sun* (New York). John Herschel was a popular explorer of the day. The public knew he was exploring Cape Good Hope and was awaiting news of his findings. Therefore, at the time of publication Herschel had no knowledge of the hoax being played on him (and the public at large) by Locke. The story claimed that a powerful telescope "twenty-four feet in diameter" and tipping the scales at "14,826 lbs. or nearly seven tons after being polished" had been built. Through the telescope Herschel had purportedly seen strange animals on the moon, and flying Lunarians.

From September 2-5, 1835, during the height of the Locke hoax, Poe's tale was republished by the New York *Transcript*. Still, Poe was not finished with balloon hoaxes and neither was *The Sun*. Nine years later, in April of 1844, *The Sun* published his "[Balloon Hoax]." February of 1849 also saw the publication of Poe's "Mellonta Tauta" in *Godey's Lady's Book* about a balloon trip that begins on April Fool's Day, 2848. Han Pfaall's adventure likewise begins on April Fool's Day.

But let's return to 1835. Right in the middle of it—July—*The Metropolitan Magazine* published "Glimpses of Other Worlds" by English author and physician, Sir Thomas Charles Morgan (husband of the popular novelist Lady Morgan). Like the others, a fantastic balloon ride played a part in the story. To be exact, "an oxyhydro-safety-high-pressure-steam-balloon, of one-thousand-and-one-elephant-power" used to reach the lunar capital, "Munchausenopolis." It is a story of many firsts in the sci-fi genre.

By using "talismanic head-gear," the protagonist visits the sun and tells of the people he finds there.

This is the first visit to the sun in a science fiction short story, as well as the first to disclose a ride on a comet controlled by "a phial or two of concentrated essence of gravitation." It further gives us the first short story to recount inhabitants at the center of the earth.

"Glimpses of Other Worlds" is published for the first time since 1835.

Glimpses of Other Worlds
(1835)

"One sun by day, by night ten thousand shine."
Young.[1]

ONE FINE STARRY night I was taking a solitary stroll, *"nescio quid meditans nugarum,"*[2] when feeling somewhat fatigued, I leaned against a grassy bank, and gazing upwards, gradually fell into a reverie. How long it lasted I cannot tell, but it seemed to be gradually sliding into a slumber, when methought it was interrupted by the appearance of a venerable old man of strange aspect, standing before me. His few scattered hairs, and his beard, were of a silvery whiteness, and Time had ploughed many a deep furrow in his brow.

But independently of baldness and wrinkles, (for these I knew were the attributes of most Octogenarians,)[3] there was a peculiar stamp of Antiquity in his physiognomy;[4] he seemed the very prosopopaeia[5] of Old Age; nor should I have been surprised to have heard that he had numbered more centuries than one. His form nevertheless was tall, and tolerably erect, and his features contemplative and regular—save that his nose seemed, by some unaccountable accident, to have been curtailed of its original fair proportions.

"What are you staring at?" he somewhat unceremoniously asked.

---

[1] Edward Young (1681-1765), "Night Thoughts," Section IX, Line 728
[2] "Thinking about nonsense"
[3] Elderly
[4] Physical appearance
[5] Personification

A little startled by the abruptness of the interrogatory, I replied that I delighted to indulge in a survey of the nocturnal sky, and to admire

> "Those bright millions of the heavens
> Of which the least full Godhead had proclaimed
> And thrown the gazer on his knee.
>   All on wing,
> In motion all, yet what profound repose!
> What fervid action—yet no noise—as awed
> To silence by the presence of their Lord!"

"Twaddledum-dee,"[6] replied he with a contemptuous drawl; "and pray how much do you know about 'those bright millions?' how much------"

"Perhaps," retorted I, waxing indignant, "perhaps all that I do know, and all that you do not know, would make together a very thick book."

Hereupon a sort of chuckling sound, like a hysterical giggle, proceeded from his lips, (or rather, his throat,) and fell with so demoniacal an insolence upon my ear, that the tips of my fingers tingled with a longing to give his epitomized nose a hearty tweak.

"Boy!" said he, "you know not what you say, nor whom you address. Before your great grandfather was christened, I had unraveled more of the celestial arcana than Copernicus,[7] Tycho Brahe,[8] or Newton.[9] They sat ensconced in their closets and observatories to watch through their telescopes the motions of distant worlds. I took a nearer station, and required but my naked eye. Nature herself intended me to be

---

[6] Lady Morgan (1781-1859)—the wife of the author, Sir Thomas Morgan (1783-1843)—used a character named Lord Mount-Twaddledum in her 1833 play *Dramatic Scenes from Real Life*, published two years before "Glimpses of Other Worlds"
[7] Nicolaus Copernicus (1473-1543) was a mathematician and astronomer during the Renaissance Age
[8] Tycho Brahe (1546-1601) was a Danish astronomer
[9] Isaac Newton (1642-1727) was an English mathematician and physicist who formulated the laws of motion and gravity

the phoenix of travellers and discoverers. At my birth the bumps of inquisitiveness and locomotiveness were so fully developed in my phrenological conformation,[10] that I narrowly escaped being exhibited as a *lusus naturae* with two heads. What are all the wanderings of your travellers and navigators compared with my peregrinations? Your travels in Bokhara, forsooth—your tours of Spain and Italy—your wanderings in New South Wales—your overland journeys to India—or your over ice journeys to the North Pole? Why before I was out of my teens, I had explored every nook of our little globe, and then—as Alexander[11] wept because there were no more worlds to conquer—I wept because there were no more to visit."

"Quite a toss up which of you was the greater baby," said I, nettled at his conceit.

"The Fates had decreed, however," he continued, "that my travelling mania should not be balked. My guardian genius appeared to me, and presented me with this cap, *ycleped a GOLGOTHA, videlicet*, the place of a skull." (Here he pulled from his head a very odd-shaped concern, apparently made of Indian rubber, with a poke or leaf behind and before.) "This was to be a preservative against all sudden and extreme changes of temperature, according as this leaf—or that—was worn in front; the leaves being, as you see, marked 'hot' and 'cold,' like the spouts of a bath."

"Well!" said I, "I have seen many varieties of travelling-caps, but never aught like this. Your guardy should have taken out a patent for his invention, and advertised its wonderful properties in the *Times* or the *Morning Herald*."

"I forgot to add," he continued, "that my genius, in promising to gratify my taste for travelling, furnished me with a time-glass,[12] warning me that the running

---

[10] Study of the shape of the skull that purported to evidence superior metal capacities in certain areas of science and the arts
[11] Alexander the Great (356-323 B.C.) was a Macedonian conqueror who never lost in battle
[12] Hourglass

out of its sands should mark the period of my sojourn in each world. We happened just then to be standing on the shores of the Lake of Geneva; a boat crowded with people was just pushing off. 'Jump into that boat,' said my genius, 'and when you are half way over—fear not—and upset it.'"

("O! the savage!" said I aside.)

"I followed my instructions to the letter, and presently some score of poor devils were struggling for their lives in the blue waters of the Leman Lake. For my own part I felt myself sinking rapidly through the eddying abyss—deeper and more deep······"

"Facilis descensus Averni!"[13] I exclaimed; "you must have thought yourself in a fair way indeed of visiting another world!"

"For myself," he replied, "I had little apprehension; but I much fear my ill-fated fellow-passengers very soon found themselves in a world, which amid all my various pilgrimages I have not yet visited. Ere long, I reached my destination—even the interior of our own earth, a world undreamt of by the most fanciful of our theorists—unsuspected by the profoundest of our philosophers;—though we have carried it in our bosom since first our orb was sent whirling through space. And yet—is its existence any thing to be marvelled at? Shall each drop of water teem throughout with life and motion, while the globe itself is animated but at its external shell?"

"Pshaw!" said I somewhat impatiently, "a truce to philosophizing. Tell me what you saw. What were the inhabitants like? 'Anthropophagi,[14] and men whose heads do grow beneath their shoulders.'"

"Not at all," he replied; "they very much resemble ourselves—perhaps a better-looking race of men. The complexions, especially of the subterranean ladies, are brilliantly fair. There is no sun to scorch by day, nor moon to smite by night!"

---

[13] Easy is the descent

[14] Mythical race of cannibals whose face is on their chests

"Faith," said I, "notwithstanding the resulting improvement to the complexions of the natives, I can scarcely conceive the absence of those luminaries a mighty blessing."

"Your remark only shows your ignorance, my friend," observed the old gentleman coolly. "What should they want with a great flaring sun, I should like to know? Their world is a snug amphitheatre, not more than a hundred miles broad—you may see across on a fine day—so that it may be imagined the crust which envelopes them is of no slight thickness, and as good as an extra blanket. Besides, it would do your heart good to see the fires they keep up in their natural stoves—of a magnitude undreamt of in your philosophy. You may have seen indeed the tops of their chimney funnels, called by learned men in these upper regions Ætna, Vesuvius, and Hecla. When that mighty eruption buried in ruins the cities of Herculaneum and Pompeii, the innocent subterranean natives had only piled on a few additional sticks to commemorate the birth of an heir apparent to the throne."

"By Jupiter! Then," exclaimed I, "it is to be hoped you gave them a hint to make no more such bonfires. What may be sport to them is death to us! But tell me—how do they manage to illumine your lower world?"

"It illuminates itself," he replied, "without the aid of sunbeams or gaspipes—oil lamps or tallow candles. The whole arched ceiling of the internal empire is studded with diamonds, carbuncles,[15] and the rarest gems; while in the midst is suspended a colossal chandelier 'of one entire and perfect chrysolite,'[16] which emits and reflects a splendour, that would dim the glories of our meridian sun."

"Still," said I, "this artificial glare must be very inferior to our glorious sunshine."

---

[15] Cut jewel

[16] Green-yellow gemstone

"All moonshine!" returned he contemptuously. "Verily in this fair and happy world my time sped on rapid wings; but—do not laugh at me—shall I confess my weakness?—I fell in love! Ere I was on my guard the bright form of a subterranean houri[17] captivated my too, too susceptible heart! Ah! she was in truth passing lovely—such as your gross senses can never picture—her soft eyes of cerulean blue—her skin whiter than drifted snow, and smooth as monumental alabaster—her lips—"

"As red as a peony, and her hair as dark and glossy as Warren's blacking,"[18] I chimed in, cutting short the matter; for the old beau was getting intolerably commonplace and sentimental. "There are similes for your paragon of loveliness. I haven't a doubt she was excessively pretty; but pray spare me the detail of her charms."

"So be it, then," said he, sighing most heart-breakingly, from the very depths of his stomach. "It is very certain I was an egregious ass thus to plunge head over ears in love. Full well I knew that the years of my brief sojourn were numbered from the beginning. The sands of my glass had already well nigh run out, and my genius appeared to prepare me for my departure. Mine was indeed a cruel, but inevitable lot! I beheld my ladylove for the last time—our interview was heart-rending—we bade each other a long—an agonizing farewell, and exchanged vows of eternal love, and locks of hair. My genius reconducted me to these upper regions, through a well-concealed trap-door, which opens among the newly-discovered caves near Mitchelstown, County of Cork, Ireland."

"I dare say" (was my most unfeeling remark) "you were extremely glad to return, and quickly forgot your vows and your ladylove."

---

[17] Type of pure, ideal young woman who does not age

[18] Warren's Blacking Warehouse was a notorious boot polish sweatshop where many children and indigent worked in England, including Charles Dickens (1812-1870) when he was only 12 years old in 1824

"You do me grievous wrong," he replied with earnestness. "Those scenes—that face (though full more than a century has since elapsed) still live vividly in my recollection.

> 'The hallowed form is ne'er forgot
> Which first love traced,
> Still it lingering haunts the greenest spot
> On memory's waste!'

If I thought, by upsetting another bark—ay, were it on the deepest of lakes—that I should be enabled to revisit those lovely regions, upset it I would, though it were freighted with all England!"

"By the powers!" said I, "then, thank you for the hint. I shall take especial care, my friend, how you and I are ever fellow-voyagers in the same wherry!"[19]

"To drive away my melancholy," resumed the traveller, "I projected a trip to the moon. The diversion was very *à propos;* for such was my despondency, I fear I might otherwise have become a *lunatic.* My indefatigable genius speedily provided me with a mode of conveyance in the shape of an oxyhydro-safety-high-pressure-steam-balloon, of one-thousand-and-one-elephant-power. Accordingly, on a fine evening in the merry month of May, I set out on my aerial voyage, with a fair breeze, high spirits, and three days' prog.[20] At daybreak on the third morning the pale cliffs of the Moon hove in sight on my weatherbow. I can see them now," he continued, looking upward at the bright orb; "do you not see the corner of that island-like spot near the centre? Before noon I was safely moored at the foot of Mons Pentakusiakron, in north latitude 53° 47', and in longitude 25' west of Munchausenopolis, the Lunar capital. I proceeded to the city, and having delivered my letters of introduction, I was soon most comfortably established in the forty-second story of

---

[19] Small row boat for shuttling passengers
[20] British slang for scrounged food

one of the grandest mansions which the metropolis could boast."

"Pardon the interruption," said I; "pray where did you obtain your letters of introduction?"

"Forged by my genius," said my narrator, coolly. "My first care was to take a survey of the Lunar Lions. I was immeasurably astonished at the inconceivable richness and fertility of the soil. Half an acre of land abundantly sufficed to support half a dozen families in affluence. Ten crops per annum were esteemed but a moderate number. Every where might be seen towering trees, producing fruits, daintier far than the pine or the pomegranate; every where there sprung up spontaneously the rarest exotics of most varied hue, and richest perfume. Nor was the amazing fecundity confined to any isolated spot; formerly the whole moon was an Arabia Felix.[21] But, alas! for the uncertainty of all lunary (as well as all sublunary) things; after ages had rolled peacefully by, of a sudden, convulsing earthquakes and vomiting volcanoes, till then smouldering and unsuspected, burst forth in almost every part with dire effect: like the outburst of some hereditary disease, which has lain for years slumbering in the constitution. Nearly the whole surface of the devoted orb was desolated and destroyed, and not more than one in a hundred of her inhabitants escaped the wholesale destruction, and lived to tell the dreadful tale. And now that surface, once so bright and beauteous, and which to us still looks so mild, so calm, and happy, is in reality blotched, and furrowed, and desolated by floods of lava—like some fair soft face, seamed and scarred by the ravages of relentless small-pox."

"Pity it is," said I, feelingly, "they cannot discover some mode of vaccination."

"But there is still," he continued, "there is still one bright redeeming spot—an oasis, which seems the more beautiful in contrast with the surrounding wreck.

---

[21] Ancient section of Arabia with ideal growing conditions

Here it was that I sojourned, here still stood the capital, and here lived that little remnant which the volcano and the earthquake had spared. But their existence was one of uncertainty and dread. Alas! even now, my kind friends may be numbered with those who have been." Here he thrust his little finger into his eye, and attempted, but in vain, to manufacture a tear. "On our earth we have one instance of large cities similarly destroyed, and their fate excites abundant sympathy and curiosity among the learned of every age and country. In the moon a Herculaneum is annually added to the hecatombs[22] which have already fallen. A feeble barrier is indeed opposed to the inroads of the resistless lava, by raising vast embankments"

"Just as the Hollanders build their mud walls to keep the sea out," suggested I, aptly.

"But the unequal warfare," he continued, "cannot last long. The molten flood is but a type of our own deluge. Ere this, doubtless, the last page of lunar history has been recorded; perchance the actual destiny of some lunar inhabitant is even now realizing the imaginary doom of Lionel Verney, the last man!"[23]

"If so," said I, struck with the happy coincidence which occurred to me, "we may speak with great appropriateness of the man in the moon. But perhaps some Noah, with his family, may have been found worthy of an ark?"

"All of my acquaintance," he replied, "I can testify were persons of the most amiable disposition and noble character. By-the-bye," continued he, in a livelier strain, "their humour and hospitality reminded me not a little of the inhabitants of our neighbouring isle,[24]

"'The emerald gem of the western world.'

---

[22] Extensive loss of life

[23] Lionel Verney was the only remaining man on earth in Mary Shelley's (1797-1851) post-apocalyptic novel published in 1826 and titled *The Last Man*

[24] Ireland

"A popular rumour, moreover, was prevalent, that 'once in the flight of ages past,' the moon was uninhabited, and that a balloon from earth, freighted with aerial voyagers, had, by some unknown fatality, escaped the sphere of terrestrial attraction, and approached within the range of the lunar gravitation. From this tradition, and from other circumstances, especially from meeting with a curious collection of lunar melodies, I was led to the theory that the moon had been colonized by a balloonfull of Milesian progenitors."

"Doubtless," said I, "quite sufficient *data* to furnish so interesting a conclusion."

"I was anxious," he resumed, "to project a tour of discovery; with this view I notified my plans to the principal lunar *literati,* and suggested that we should form a caravan among ourselves, for the purpose of exploring distant regions, and perhaps on our return recording the result of our travels, for the edification of all whom it might concern, in three volumes post octavo."[25]

"I should think it a very doubtful question," said I, "whether you ever *would* return. The boiling mountains spitting around you, like so many roasting apples, must have been rather unfavourable to your picnic party."

"In truth, we were not blind to the probable dangers of the attempt. Nevertheless, in the glorious cause of science, a small band of enthusiasts were found, willing to undertake the arduous duty, and steel their souls to the perils of the way. Government had guaranteed in the event of our not returning within a prescribed period, to send out a party, headed by one Captain Forward, to search for our bodies, and provide us with a decent burial. Cheered by this assurance we set forth boldly. I will not attempt a detail of the perilous, soul-stirring adventures we met with; suffice

---

[25] Book where each sheet is folded into 8 leaves

it to say, one-fifteenth of our number returned in safety, highly gratified by the wonderful discoveries which had rewarded our toils. I regret I cannot even satisfy your curiosity in particular, and mankind's in general, regarding the statistical phenomena of the moon, as my period of stay had elapsed before the first edition of our Travels came from the press, otherwise I should certainly have provided myself with a copy."

"Mankind have indeed sustained a loss," said I.

"I was very much struck with the extraordinary number and elevation of the lunar mountains. The earth has nothing like their lowest. Compared to the moon, it is a dead flat. Wales, Scotland, Switzerland, are as flat as pancakes."

"You surely forget Mont Blanc?" said I.

"A molehill!" said he

"Chimborazo?" said I.

"An anthill!" said he.

"Cotopaxi?" said I.

"A dunghill!" said he. "On the side turned away from us I observed one very lofty and peculiarly-shaped mountain, exactly like a nose, with a sarcastic turn upward. On closer observation, I discovered a remarkable fact. The rising and falling of the surface are there so alternated and proportioned, that when thrown in relief against the sky, it exhibits an exact counterpart of the profile of the ex-chancellor!"[26]

"Indeed!" said I, "then that very probably is the reason why the moon is ashamed to show us that side of her physiognomy. Philosophers have ever wondered why she always takes such especial care to keep the same position of her face eternally grinning upon us,

---

[26] The ruling chancellor prior to this story's publication was Henry Peter Brougham (1778-1868), founder of the *Edinburgh Review*, who decried scientific principles found by Sir William Herschel (1738-1822), the explorer hoax in 1835 by Richard Adams Locke's (1800-1871) publication of "Great Astronomical Discoveries Lately Made by Sir John Herschel, L.L.D. F.R.S. &C. at the Cape of Good Hope"

by twirling on her axis in exactly the same period of time as she revolves in her orbit."

"I did not trouble myself," replied the traveller, "with speculating upon the cause of the odd coincidence. But now my visit was drawing to a close, and, to tell you the truth, this did not cause me unalloyed regret; for highly as I was delighted with the kindness, and charmed by the affability of my little circle of friends, I could not but feel the insecurity of my position; and my philanthropy did not go quite so far as to reconcile me to the idea of being boiled alive in their company.

"Accordingly I prepared to visit the grand centre of our system—the sun. I must say, my anticipations were raised high indeed. When I considered how gigantic in size, and how unrivalled in splendour the solar orb appears even at the great distance at which we are placed, when I considered that it was the almost immoveable centre of light, and life, and motion, around which numerous and vast planets were borne unerringly in their concentric orbits, I expected to behold a spectacle of magnificence, such as no dream, no imagination had shadowed forth, and which the boldest eye and the stoutest heart could not regard without quailing."

"Of course," said I, "you took care to adjust your cap accordingly; or else the heat might chance to prove a damper to your delight?"

"I very naturally thought as you do," he replied. "I was fully prepared for a degree of heat which would put the virtues of my talismanic head-gear to the severest test. But, alas! 'Sad was the hour, and luckless was the day.'"

"What in the name of fortune happened to you," interrupted I; "were you trussed and spitted like a Christmas turkey?"

"Pray," asked he, abruptly, "do you perceive any thing peculiar in my face—in my features?"

"Why—ahem!" said I, wishing to shirk the delicate query; "really—ahem—perhaps if I were asked my opinion—ahem."

"I beg you won't mince the matter," said he.

"Why then, I should—ahem—very delicately hint that—the end of your nasal organ was absent without leave."

"And how do you suppose I lost it?" he asked.

"Can't guess," said I.

"Mortified by frost in the sun," he replied.

"Haw! haw! haw!" affecting to humour the joke, "A very novel idea—frost in the sun! You are pleased to wax facetious, he! he! he!"

"I speak in sober sadness," returned the old gent, gravely; "no giggling matter, I assure you. So sudden, and so intense was the change of temperature, that before I could twirl round my cap on my head, the tip of my nose turned the colour of a blue-bottle fly, and falling at my feet, with one snivel gave up the ghost. Conceive my feelings when I witnessed the irremediable catastrophe. You may grin, if you choose; but let me tell you, before the loss of the much lamented tip, I was the 'glass of fashion and the mould of form.'"

"Nay, my friend, I haven't the slightest doubt of the fact," said I, looking as serious as possible, and thrusting my tongue into the cheek, turned away from him. "But you have not yet explained the riddle."

"There is no riddle to explain," he replied. "The sun, indeed, emits heat, but retains none. His rays are icy until they have been rubbed hot by passing through our air. Do you not observe that the top of a mountain, though nearer the sun, is colder than the valley below? Do not always trust to mere appearances. Look at the moon and stars. They seem bright enough from here; if you could take a closer view, you would find them duller than the eye of a boiled salmon. Then consider the case of *gravitation.* Philosophers say all bodies tend to the centre; would not that point seem to contain the accumulated aggregate of all attraction and weight? Yet they tell us again, a body *at* the centre would have no weight at all. I tell you, the little warmth which the sun can boast at home, is squeezed from his own rays, when reflected back by the earth and the moon."

"That's passing odd!" said I, utterly bewildered by the subtle web of reasoning, and the erudite illustrations of my travelled friend. "One would have thought, in sooth, that sending rays to warm the sun, would be sending coals to Newcastle with a vengeance."

"Such is the fact, nevertheless," he replied, "as I learned to my cost. *Experto crede!*[27] You can form but a meagre idea of the intensity of cold, unless you can conceive five thousand degrees below zero of Fahrenheit; unless you can imagine a lump of solid mercury or frozen alcohol feeling in your hand hotter than a live coal; unless you can fancy the North Pole blazing like a kitchen fire—unless—"

"Grammercy!" I exclaimed, "I give it up in despair; the stretch of imagination is beyond me. On this view of the matter I wonder no longer that one end of your nose fell off, but that the other end stayed on."

"And when at last," he continued, "I was domiciled in the solar world, what was there to repay me for the catastrophe of my first *debut?* The best lodging which gold or grumbling could procure, was such that any pig would have rejected with an indignant grunt. And then the natives! I thought, at first, I had been transplanted among a nation of baboons; but in verity, to a genuine, gentlemanly, well-behaved baboon the comparison is most unfair. In intellect and person they appeared to me a remove below the ugliest and stupidest of monkey-race. During one half of the year all were in a state of the most besotted drunkenness, and during the other half, all lay torpid like so many moles or bats. Yet here was I doomed to drag out the full period of my appointed sojourn. Miserable as it was, I could not abridge, by a single hour, the fixed duration of this hated imprisonment."

---

[27] Exemplary proposition

"You have no reason to complain," interrupted I, "this was the tax you were destined to pay for your privileges. The course of your travels, like that of true love, was not to run smooth."

"If you had been in my place, my friend," he replied, "I calculate you would not have practised the philosophy you preach. In vain did I shake my glass, and curse my genius, for making its neck so infernally narrow. Each obstinate grain of sand dropped deliberately and methodically through—much more slowly, I am very sure, than usual. No Siberian exile ever exulted half so much at the dawning of the day which was to restore him to his long-lost home, as did I, when the last gram had run out, and released me from my odious thraldom.[28] 'With curses not loud but deep,' I departed, and as I went, I shook the dust from off my feet!—

"To wind up my tour of our own system, I next resolved to pay a visit to one of those strange bodies called comets. It was about the middle of the last century, and a huge fellow was then bowling away towards the sun, but as yet some couple of billions of miles distant. I found all the inhabitants of the Nucleus busily preparing for the gaieties of the approaching carnival—that is their passage of the perihelion, which, occurring in the comet I speak of only once in seventy years, was of course made a season of the most boisterous hilarity."

"I should think so, indeed," said I, "seventy Christmas-days rolled into one! Our ballad says, Christmas comes but once a-year,[29] &c. what should we say, if it came only once in seventy years?"

"We should say it was rather long in coming," said the old gentleman, with *naivete.* "I should mention, moreover, that this was the only holiday kept at all, nor was it less ardently longed for, than chimney-sweeps anticipate May-day.[30]

---

[28] State of being under the bondage of another
[29] Early English ballad, author unknown
[30] May 1st

"During this long period," continued he, "they had had abundance of time to spin a new tail; the old one having paid toll in the former passage; for, you must know, the sun, as lord of the manor, levies this his tribute in proportion as the comets trespass upon his domain. On we came with the glorious appendage, 'streaming like a meteor in the troubled *space!*' I will not shock your credulity, by attempting to give an accurate estimate of its computed magnitude. The cometists were justly proud of it, as they had spared neither labour nor expense in its creation, and certainly they had exceeded their most sanguine expectations. All other rivals, including the Safety-Opposition Comet,[31] which appeared at the end of last year may hide their diminished tails. I speak within bounds, when I say the tail was many hundred times as large as itself!"

"I don't doubt it at all," said I. "Why, we have a comet attached to our own earth, ay, even to our own little corner of it, a very queer and very mischievous comet too, whose *tail* is computed to be *forty* times the size of itself! But what, after all, is the use of your mighty tails?"

"Ah! thereby hangs a tale," said my traveller. "Of what use is the rudder to a ship? Such unsubstantial aerial things are comets, that had it not been for this providential appendage, and for the consummate skill of the cometists themselves, every stray star in the heavens would have jostled us, by his attraction, from our course, and sent us floundering Heaven knows whither! I laughed when I thought of your conceited astronomers peeping through their puny telescopes, and calculating the laws of our motion, and the elements of our orbit! With the aid of a phial or two of concentrated essence of gravitation, we could accelerate or retard our speed, and with the help of our redoubled tail we regulated our course almost at pleasure."

---

[31] Reference to Halley's Comet that appears every 75 years, which it did in 1834

"And in what direction *did* you please to regulate it?"

"At first we steered right for the sun's eye, but apprehending the danger of too close a contact, we suddenly put the helm hard-a-lee,[32] and passed our perihelion[33] at about two comets' length. For my own part, I found nothing so very delightful in these vaunted halcyon-days. It was fiery hot, as you may well imagine, and the sun's atmosphere, being composed of extract of comets' tails, was so close and suffocating, that I fancied, all the time, my head was dipped in a tureen of pea-soup. A London fog in November is *vacuum* compared to it."

"It only proves," I sagely observed, "that the *comical* natives have the same failings as we earthites. They prize things, valueless in themselves, in proportion to their rarity. I suppose that what they deemed Paradise, because it happened once in seventy years, they would have thought Purgatory had it happened once a week!"

"I suppose so. Well, the infatuated people revelled in their fancied happiness, little recking of the catastrophe in store for them. All this time, you may be sure, the sun's absorbing powers were not idle. No sooner had we emerged from the *soupy* atmosphere, whose amazing density had put in requisition our whole stock of quintessence of gravity, to work our way onward, than we found ourselves in a lamentable plight indeed, sweeping 'through the horizontal misty air, shorn of our *tail.*' So immoderately had the foolish people been intoxicated with their imaginary joy during the continuance of these *Saturnalia,*[34] that the depression which usually succeeds uncommon excitement would have been sufficient alone to impart a very woe-begone expression to the phizzes of every one. Away then we slunk with our tail between our legs, like—"

---

[32] Side away from the wind

[33] Point in the orbit of a comet when it is closest to the sun

[34] Wild partying

"How now, old gentleman!" said I tartly, "'twas but a minute ago you said, that like Bopeep's sheep,[35] you had left your tail behind you; and now you tell me—"

"Don't be snappish, my friend," said the veteran, gravely. "I spoke but figuratively, to express our consummate discomfiture. And besides we still had a remnant—a small apology for a tail."

"Enough to swear by, I suppose," said I.

"Yes, but not enough to steer by, as the sequel will show. A cabinet council had been convened in our emergency, and a venerable elder, whose thin hairs, twelve passages of the perihelion had silvered, was impressively haranguing his listening brethren. I found that the whole upshot of his eloquent discourse was to beseech them not to lose an hour in spinning a new tail. In the midst of his address an interruption occurred—'Planet a-head!' shouted the astronomer on the lookout, at the mizentop[36] of the observatory. 'Planet a-head!' echoed the first-lieutenant. Forthwith all was confusion and dismay, scampering hither and thither; every one speaking, no one listening! I was cool as a cucumber, but joined in the row through sympathy. During the confusion I took an opportunity of peering through the gigantic national telescope, whose powerful optics had detected the dreaded object, and sure enough I saw, apparently not very far distant, a huge Leviathan[37] of space, accompanied by four smaller fry, dancing as if they were mad through the regions of vacuity. I was presently informed that this was the planet Jupiter, with his four attendant moons, and that the astronomer royal had just announced, as the result of his calculations, that according to our respective courses, we bade fair, in the space of a few hours, to come with a deuce of a *bump* against the very heart of the planet."

---

[35] "Little Bo Peep" is a traditional English nursery Rhyme
[36] Lookout platform secured to the top of the lower mast
[37] Monster

"In truth," said I, "a most interesting and consolatory fact for the edification of your luckless inhabitants of the lesser body."

"I confess, it seemed to me a very embarrassing situation," replied the traveller, "to say the least of it. Nevertheless the energies of the cometists, instead of being paralyzed, seemed even invigorated by the dangers that threatened. By the dint of working our fragment of a tail so vigorously and intermittingly that I thought we should have worked it fairly off, and diminishing our specific gravity, by throwing over a quantity of ballast and heavy material, principally some ponderous quartos of metaphysical treatises, we escaped the more formidable evil, and only ran foul of the rearmost moon. This had been provided for; so giving three hearty cheers, we soon pushed off again, with the help of several long wooden poles, and without any serious accident, except that the astronomer royal, who happened to be picking his teeth at the time with a pair of compasses, nearly broke his principal grinder by the suddenness of the shock. However the collision had the effect of materially altering our course, for the orbit, which before was a very elongated ellipse, suddenly became a hyperbola, and the astronomers informed us we were on the high road to some other system. This reminded me that it was high time I too should extend my peregrinations[38] beyond the narrow limits of our own system. Accordingly—"

But at this point of my traveller's narration, I felt myself smartly hit on various parts of the face. I fancied the old fellow was peppering me for his amusement with a *peaspitter,*[39] and in incipient wrath, I was taking off my shoe to hurl at his fragment of a nose, but a blow, sharper than any, struck my right eyelid; when lo! on a sudden, the stars had disappeared, and with them my venerable friend! I looked up—the heavens were overcast and

---

[38] Traveling from place-to-place

[39] Hollow tube through which hard peas are blown out

threatening, and the big hailstones fell thick upon me. I rushed homeward, musing on what I had heard, and wondering what adventures might have befallen our traveller in his tour to other systems.

LYDIA MARIA CHILD
(1802-1880)

Introduction
Hilda Silfverling, A Fantasy

Lydia Maria Child is best known today for her stand against slavery and promotion of the rights of American Indians. The musical version of her Thanksgiving poem, "Over the River and Through the Woods," is still sung by children.

She is seldom mentioned as a female pioneer in the science fiction genre; perhaps due to the large shadow Mary Shelley casts in this space. Yet this American writer deserves a prominent place in the genre due to two groundbreaking short stories of hers: "Hilda Silfverling, A Fantasy" and "The Rival Mechanicans." Both are included in this collection and were published in the 1840s.

"Hilda Silfverling, A Fantasy" was her first sci-fi tale. It was published in 1845 in *The Columbian Magazine*. And, assuming none of the anonymously published sci-fi stories before it were penned by a female, Lydia Maria Child wrote the first science fiction short story by a woman as Catherine Crowe did with her werewolf tale in *Shifters: The Best Werewolf Short Stories 1800-1849.*

That alone is enough to place Child on a pedestal, but the story holds another first in science fiction. "Hilda Silfverling, A Fantasy," set in 1740, is the first short story involving cryopreservation. In it the chemist can "suspend animation in living creatures, and restore it at any prescribed time."

Rightfully, "Hilda Silfverling, A Fantasy," had a good run in the 19th century; being republished a number of times. In the following century it inexplicably fell off the radar screen of sci-fi anthologists.

It deserves to be in the forefront again.

Hilda Silfverling
A Fantasy
(1845)

"THOU HAST NOR YOUTH NOR AGE;
BUT, AS IT WERE, AN AFTER DINNER'S SLEEP.
DREAMING ON BOTH."—MEASURE FOR MEASURE.[1]

HILDA GYLLENLOF WAS the daughter of a poor Swedish clergyman. Her mother died before she had counted five summers. The good father did his best to supply the loss of maternal tenderness; nor were kind neighbors wanting, with friendly words, and many a small gift for the pretty little one. But at the age of thirteen, Hilda lost her father also, just as she was receiving rapidly from his affectionate teachings as much culture as his own education and means afforded.

The unfortunate girl had no other resource than to go to distant relatives, who were poor, and could not well conceal that the destitute orphan was a burden. At the end of a year, Hilda in sadness and weariness of spirit, went to Stockholm, to avail herself of an opportunity to earn her living by her needle and some light services about the house. She was then in the first blush of maidenhood, with a clear innocent look, and exceedingly fair complexion. Her beauty soon attracted the attention of Magnus Hansteen, mate of a Danish vessel then lying at the wharves of Stockholm.

He could not be otherwise than fascinated with her budding loveliness; and alone as she was in the world, she was naturally prone to listen to the first words of warm affection she had heard since her father's death.

---

[1] Quote from William Shakespeare's (1564-1616) *Measure for Measure*, Act III, Sc. 1

What followed is the old story, which will continue to be told as long as there are human passions and human laws. To do the young man justice, though selfish, he was not deliberately unkind; for he did not mean to be treacherous to the friendless young creature who trusted him. He sailed from Sweden with the honest intention to return and make her his wife; but he was lost in a storm at sea, and the earth saw him no more.

Hilda never heard the sad tidings; but, for another cause, her heart was soon oppressed with shame and sorrow. If she had had a mother's bosom on which to lean her aching head, and confess all her faults and all her grief, much misery might have been saved. Cut there was none to whom she dared to speak of her anxiety and shame. Her extreme melancholy attracted the attention of a poor old woman, to whom she sometimes carried clothes for washing. The good Virika, after manifesting her sympathy in various ways, at last ventured to ask outright why one so young was so very sad.

The poor child threw herself on the friendly bosom, and confessed all her wretchedness. After that, they had frequent confidential conversations; and the kind-hearted peasant did her utmost to console and cheer the desolate orphan. She said she must soon return to her native village, in the Norwegian Valley of Westfjordalen; and as she was alone in the world, and wanted something to love, she would gladly take the babe, and adopt it for her own.

Poor Hilda thankful for any chance to keep her disgrace a secret, gratefully accepted the offer. When the babe was ten days old, she allowed the good Virika to carry it away; though not without hitter tears, and the oft repeated promise that her little one might be reclaimed, whenever Magnus returned and fulfilled his promise of marriage. But though these arrangements were managed with great caution, the young mother did not escape suspicion. It chanced, very unfortunately, that soon after Virika's departure, an infant was found in the water, strangled with a sash very like one Hilda had been accustomed to wear. A train of circumstantial evidence seemed to connect the child with her, and she was arrested. For some time, she contented herself with assertions of innocence, and obstinately refused to tell anything more. But at last, having the fear of death before her eyes, she acknowledged that she had given birth to a daughter, which had been carried away by Virika Gjetter, to her native place, in the parish of Tind in the Valley of Westljordalen. Inquiries were accordingly made in Norway, but the answer obtained was that Virika had not been heard of in her native valley, for many years. Through weary months, Hilda lingered in prison, waiting in vain for favorable testimony; and at last, on strong circumstantial evidence, she was condemned to die.

It chanced there was at that time a very learned chemist in Stockholm; a man whose thoughts were all gas, and his hours marked only by combinations and explosions. He had discovered a process of artificial cold, by which he could suspend animation in living creatures, and restore it at any prescribed time. He had in one apartment of his laboratory a bear that had been in a torpid state five years, a wolf two years, and so on. This of course excited a good deal of attention in the scientific world.

A metaphysician suggested how extremely interesting it would be to put a human being asleep thus, and watch the reunion of soul and body, after the lapse of a hundred years. The chemist was half wild with the magnificence of the idea; and he forthwith petitioned that Hilda instead of being beheaded, might be delivered to him, to be frozen for a century. He urged that her extreme youth demanded pity; that his mode of execution would be a very gentle one, and, being so strictly private, would be far less painful to the poor young creature than exposure to the public gaze.

His request, being seconded by several men of science, was granted by the government; for no one suggested a doubt of its divine right to freeze human hearts, instead of chopping off human heads, or choking human lungs. This change in the mode of death was much lauded as an act of clemency, and poor Hilda tried to be as grateful as she was told she ought to be.

On the day of execution, the chaplain came to pray with her, but found himself rather embarrassed in using the customary form. He could not well allude to her going in a few hours to meet her final judge; for the chemist said she would come back in a hundred years, and where her soul would be meantime was more than theology could teach.

The subject of this curious experiment was conveyed in a close carriage from the prison to the laboratory. A shudder ran through soul and body, as she entered the apartment assigned her. It was built entirely of stone, and rendered intensely cold by an artificial process. The light was dim and spectral, being admitted from above through a small circle of blue glass. Around the sides of the room, were tiers of massive stone shelves, on which reposed various objects in a torpid state.

A huge bear lay on his back, with paws crossed on his breast, as devoutly as some pious knight of the fourteenth century. There was in fact no inconsiderable resemblance in the proceedings by which both these characters gained their worldly possessions; they were equally based on the maxim that "might makes right." It is true, the Christian obtained a better name, inasmuch as he paid a tithe of his gettings to the holy church, which the bear never had the grace to do. But then it must be remembered that the bear had no soul to save, and the Christian knight would have been very unlikely to pay fees to the ferrymen, if he likewise had had nothing to send over.

The two public functionaries, who had attended the prisoner, to make sure that justice was not defrauded of its due, soon begged leave to retire, complaining of the unearthly cold. The pale face of the maiden became still paler, as she saw them depart. She siezed the arm of the old chemist, and said, imploringly, "You will not go away, too, and leave me with these dreadful creatures?"

He replied, not without some touch of compassion in his tones, "You will be sound asleep, my dear, and will not know whether I am here or not. Drink this; it will soon make you drowsy."

"But what if that great bear should wake up?" asked she, trembling.

"Never fear. He cannot wake up," was the brief reply. "And what if I should wake up all alone here?"

"Don't disturb yourself," said he, "I tell you that you will not wake up. Come, my dear, drink quick; for I am getting chilly myself."

The poor girl cast another despairing glance round the tomb-like apartment, and did as she was requested. "And now," said the chemist, "let us shake hands, and say farewell; for you will never see me again."

"Why, wont you come to wake me up?" inquired the prisoner; not reflecting on all the peculiar circumstances of her condition.

"My great-grandson may," replied he, with a smile. "Adieu, my dear. It is a great deal pleasanter than being beheaded. You will fall asleep as easily as a babe in his cradle." She gazed in his face, with a bewildered drowsy look, and big tears rolled down her cheeks. "Just step up here, my poor child," said he; and he offered her his hand.

"Oh, don't lay me so near the crocodile!" she exclaimed. "If he should wake up!"

"You wouldn't know it, if he did," rejoined the patient chemist; "but never mind. Step up to this other shelf, if you like it better." He handed her up very politely, gathered her garments about her feet, crossed her arms below her breast, and told her to be perfectly still. He then covered his face with a mask, let some gasses escape from an apparatus in the centre of the room, and immediately went out, locking the door after him.

The next day, the public functionaries looked in, and expressed themselves well satisfied to find the maiden lying as rigid and motionless as the bear, the wolf, and the snake. On the edge of the shelf where she lay was pasted an inscription: "Put to sleep for infanticide,[2] Feb. 10, 1740, by order of the king. To be wakened Feb. 10, 1840."

The earth whirled round on its axis, carrying with it the Alps and the Andes, the bear, the crocodile, and the maiden. Summer and winter came and went; America took place among the nations; Bonaparte[3] played out his great game, with kingdoms for pawns; and still the Swedish damsel slept on her stone shelf with the bear and the crocodile.

When ninety-five years had passed, the bear, having fulfilled his prescribed century, was waked according to agreement. The curious flocked round him to see him eat, and hear whether he could growl as well as other bears. Not liking such close observation, he broke his chain one night, and made off for the hills. How he seemed to his comrades, and what mistakes he made in his recollections, there were never any means of ascertaining. But bears, being more strictly conservative than men, happily escape the influence of French revolutions, German philosophy, and reforms of all sorts; therefore Bruin doubtless found less change in his fellow citizens, than an old knight or Viking might have done, had he chanced to sleep so long.

At last, came the maiden's turn to be resuscitated. The populace had forgotten her and her story long ago; but a select scientific few were present at the ceremony, by special invitation. The old chemist and his children all "slept the sleep that knows no waking."

---

[2] Killing of an infant

[3] Napoléon Bonapart (1769-1821), first French emperor and military commander

But carefully written orders had been transmitted from generation to generation; and the duty finally devolved on a great grandson, himself a chemist of no mean reputation. Life returned very slowly; at first by almost imperceptible degrees, then by a visible shivering through the nerves. When the eyes opened, it was as if by the movement of pulleys, and there was something painfully strange in their marble gaze. But the lamp within the inner shrine lighted up, and gradually shone through them, giving assurance of the presence of a soul. As consciousness returned, she looked in the faces round her, as if seeking for some one; for her first dim recollection was of the old chemist.

For several days, there was a general sluggishness of soul and body; an overpowering inertia, which made all exertion difficult, and prevented memory from rushing back in too tumultuous a tide. For some time, she was very quiet and patient; but the numbers who came to look at her, their perpetual questions how things seemed to her, and what was the state of her appetite and her memory, made her restless and irritable. Still worse was it when she went into the street. Her numerous visitors pointed her out to others, who ran to doors and windows to stare at her, and this soon attracted the attention of boys and lads.

To escape such annoyances, she one day walked into a little shop, bearing the name of a woman she had formerly known. It was now kept by her granddaughter, an aged woman, who was evidently as afraid of Hilda, as if she had been a witch or a ghost. This state of things became perfectly unendurable. After a few weeks, the forlorn being made her escape from the city, at dawn of day, and with money which had been given her by charitable people, she obtained a passage to her native village, under the new name of Hilda Silfverling. But to stand, in the bloom of sixteen, among well remembered hills and streams, and not recognize a single human face, or know a single human voice, this was the most mournful of all; far worse than loneliness in a foreign land; sadder than sunshine on a ruined city.

And all these suffocating emotions must be crowded back on her own heart; for if she revealed them to any one, she would assuredly be considered insane or bewitched. As the thought became familiar to her that even the little children she had known were all dead long ago, her eyes assumed an indescribably perplexed and mournful expression, which gave them an appearance of supernatural depth. She was seized with an inexpressible longing to go where no one had ever heard of her, and among scenes she had never looked upon. Her thoughts often reverted fondly to old Virika Gjetter, and the babe for whose sake she had suffered so much; and her heart yearned for Norway.

But then she was chilled by the remembrance that even if her child had lived to the usual age of mortals, she must have been long since dead; and if she had left descendants, what would they know of her? Overwhelmed by the complete desolation of her lot on earth, she wept bitterly. But she was never utterly hopeless; for in the midst of her anguish, something prophetic seemed to beckon through the clouds, and call her into Norway.

In Stockholm, there was a white-haired old clergyman, who had been peculiarly kind, when he came to see her, after her centennial slumber. She resolved to go to him, to tell him how oppressively dreary was her restored existence, and how earnestly she desired to go under a new name to some secluded village in Norway, where none would be likely to learn her history, and where there would be nothing to remind her of the gloomy past. The good old man entered at once into her feelings, and approved her plan. He had been in that country himself, and had staid a few days at the house of a kind old man, named Hans Oberg. He furnished Hilda with means for the journey, and gave her an affectionate letter of introduction, in which he described her as a Swedish orphan, who had suffered much, and would be glad to earn her living in any honest way that could be pointed out to her.

It was the middle of June when Hilda arrived at the house of Hans Oberg. He was a stout, clumsy, red-visaged old man, with wide mouth, and big nose, hooked like an eagle's beak; but there was a right friendly expression in his large eyes, and when he had read the letter, he greeted the young stranger with such cordiality, she felt at once that she had found a father. She must come in his boat, he said, and he would take her at once to his island home, where his good woman would give her a hearty welcome. She always loved the friendless; and especially would she love the Swedish orphan, because her last and youngest daughter had died the year before. On his way to the boat, the worthy man introduced her to several people, and when he told her story, old men and young maidens took her by the hand, and spoke as if they thought Heaven had sent them a daughter and a sister. The good Brenda received her with open arms, as her husband had said she would. She was an old weather-beaten woman, but there was a whole heart full of sunshine in her honest eyes.

And this new home looked so pleasant under the light of the summer sky! The house was embowered in the shrubbery of a small island, in the midst of a fiord,[4] the steep shores of which were thickly covered with pine, fir, and juniper, down to the water's edge.

The fiord went twisting and turning about, from promontory to promontory, as if the Nereides,[5] dancing up from the sea, had sportively chased each other into nooks and corners, now hiding away behind some bold projection of rock, and now peeping out suddenly, with a broad sunny smile. Directly in front of the island, the fiord expanded into a broad bay, on the shores of which was a little primitive romantic-looking village. Here and there, a sloop was at anchor, and picturesque little boats tacked off and on from cape to

---

[4] Sea inlet formed in a valley with high cliffs
[5] Sea nymphs of Greek mythology

cape, their white sails glancing in the sun. A range of lofty blue mountains closed in the distance. One giant, higher than all the rest, went up perpendicularly into the clouds, wearing a perpetual crown of glittering snow. As the maiden gazed on this sublime and beautiful scenery, a new and warmer tide seemed to flow through her stagnant heart. Ah, how happy might life be here among these mountain homes, with a people of such patriarchal simplicity, so brave and free, so hospitable, frank, and hearty!

The house of Hans Oberg was built of pine logs, neatly whitewashed. The roof was covered with grass, and bore a crop of large bushes. A vine, tangled among these, fell in heavy festoons that waved at every touch of the wind. The door was painted with flowers in gay colors, and surmounted with fantastic carving. The interior of the dwelling was ornamented with many little grotesque images, boxes, bowls, ladles, &c., curiously carved in the close grained and beautifully white wood of the Norwegian fir. This was a common amusement with the peasantry, and Hans Oberg, being a great favorite among them, received many such presents during his frequent visits in the surrounding parishes. But nothing so much attracted Hilda's attention, as a kind of long trumpet, made of two hollow half cylinders of wood, bound tightly together with birch bark. The only instrument of the kind she had ever seen was in the possession of Virika Gjetter, who called it a luhr, and said it was used to call the cows home in her native village, in Upper Tellemarken. She showed how it was used, and Hilda, having a quick ear, soon learned to play upon it with considerable facility.

And here in her new home, this rude instrument reappeared; forming the only visible link between her present life and that dreamy past! With strange feelings, she took up the pipe, and began to play one of the old tunes. At first, the tones flitted like phantoms in and out of her brain; but at last, they all came back, and took their places rank and file. Old

Brenda said it was a pleasant tune, and asked her to play it again; but to Hilda it seemed awfully solemn, like a voice warbling from the tombs. She would learn other tunes to please the good mother, she said; but this she would play no more; it made her too sad, for she had heard it in her youth.

"Thy youth!" said Brenda, smiling. "One sees well that must have been a long time ago. To hear thee talk, one might suppose thou wert an old autumn leaf, just ready to drop from the bough, like myself."

Hilda blushed, and said she felt old, because she had had much trouble.

"Poor child," responded the good Brenda: "I hope thou hast had thy share."

"I feel as if nothing could trouble me here," replied Hilda, with a grateful smile; "all seems so kind and peaceful." She breathed a few notes through the luhr, as she laid it away on the shell where she had found it. "But, my good mother," said she, "how clear and soft are these tones. The pipe I used to hear was far more harsh."

"The wood is very old," rejoined Brenda: "They say it is more than a hundred years. Alerik Tuorilii gave it to me, to call my good man when he is out in the boat. Ah, he was such a Berserker[6] of a boy! And in truth he was not much more sober when he was here three years ago. But no matter what he did; one could never help loving him."

"And who is Alerik?" asked the maiden.

Brenda pointed to an old house, seen in the distance, on the declivity of one of the opposite hills. It overlooked the broad bright bay, with its picturesque little islands, and was sheltered in the rear by a noble pine forest. A waterfall came down from the hillside, glancing in and out among the trees; and when the sun kissed it as he went away, it lighted up with a smile of rainbows.

---

[6] A warrior famous in the Northern Sagas for his stormy and untamable character

"That house," said Brenda, "was built by Alerik's grandfather. He was the richest man in the village. But his only son was away among the wars for a long time, and the old place has been going to decay. But they say Alerik is coming back to live among us; and he will soon give it a different look. He has been away to Germany and Paris, and other outlandish parts, for a long time. Ah! The rogue! There was no mischief he didn't think of. He was always tying cats together under the windows, and barking in the middle of the night, till he set all the dogs in the neighborhood a howling. But as long as it was Alerik that did it, it was all well enough: for everybody loved him, and he always made one believe just what he liked. If he wanted to make thee think thy hair was as black as Noeck's[7] mane, he would make thee think so."

Hilda smiled, as she glanced at her flaxen hair, with here and there a gleam of paly gold, where the sun touched it. "I think it would be hard to prove that this was black," said she.

"Nevertheless," rejoined Brenda, "if Alerik undertook it, he would do it. He always has his say, and does what he will. One may as well give in to him first as last."

This account of the unknown youth carried with it that species of fascination, which the idea of uncommon power always has over the human heart. The secluded maiden seldom touched the luhr without thinking of the giver; and not infrequently she found herself conjecturing when this wonderful Alerik would come home.

Meanwhile, constant but not excessive labor, the mountain air, the quiet life, and the kindly hearts around her, restored to Hilda more than her original loveliness. In her large blue eyes, the inward-looking sadness of experience now mingled in strange beauty with the out-looking clearness of youth. Her fair complexion was tinged with the glow of health, and her

---

[7] An elfish spirit, which, according to popular tradition in Norway, appears in the form of a coal-black horse

motions had the airy buoyancy of the mountain breeze. When she went to the mainland, to attend church, or rustic festival, the hearts of young and old greeted her like a May blossom. Thus with calm cheerfulness her hours went by, making no noise in their flight, and leaving no impress. But here was an unsatisfied want! She sighed for hours that did leave a mark behind them. She thought of the Danish youth, who had first spoken to her of love; and plaintively came the tones from her luhr, as she gazed on the opposite hills, and wondered whether the Alerik they talked of so much, was indeed so very superior to other young men.

Father Oberg often came home at twilight with a boat full of juniper boughs, to be strewed over the floors, that they might diffuse a balmy odor, inviting to sleep. One evening, when Hilda saw him coming with his verdant load, she hastened down to the water's edge to take an armful of the fragrant boughs. She had scarcely appeared in sight, before he called out, "I do believe Alerik has come! I heard the organ up in the old house. Somebody was playing on it like a Northeast storm; and surely, said I, that must be Alerik."

"Is there an organ there?" asked the damsel, in surprise.

"Yes. He built it himself, when he was here three years ago. He can make anything he chooses. An organ, or a basket cut from a cherry stone is all one to him."

When Hilda returned to the cottage, she of course repeated the news to Brenda, who exclaimed joyfully, "Ah, then we shall see him soon! If he does not come before, we shall certainly see him at the weddings in the church tomorrow."

"And plenty of tricks we shall have now," said Father Oberg, shaking his head, with a good-natured smile. "There will be no telling which end of the world is uppermost, while he is here."

"Oh yes, there will, my friend," answered Brenda, laughing; "for it will certainly be whichever end Alerik stands on. The handsome little Bersherker! How I should like to see him."

The next day there was a sound of lively music on the waters, for two young couples from neighboring islands were coming up the fiord, to be married at the church in the opposite village. Their boats were ornamented with gay little banners, friends and neighbors accompanied them, playing on musical instruments, and the rowers had their hats decorated with garlands. As the rustic band floated thus gaily over the bright waiters, they were joined by Father Oberg, with Brenda and Hilda in his boat.

Friendly villagers had already decked the simple little church with evergreens and flowers, in honor of the bridal train. As they entered, Father Oberg observed that two young men stood at the door with clarinets in their hands. But he thought no more of it, till, according to immemorial custom, he, as clergyman's assistant, began to sing the first lines of the hymn that was given out. The very first note he sounded, up struck the clarinets at the door. The louder they played, the louder the old man bawled; but the instruments gained the victory. When he essayed to give out the lines of the next verse, the merciless clarinets brayed louder than before.

His stentorian voice had become vociferous and rough, from thirty years of hallooing across the water, and singing of psalms in four village churches. He exerted it to the utmost, till the perspiration poured down his rubicund visage; but it was of no use. His rivals had strong lungs, and they played on clarinets in F. If the whole village had screamed fire, to the shrill accompaniment of railroad whistles, they would have over-topped them all. Father Oberg was vexed at heart, and it was plain enough that he was so. The congregation held down their heads with suppressed laughter; all except one tall vigorous young man, who sat up very serious and dignified, as if he were reverently listening to some new manifestation of musical genius.

When the people left church, Hilda saw this young stranger approaching toward them, as fast as numerous handshakings by the way would permit. She had time to observe him closely. His noble figure, his strong agile motions, his expressive countenance, hazel eyes with strongly marked brows, and abundant brown hair, tossed aside with a careless grace, left no doubt in her mind that this was the famous Alerik Thorild; but what made her heart beat more wildly was his strong resemblance to Magnus the Dane. He went up to Brenda and kissed her, and threw his arms about Father Oberg's neck, with expressions of joyful recognition. The kind old man, vexed as he was, received these affectionate demonstrations with great friendliness. "Ah, Alerik," said he, after the first salutations were over, "that was not kind of thee."

"Me! What!" exclaimed the young man with well-feigned astonishment.

"To put up those confounded clarinets to drown my voice," rejoined he, bluntly. "When a man has led the singing thirty years in four parishes, I can assure thee it is not a pleasant joke to be treated in that style. I know the young men are tired of my voice, and think they could do things in better fashion, as young fools always do; but I may thank thee for putting it into their heads to bring those detestable clarinets."

"Oh, dear Father Oberg," replied the young man, in the most coaxing tones, and with the most caressing manner, "you couldn't think I would do such a thing!"

"On the contrary, it is just the thing I think thou couldst do," answered the old man. "Thou need'st not think to cheat me out of my eyeteeth, this time. Thou hast often enough made me believe the moon was made of green cheese. But I know thy tricks. I shall be on my guard now; and mind thee, I am not going to be bamboozled by thee again."

Alerik smiled mischievously; for he, in common with all the villagers, knew it was the easiest thing in the world to gull the simple-hearted old man. "Well, come Father Oberg," said he, "shake hands and be friends. When you come over to the village, tomorrow, we will drink a mug of ale together, at the Wolf's Head."

"Oh yes, and be played some trick for his pains," said Brenda.

"No, no," answered Alerik, with great gravity; "he is on his guard now, and I cannot bamboozle him again." With a friendly nod and smile, he bounded off, to greet someone whom he recognized. Hilda had stepped back to hide herself from observation. She was a little afraid of the handsome Berserker; and his resemblance to the Magnus of her youthful recollections made her sad.

The next afternoon, Alerik met his old friend, and reminded him of the agreement to drink ale at the Wolf's Head. On the way, he invited several young companions. The ale was excellent, and Alerik told stories and sang songs, which filled the little tavern with roars of laughter. In one of the intervals of merriment, he turned suddenly to honest Hans, and said, "Father Oberg, among the many things I have learned and done in foreign countries, did I ever tell you that I had made a league with the devil, and am shot-proof?"

"One might easily believe thou hadst made a league with the devil, before thou wert born," replied Hans, with a grin at his own wit; "but as for being shot-proof, that is another affair."

"Try and see," rejoined Alerik. "These friends are witnesses that I tell you it is perfectly safe to try. Come, I will stand here; fire your pistol, and you will soon see that the evil one will keep the bargain he made with me."

"Be done with thy nonsense, Alerik," rejoined his old friend.

"Ah, I see how it is," replied Alerik, turning towards the young men. "Father Oberg used to be a famous shot. Nobody was more expert in the bear or the wolf hunt than he; but old eyes grow dim, and old hands will tremble. No wonder he does not like to have us see how much he fails." This was attacking honest Hans on his weak side. He was proud of his strength, and skill in shooting, and he did not like to admit that he was growing old.

"I not hit a mark!" exclaimed he, with indignation. "When did I ever miss a thing I aimed at?"

"Never, when you were young," answered one of the company; "but it is no wonder you are afraid to try now."

"Afraid!" exclaimed the old hunter, impatiently. "Who the devil said I was afraid?"

Alerik shrugged his shoulders, and replied carelessly, "It is natural enough that these young men should think so, when they see you refuse to aim at me, though I assure you that I am shot-proof, and that I will stand perfectly still."

"But art thou really shot-proof?" inquired the guileless old man. " The devil has helped thee to do so many strange things, that one never knows what he will help thee to do next."

"Really, Father Oberg, I speak in earnest. Take up your pistol and try, and you will soon see with your own eyes that I am shot-proof."

Hans Oberg looked round upon the company like one perplexed. His wits, never very bright, were somewhat muddled by the ale. "What shall I do with this wild fellow?" inquired he. "You see he will be shot."

"Try him, try him," was the general response. "He has assured you he is shot-proof; what more do you need?" The old man hesitated awhile, but after some further parley, took up his pistol and examined it.

"Before we proceed to business," said Alerik, "let me tell you that if you do not shoot me, you shall have a gallon of the best ale you ever drank in your life. Come and taste it, Father Oberg, and satisfy yourself that it is good." While they were discussing the merits of the ale, one of the young men took the ball from the pistol.

"I am ready now," said Alerik. "Here I stand. Now don't lose your name for a good marksman."

The old man flred, and Alerik fell back with a deadly groan. Poor Father Oberg stood like a stone image of terror. His arms adhered rigidly to his sides, his jaw dropped, and his great eyes seemed starting from their sockets. "Oh Father Oberg, how could you do it!" exclaimed the young men.

The poor horrified Hans stared at them wildly, and gasping and stammering replied, "Why he said he was shot-proof; and you all told me to do it."

"Oh yes," said they; "but we supposed you would have sense enough to know it was all in fun. But don't take it too much to heart. You will probably forfeit your life; for the government will of course consider it a poor excuse when you tell them that you fired at a man merely to oblige him, and because he said he was shot-proof. But don't be too much cast down, Father Oberg. We must all meet death in some way; and if worst comes to worst, it will be a great comfort to you and your good Brenda that you did not intend to commit murder." The poor old man gazed at them with an expression of such extreme suffering, that they became alarmed, and said, "Cheer up, cheer up. Come, you must drink something to make you feel better." They took him by the shoulders, and as they led him out, he looked back wistfully on the body.

The instant he left the apartment, Alerik sprang up and darted out of the opposite door; and when Father Oberg entered the other room, there he sat, as composedly as possible, reading a paper, and smoking his pipe.

"There he is!" shrieked the old man, turning paler than ever.

"Who is there?" inquired the young men. "Don't you see Alerik Thorild?" exclaimed he, pointing, with an expression of intense horror.

They turned to the landlord, and remarked, in a compassionate tone, "Poor Father Oberg has shot Alerik Thorild, whom he loved so well; and the dreadful accident has so affected his brain, that he imagines he sees him."

The old man pressed his broad hand hard against his forehead, and again groaned out, "Oh don't you see him?"

The tones indicated such agony, that Alerik had not the heart to prolong the scene. He sprang on his feet, and exclaimed, "Now for your gallon of ale, Father Oberg! you see the devil did keep his bargain with me."

"And are you alive?" shouted the old man. The mischievous fellow soon convinced him of that, by a slap on the shoulder, that made his bones ache. Hans Oberg capered like a dancing bear. He hugged Alerik, and jumped about, and clapped his hands, and was altogether beside himself. He drank unknown quantities of ale, and this time sang loud enough to drown a brace of clarinets in F.

The night was far advanced when he went on board his boat to return to his island home. He pulled the oars vigorously, and the boat shot swiftly across the moonlighted waters. But on arriving at the customary landing, he could discover no vestige of his whitewashed cottage. Not knowing that Alerik, in the full tide of his mischief, had sent men to paint the house with a dark brown wash, he thought he must have made a mistake in the landing; so he rowed round to the other side of the island, but with no better success. Ashamed to return to the mainland, to inquire for a house that had absconded, and a little suspicious that the ale had hung some cobwebs in his brain, he continued to row hither and thither, till his strong muscular arms fairly ached with exertion. But the moon was going down, and all the landscape settling into darkness; and he at last reluctantly concluded that it was best to go back to the village inn.

Alerik, who had expected this result much sooner, had waited there to receive him. When he had kept him knocking a sufficient time, he put his head out of the window, and inquired who was there.

"Father Oberg," was the disconsolate reply. "For the love of mercy let me come in and get a few minutes sleep, before morning. I have been rowing about the bay these four hours, and I can't find my house any where."

"This is a very bad sign," replied Alerik, solemnly. "Houses don't run away, except from drunken men. Ah, Father Oberg! Father Oberg! What will the minister say?" But he did not have a chance to persecute the weary old man much longer; for scarcely had he come under the shelter of the house, before he was snoring in a profound sleep.

Early the next day, Alerik sought his old friends in their brown-washed cottage. He found it not so easy to conciliate them as usual. They were really grieved; and Brenda even said she believed he wanted to be the death of her old man.

But he had brought them presents, which he knew they would like particularly well; and he kissed their hands, and talked over his boyish days, till at last he made them laugh. "Ah now," said he, "you have forgiven me, my dear old friends. And you see, father, it was all your own fault. You put the mischief into me, by boasting before all those young men that I could never bamboozle you again."

"Ah thou incorrigible rogue!" answered the old man. "I believe thou hast indeed made a league with the devil and he gives thee the power to make everybody love thee, do what thou wilt."

Alerik's smile seemed to express that he always had a pleasant consciousness of such power. The luhr lay on the table beside him, and as he took it up, he asked, "Who plays on this? Yesterday, when I was out in my boat, I heard some very wild pretty little variations."

Brenda instead of answering called, "Hilda! Hilda!" and the young girl came from the next room, blushing as she entered.

Alerik looked at her with evident surprise. "Surely, this is not your Gunilda?" said he.

"No," replied Brenda, "she is a Swedish orphan, whom the all-kind Father sent to take the place of our Gunilda, when she was called hence." After some words of friendly greeting, the visitor asked Hilda if it was she who played so sweetly on the luhr.

She answered timidly, without looking up. Her heart was throbbing; for the tones of his voice were like Magnus the Dane.

The acquaintance thus begun, was not likely to languish on the part of such an admirer of beauty as was Alerik Thorild. The more he saw of Hilda, during the long evenings of the following winter, the more he was charmed with her natural refinement of look, voice, and manner. There was, as we have said, a peculiarity in her beauty, which gave it a higher character than mere rustic loveliness. A deep, mystic, plaintive expression in her eyes; a sort of graceful bewilderment in her countenance, and at times in the carriage of her head, and the motions of her body; as if her spirit had lost its way, and was listening intently.

No wonder he was charmed by her spiritual beauty, her simple untutored modesty. No wonder she was delighted with his frank strong exterior, his cordial caressing manner, his expressive eyes, now tender and earnest, and now sparkling with merriment, and his "smile most musical," because always so in harmony with the inward feeling, whether of sadness, fun, or tenderness. Then his moods were so bewitchingly various. Now powerful as the organ, now gentle as the flute, now naïve as the oboe.

Brenda said everything he did seemed to be alive. He carved a wolf's head on her old man's cane, and she was always afraid it would bite her. Brenda, in her simplicity, perhaps gave as good a description of genius as could be given, when she said everything it did seemed to be alive.

Hilda thought it certainly was so with Alerik's music. Sometimes all went madly with it, as if fairies danced on the grass, and ugly gnomes came and made faces at them, and shrieked, and clutched at their garments; the fairies pelted them off with flowers, and then all died away to sleep in the moonlight. Sometimes, when he played on flute or violin, the sounds came mournfully as the midnight wind through ruined towers; and they stirred up such sorrowful memories of the past, that Hilda pressed her hand upon her swelling heart, and said, "Oh not such strains as that, dear Alerik." But when his soul overflowed with love and happiness, oh, then how the music gushed and nestled!

> "The lark could scarce get out his notes for joy,
> But shook his song together, as he neared
> His happy home, the ground."

The old luhr was a great favorite with Alerik; not for its musical capabilities, but because it was entwined with the earliest recollections of his childhood. "Until I heard thee play upon it," said he, "I half repented having given it to the good Brenda. It has been in our family for several generations, and my nurse used to play upon it when I was in my cradle. They tell me my grandmother was a foundling. She was brought to my great-grandfather's house by an old peasant woman, on her way to the valley of Westfjordalen. She died there, leaving the babe and the luhr in my great-grandmother's keeping. They could never find out to whom the babe belonged; but she grew up very beautiful, and my grandfather married her.

"What was the old woman's name?" asked Hilda; and her voice was so deep and suppressed, that it made Alerik start. "Virika Gjetter, they have always told me," he replied. "But, my dearest one, what is the matter?"

Hilda, pale and fainting, made no answer. But when he placed her head upon his bosom, and kissed her forehead, and spoke soothingly, her glazed eyes softened, and she burst into tears. All his entreaties, however, could obtain no information at that time.

"Go home now," she said, in tones of deep despondency. "Tomorrow I will tell thee all. I have had many unhappy hours; for I have long felt that I ought to tell thee all my past history; but I was afraid to do it, for I thought thou wouldst not love me any more; and that would be worse than death. But come tomorrow, and I will tell thee all."

"Well, dearest Hilda, I will wait," replied Alerik; "but what my grandmother, who died long before I was born, can have to do with my love for thee, is more than I can imagine."

The next day, when Hilda saw Alerik coming to claim the fulfillment of her promise, it seemed almost like her death-warrant. "He will not love me any more," thought she, "he will never again look at me so tenderly; and then what can I do, but die?"

With much embarrassment, and many delays, she at last began her strange story. He listened to the first part very attentively, and with a gathering frown; but as she went on, the muscles of his face relaxed into a smile; and when she ended by saying, with the most melancholy seriousness, "So thou seest, dear Alerik, we cannot be married, because it is very likely that I am thy great-grandmother," he burst into immoderate peals of laughter.

When his mirth had somewhat subsided, he replied, "Likely as not thou art my great-grandmother, dear Hilda; and just as likely I was thy grandfather, in the first place. A great German scholar[8] teaches that our souls keep coming back again and again into new bodies. An old Greek philosopher is said to have come back for the fourth time, under the name of

---

[8] Gotthold Ephraim Lessing (1727-1781) was a German author, philosopher and art critic who was a leading voice in the Enlightenment Age and believed in reincarnation of the soul

Pythagoras.[9] If these things are so, how the deuce is a man ever to tell whether he marries his grandmother or not?"

"But, dearest Alerik, I am not jesting," rejoined she. "What I have told thee is really true. They did put me to sleep for a hundred years."

"Oh, yes," answered he, laughing, "I remember reading about it in the Swedish papers; and I thought it a capital joke. I will tell thee how it is with thee, my precious one. The elves sometimes seize people, to carry them down into their subterranean caves; but if the mortals run away from them, they, out of spite, forever after fill their heads with gloomy insane notions. A man in Drontheim ran away from them, and they made him believe he was an earthen coffeepot. He sat curled up in a corner all the time, for fear somebody would break his nose off."

"Nay, now thou art joking, Alerik; but really"—

"No, I tell thee as thou hast told me, it was no joke at all," he replied. "The man himself told me he was a coffee-pot."

"But be serious, Alerik," said she, "and tell me dost thou not believe that some learned men can put people to sleep for a hundred years!"

"I don't doubt some of my college professors could," rejoined he; "provided their tongues could hold out so long."

"But, Alerik, dost thou not think it possible that people may be alive, and yet not alive?"

"Of course I do," he replied; "the greater part of people are in that condition."

"Oh, Alerik, what a tease thou art! I mean is it not possible that there are people now living, or staying somewhere, who were moving about on this earth ages ago?"

"Nothing more likely;" answered he, "for instance, who knows what people there may be under the ice-sea of Folgefond? They say the cocks are heard

____

[9] Pythagoras (570-490 B.C.) was a Greek philosopher and mathematician who believed his soul had lived before in other bodies

crowing down there, to this day. How a fowl of any feather got there is a curious question; and what kind of atmosphere he had to crow in, is another puzzle. Perhaps they are poor ghosts, without sense of shame, crowing over the recollection of sins committed in the human body. The ancient Egyptians thought the soul was obliged to live three thousand years, in a succession of different animals, before it could attain to the regions of the blest. I am pretty sure I have already been a lion and a nightingale. What I shall be next, the Egyptians know as well as I do. One of their sculptors made a stone image, half woman and half lioness. Doubtless his mother had been a lioness, and had transmitted to him some dim recollection of it. But I am glad, dearest, they sent thee back in the form of a lovely maiden; for if thou hadst come as a wolf, I might have shot thee; and I shouldn't like to shoot my—great-grandmother. Or if thou hadst come as a red herring, Oberg might have eaten thee in his soup; and then I should have had no Hilda Silfverling."

Hilda smiled, as she said, half reproachfully, "I see well that thou dost not believe one word I say."

"Oh yes. I do, dearest," rejoined he, very seriously, "I have no doubt the fairies carried thee off some summer's night, and made thee verily believe thou hadst slept for a hundred years. They do the strangest things. Sometimes they change babies in the cradle; leave an imp, and carry off the human to the metal mines, where he hears only clink! clink! Then the fairies bring him back, and put him in some other cradle. When he grows up, how he does hurry skurry after the silver! He is obliged to work all his life, as if the devil drove him. The poor miser never knows what is the matter with him; but it is all because the gnomes brought him up in the mines, and he could never get the clink out of his head. A more poetic kind of fairies sometimes carry a babe to Æolian caves, full of wild dreamy sounds; and when he is brought back to upper earth, ghosts of sweet echoes keep beating time in some corner of his brain, to something which they hear, but which nobody else is the wiser for. I know that is true, for I was brought up in those caves myself."

Hilda remained silent for a few minutes, as he sat looking in her face with comic gravity. "Thou wilt do nothing but make fun of me," at last she said. "I do wish I could persuade thee to be serious. What I told thee was no fairy story. It really happened. I remember it as distinctly as I do our sail round the islands yesterday. I seem to see that great bear now with his paws folded up, on the shelf opposite to me."

"He must have been a great bear to have staid there," replied Alerik, with eyes full of roguery. "If I had been in his skin, may I be shot if all the drugs and gasses in the world would have kept me there, with my paws folded on my breast." Seeing a slight blush pass over her cheek, he added, more seriously, "After all, I ought to thank that wicked elf, whoever he was, for turning thee into a stone image; for otherwise thou wouldst have been in the world a hundred years too soon for me, and so I should have missed my life's best blossom." Feeling her tears on his hand, he again started off into a vein of merriment. "Thy case was not so very peculiar," said he. "There was a Greek lady, named Niobe,[10] who was changed to stone. The Greek gods changed women into trees, and fountains, and all manner of things. A man couldn't chop a walking-stick in those days, without danger of cutting off some lady's finger. The tree might be his great-grandmother, and she of course would take it very unkindly of him."

"All these things are like the stories about Odin and Frigga,"[11] rejoined Hilda. "They are not true, like the Christian religion. When I tell thee a true story, why dost thou always meet me with fairies and fictions?"

"But tell me, best Hilda," said he, "what the Christian religion has to do with penning up young maidens with bears and crocodiles? In its marriage

---

[10] In Greek mythology Niobe's fourteen children died and she was turned to stone for her haughtiness

[11] Frigga is the wife of Odin in Norse mythology and queen of the gods

ceremonies, I grant that it sometimes does things not very unlike that, only omitting the important part of freezing the maiden's heart. But since thou hast mentioned the Christian religion, I may as well give thee a hit of consolation from that quarter. I have read in my mother's big Bible, that a man must not marry his grandmother; but I do not remember that it said a single word against his marrying his great-grandmother."

Hilda laughed, in spite of herself. But after a pause, she looked at him earnestly, and said, "Dost thou indeed think there would be no harm in marrying, under these circumstances, if I were really thy great-grandmother? Is it thy earnest? Do be serious for once, dear Alerik!"

"Certainly there would be no harm," answered he. "Physicians have agreed that the body changes entirely once in seven years. That must be because the soul outgrows its clothes; which proves that the soul changes every seven years, also. Therefore, in the course of one hundred years, thou must have had fourteen complete changes of soul and body; and it is as plain as daylight that if thou wert my great-grandmother when thou fell asleep, thou couldst not have been my great-grandmother when they waked thee up."

"Ah, Alerik," she replied, "it is as the good Brenda says, there is no use in talking with thee. One might as well try to twist a string that is not fastened at either end."

He looked up merrily in her face. The wind was playing with her ringlets, and freshened the color on her cheeks. "I only wish I had a mirror to hold before thee," said he; "that thou couldst see how very like thou art to a—great-grandmother."

"Laugh at me as thou wilt," answered she; "but I assure thee I have strange thoughts about myself sometimes. Dost thou know," added she, almost in a whisper, "I am not always quite certain that I have not died, and am now in heaven?" A ringing shout of laughter burst from the lighthearted lover.

"Oh, I like that! I like that!" exclaimed he. "That is good! That a Swede coming to Norway does not know certainly whether she is in heaven or not."

"Do be serious, Alerik," said she, imploringly. "Don't carry thy jests too far."

"Serious? I am serious. If Norway is not heaven, one sees plainly enough that it must have been the scaling place, where the old giants got up to heaven; for they have left their ladders standing. Where else wilt thou find clusters of mountains running up perpendicularly thousands of feet right into the sky? If thou wast to see some of them, thou couldst tell whether Norway is a good climbing place into heaven."

"Ah, dearest Alerik, thou hast taught me that already," she replied, with a glance full of affection; "so a truce with thy joking. Truly one never knows how to take thee. Thy talk sets everything in the world, and above it, and below it, dancing together in the strangest fashion."

"Because they all do dance together," rejoined the perverse man.

"Oh, be done! be done, Alerik!" she said, putting her hand playfully over his mouth. "Thou wilt tie my poor brain all up into knots."

He seized her hand and kissed it, then busied himself with braiding the wild spring flowers into a garland for her fair hair. As she gazed on him earnestly, her eyes beaming with love and happiness, he drew her to his breast, and exclaimed fervently, "Oh, thou art beautiful as an angel; and here or elsewhere, with thee by my side, it seemeth heaven."

They spoke no more for a long time. The birds now and then serenaded the silent lovers with little twittering gushes of song. The setting sun, as he went away over the hills, threw diamonds on the bay, and a rainbow ribbon across the distant waterfall. Their hearts were in harmony with the peaceful beauty of Nature. As he kissed her drowsy eyes, she murmured,

"Oh, it was well worth a hundred years with bears and crocodiles, to fall asleep thus on thy heart."

* * * * *

The next autumn, a year and a half after Hilda's arrival in Norway, there was another procession of boats, with banners, music and garlands. The little church was again decorated with evergreens; but no clarinet players stood at the door to annoy good Father Oberg. The worthy man had in fact taken the hint, (though somewhat in the cross) and had good-naturedly ceased to disturb modern ears with his clamorous vociferation of the hymns. He and his kind-hearted Brenda were happy beyond measure at Hilda's good fortune. But when she told her husband anything he did not choose to believe, they could never rightly make out what he meant by looking at her so slyly, and saying, "Pooh! Pooh! Tell that to my great-grandmother."

NATHANIEL HAWTHORNE
(1804-1864)

Introduction
Rappaccini's Daughter
This fascinating story was first published under the title "The Writings of Aubépine: Rappaccini's Daughter." "Aubépine" is the French term for Hawthorn and the plant is purported to repair heart disease. When originally published, "Rappaccini's Daughter" contained a foreword introducing the fictitious French author, M. de l'Aubépine, to the American public. It was supposed to be an English translation of his French story titled *"Beatrice; ou La Belle Empoisonneuse,"* ("Beatrice; or the Beautiful Poisoner") that had been recently published in the equally fictitious French journal *La Revue Anti-Aristocratique.*

The tale was popular among readers of the day. In a September, 1846 essay on Hawthorne's works by Charles Wilkins Webber in the *American Whig Review*, valid questions were asked about the story. "Who of our Poets can point to a deeper Poetry than is expressed in 'Rappaccini's Daughter'? Where, out of Hell or Byron, will you find anything to compass the cold, intellectual diabolicism of the famous Doctor 'Giacomo Rappaccini?' And where—certainly *not* in Byron!—will you find a sublimer retribution visited upon that presumptuous Thought, which dared the Ineffable and died!—than he there quietly gives?"

In December of 1844, "Rappaccini's Daughter," was published by Nathaniel Hawthorne in *The United States Magazine and Democratic Review*. In doing, so he gave the world the first biological science fiction story.

Margaret Fuller, in her review of *Mosses from an Old Manse* in the *New York Daily Tribune* (June 22, 1846), was of the opinion that "'The Birthmark' and 'Rappaccini's Daughter' embody truths of profound importance in shapes of aerial elegance."

Rappaccini's Daughter
(1844)

Foreword

WE DO NOT remember to have seen any translated specimens of the productions of M. de l'Aubépine[1]—a fact the less to be wondered at, as his very name is unknown to many of his own countrymen as well as to the student of foreign literature.[2] As a writer, he seems to occupy an unfortunate position between the Transcendentalists[3] (who, under one name or another, have their share in all the current literature of the world)[4] and the great body of pen-and-ink men who address the intellect and sympathies of the multitude.[5] If not too refined, at all events too remote, too shadowy, and unsubstantial in his modes of development to suit the taste of the latter class, and yet too popular to satisfy the spiritual or metaphysical requisitions of the former, he must necessarily find himself without an audience, except here and there an individual or possibly an isolated clique. His writing's, to do them justice, are not altogether destitute of fancy and originality; they might have won him greater

---

[1] Nathaniel Hawthorne (1804-1864) penname, which means Hawthorn in French

[2] Hawthorne is lamenting he is hardly known in the United States, let alone in foreign countries

[3] Transcendentalism is best defined as the unadulterated side of humanism that believed people should be free-thinking, self-reliant, and were inherently good; it was founded by Ralph Waldo Emerson (1803-1882) and Margaret Fuller (1810-1850), while Hawthorne, who was a neighbor of Emerson for three years, did not embrace transcendentalism

[4] For a number of years it appeared to Hawthorne that much literature was either written by transcendentalists or about transcendentalists

[5] Common fiction for the working population

reputation but for an inveterate love of allegory,[6] which is apt to invest his plots and characters with the aspect of scenery and people in the clouds, and to steal away the human warmth out of his conceptions. His fictions are sometimes historical, sometimes of the present day, and sometimes, so far as can be discovered, have little or no reference either to time or space. In any case, he generally contents himself with a very slight embroidery of outward manners,—the faintest possible counterfeit of real life,—and endeavors to create an interest by some less obvious peculiarity of the subject. Occasionally a breath of Nature, a raindrop of pathos and tenderness, or a gleam of humor, will find its way into the midst of his fantastic imagery, and make us feel as if, after all, we were yet within the limits of our native earth. We will only add to this very cursory notice that M. de l'Aubépine's productions, if the reader chance to take them in precisely the proper point of view, may amuse a leisure hour as well as those of a brighter man; if otherwise, they can hardly fail to look excessively like nonsense.

Our author is voluminous; he continues to write and publish with as much praiseworthy and indefatigable prolixity as if his efforts were crowned with the brilliant success that so justly attends those of Eugene Sue.[7] His first appearance was by a collection of stories in a long series of volumes entitled "*Contes deux fois racontées*."[8] The titles of some of his more recent works (we quote from memory) are as follows: "*Le Voyage Céleste á Chemin de Fer*,"[9] 3 tom.,

---

[6] A style of writing, practiced by Hawthorne, were there is an underlying meaning in the storyline and characters

[7] Joseph Marie Eugene Sue (1804-1857), popular French novelist and short story writer

[8] *Twice Told Tales* was Hawthorne's 1837 collection of short stories

[9] "Travels by the Celestial Railroad" was a 1838 short story by Hawthorne

1838; *"Le nouveau Père Adam et la nouvelle Mère Eve,"*[10] 2 tom., 1839; *"Roderic; ou le Serpent à l'estomac,"*[11] 2 tom., 1840; *"Le Culte du Feu,"*[12] a folio volume of ponderous research into the religion and ritual of the old Persian Ghebers,[13] published in 1841; *"La Soirée du Chateau en Espagne,"*[14] i tom., 8vo, 1842; and *"L'Artiste du Beau; ou le Papillon Mècanique,"*[15] 5 tom., 4to, 1843. Our somewhat wearisome perusal of this startling catalogue of volumes has left behind it a certain personal affection and sympathy, though by no means admiration, for M. de l'Aubepine; and we would fain do the little in our power towards introducing him favorably to the American public. The ensuing tale is a translation of his "Beatrice; ou la Belle Empoisonneuse,"[16] recently published in "La Revue AntiAristocratique."[17] This journal, edited by the Comte de Bearhaven,[18] has for some years past led the defence of liberal principles and popular rights with a faithfulness and ability worthy of all praise.

———

A YOUNG MAN, named Giovanni Guasconti, came, very long ago, from the more southern region of Italy, to pursue his studies at the University of Padua.[19] Giovanni, who had but a scanty supply of gold ducats in his pocket, took lodgings in a high and gloomy chamber of an old edifice, which looked not unworthy

---

[10] "The New Father Adam and Mother Eve" was an 1839 short story by Hawthorne

[11] "Roderick, or, the Serpent's Stomach" was an 1840 short story by Hawthorne, which is also called "Egotism, or, the Bosom-Serpent"

[12] *The Cult of Fire* was a non-fiction book published in 1841 by Hawthorne

[13] Original natives of Iran that worshipped fire

[14] "Night in a Spanish Castle" was an 1842 short story by Hawthorne

[15] "The Artist of the Beautiful; or, the Mechanical Butterfly" was an 1843 short story by Hawthorne, which is included in this anthology

[16] Beatrice; or, the Beautiful Prisoner

[17] Fictitious French journal

[18] Fictitious count

[19] City in Lombard region of northern Italy

to have been the palace of a Paduan noble, and which, in fact, exhibited over its entrance the armorial bearings[20] of a family long since extinct. The young stranger, who was not unstudied in the great poem of his country,[21] recollected that one of the ancestors of this family, and perhaps an occupant of this very mansion, had been pictured by Dante as a partaker of the immortal agonies of his Inferno. These reminiscences and associations, together with the tendency to heart-break natural to a young man for the first time out of his native sphere, caused Giovanni to sigh heavily, as he looked around the desolate and ill-furnished apartment.

"Holy Virgin, signor," cried old dame Lisabetta, who, won by the youth's remarkable beauty of person, was kindly endeavoring to give the chamber a habitable air, "what a sigh was that to come out of a young man's heart! Do you find this old mansion gloomy? For the love of heaven, then, put your head out of the window, and you will see as bright sunshine as you have left in Naples."

Guasconti mechanically did as the old woman advised, but could not quite agree with her that the Lombard sunshine was as cheerful as that of southern Italy. Such as it was, however, it fell upon a garden beneath the window, and expended its fostering influences on a variety of plants, which seemed to have been cultivated with exceeding care.

"Does this garden belong to the house?" asked Giovanni.

"Heaven forbid, signor!—unless it were fruitful of better potherbs than any that grow there now," answered old Lisabetta. "No; that garden is cultivated by the own hands of Signor Giacomo Rappaccini, the famous Doctor, who, I warrant him, has been heard of as far as Naples. It is said that he distils these plants into medicines that are as potent as a charm. Oftentimes you may see the signor Doctor at work, and

---

[20] Family crest

[21] *The Divine Comedy* by Dante Alighieri (1265-1321)

perchance the signora his daughter, too, gathering the strange flowers that grow in the garden."

The old woman had now done what she could for the aspect of the chamber, and, commending the young man to the protection of the saints, took her departure.

Giovanni still found no better occupation than to look down into the garden beneath his window. From its appearance, he judged it to be one of those botanic gardens, which were of earlier date in Padua than elsewhere in Italy, or in the world. Or, not improbably, it might once have been the pleasure-place of an opulent family; for there was the ruin of a marble fountain in the centre, sculptured with rare art, but so woefully shattered that it was impossible to trace the original design from the chaos of remaining fragments. The water, however, continued to gush and sparkle into the sunbeams as cheerfully as ever.

A little gurgling sound ascended to the young man's window, and made him feel as if a fountain were an immortal spirit, that sung its song unceasingly, and without heeding the vicissitudes around it; while one century embodied it in marble, and another scattered the perishable garniture on the soil. All about the pool into which the water subsided, grew various plants, that seemed to require a plentiful supply of moisture for the nourishment of gigantic leaves, and, in some instances, flowers gorgeously magnificent. There was one shrub in particular, set in a marble vase in the midst of the pool, that bore a profusion of purple blossoms, each of which had the lustre and richness of a gem; and the whole together made a show so resplendent that it seemed enough to illuminate the garden, even had there been no sunshine.

Every portion of the soil was peopled with plants and herbs, which, if less beautiful, still bore tokens of assiduous care; as if all had their individual virtues, known to the scientific mind that fostered them. Some were placed in urns, rich with old carvings, and others in common garden-pots; some crept serpentlike along the ground, or climbed on high, using whatever means of ascent was offered them. One plant had wreathed itself round a statue of Vertumnus,[22] which was thus quite veiled and shrouded in a drapery of hanging foliage, so happily arranged that it might have served a sculptor for a study.

While Giovanni stood at the window, he heard a rustling behind a screen of leaves, and became aware that a person was at work in the garden. His figure soon emerged into view, and showed itself to be that of no common laborer, but a tall, emaciated, sallow, and sickly-looking man, dressed in a scholar's garb of black. He was beyond the middle term of life, with grey hair, a thin grey beard, and a face singularly marked with intellect and cultivation, but which could never, even in his more youthful days, have expressed much warmth of heart.

Nothing could exceed the intentness with which this scientific gardener examined every shrub which grew in his path; it seemed as if he was looking into their inmost nature, making observations in regard to their creative essence, and discovering why one leaf grew in this shape, and another in that, and wherefore such and such flowers differed among themselves in hue and perfume. Nevertheless, in spite of the deep intelligence on his part, there was no approach to intimacy between himself and these vegetable existences. On the contrary, he avoided their actual touch, or the direct inhaling of their odors, with a caution that impressed Giovanni most disagreeably; for the man's demeanor was that of one walking among malignant influences, such as savage beasts, or deadly snakes, or evil spirits, which, should he allow them one moment of license, would wreak upon him some terrible fatality. It was strangely frightful to the young man's imagination, to see this air of insecurity in a person cultivating a garden, that most simple and innocent of human toils, and which had been alike the

---

[22] Roman god of seasons and gardens

joy and labor of the unfallen parents of the race. Was this garden, then, the Eden of the present world?—and this man, with such a perception of harm in what his own hands caused to grow, was he the Adam?

The distrustful gardener, while plucking away the dead leaves or pruning the too luxuriant growth of the shrubs, defended his hands with a pair of thick gloves. Nor were these his only armor. When, in his walk through the garden, he came to the magnificent plant that hung its purple gems beside the marble fountain, he placed a kind of mask over his mouth and nostrils, as if all this beauty did but conceal a deadlier malice. But finding his task still too dangerous, he drew back, removed the mask, and called loudly, but in the infirm voice of a person affected with inward disease:

"Beatrice!—Beatrice!"[23]

"Here am I, my father! What would you?" cried a rich and youthful voice from the window of the opposite house; a voice as rich as a tropical sunset, and which made Giovanni, though he knew not why, think of deep hues of purple or crimson, and of perfumes heavily delectable—"Are you in the garden!"

"Yes, Beatrice," answered the gardener, "and I need your help."

Soon there emerged from under a sculptured portal the figure of a young girl, arrayed with as much richness of taste as the most splendid of the flowers, beautiful as the day, and with a bloom so deep and vivid that one shade more would have been too much. She looked redundant with life, health, and energy; all of which attributes were bound down and compressed, as it were, and girdled tensely, in their luxuriance, by her virgin zone. Yet Giovanni's fancy must have grown morbid, while he looked down into the garden; for the impression which the fair stranger made upon him was as if here were another flower, the human sister of those vegetable ones, as beautiful as they—more

---

[23] Beatrice Portinari (1266-1290) was purportedly the life love of Dante Alighieri (1265-1321) though he met her only twice in his life; Beatrice guides Dante through parts of *The Divine Comedy*

beautiful than the richest of them—but still to be touched only with a glove, nor to be approached without a mask. As Beatrice came down the garden-path, it was observable that she handled and inhaled the odor of several of the plants, which her father had most sedulously avoided.

"Here, Beatrice," said the latter,—"see how many needful offices require to be done to our chief treasure. Yet, shattered as I am, my life might pay the penalty of approaching it so closely as circumstances demand. Henceforth, I fear, this plant must be consigned to your sole charge."

"And gladly will I undertake it," cried again the rich tones of the young lady, as she bent towards the magnificent plant, and opened her arms as if to embrace it. "Yes, my sister, my splendor, it shall be Beatrice's task to nurse and serve thee; and thou shalt reward her with thy kisses and perfume breath, which to her is as the breath of life!"

Then, with all the tenderness in her manner that was so strikingly expressed in her words, she busied herself with such attentions as the plant seemed to require; and Giovanni, at his lofty window, rubbed his eyes, and almost doubted whether it were a girl tending her favorite flower, or one sister performing the duties of affection to another. The scene soon terminated.

Whether Doctor Rappaccini had finished his labors in the garden, or that his watchful eye had caught the stranger's face, he now took his daughter's arm and retired. Night was already closing in; oppressive exhalations seemed to proceed from the plants, and steal upward past the open window; and Giovanni, closing the lattice, went to his couch, and dreamed of a rich flower and beautiful girl. Flower and maiden were different and yet the same, and fraught with some strange peril in either shape.

But there is an influence in the light of morning that tends to rectify whatever errors of fancy, or even of judgment, we may have incurred during the sun's decline, or among the shadows of the night, or in the less wholesome glow of moonshine. Giovanni's first movement on starting from sleep, was to throw open the window, and gaze down into the garden which his dreams had made so fertile of mysteries. He was surprised, and a little ashamed, to find how real and matter-of-fact an affair it proved to be, in the first rays of the sun, which gilded the dew-drops that hung upon leaf and blossom, and, while giving a brighter beauty to each rare flower, brought everything within the limits of ordinary experience.

The young man rejoiced, that, in the heart of the barren city, he had the privilege of overlooking this spot of lovely and luxuriant vegetation. It would serve, he said to himself, as a symbolic language, to keep him in communion with nature. Neither the sickly and thought-worn Doctor Giacomo Rappaccini, it is true, nor his brilliant daughter, were now visible; so that Giovanni could not determine how much of the singularity which he attributed to both, was due to their own qualities, and how much to his wonder-working fancy. But he was inclined to take a most rational view of the whole matter.

In the course of the day, he paid his respects to Signor Pietro Baglioni, professor of medicine in the University, a physician of eminent repute, to whom Giovanni had brought a letter of introduction. The professor was an elderly personage, apparently of genial nature, and habits that might almost be called jovial; he kept the young man to dinner, and made himself very agreeable by the freedom and liveliness of his conversation, especially when warmed by a flask or two of Tuscan wine. Giovanni, conceiving that men of science, inhabitants of the same city, must needs be on familiar terms with one another, took an opportunity to mention the name of Dr. Rappaccini. But the professor did not respond with so much cordiality as he had anticipated.

"Ill would it become a teacher of the divine art of medicine," said Professor Pietro Baglioni, in answer to a question of Giovanni, "to withhold due and well-considered praise of a physician so eminently skilled as Rappaccini. But, on the other hand, I should answer it but scantily to my conscience, were I to permit a worthy youth like yourself, Signor Giovanni, the son of an ancient friend, to imbibe erroneous ideas respecting a man who might hereafter chance to hold your life and death in his hands. The truth is, our worshipful Doctor Rappaccini has as much science as any member of the faculty—with perhaps one single exception—in Padua, or all Italy. But there are certain grave objections to his professional character."

"And what are they?" asked the young man.

"Has my friend Giovanni any disease of body or heart, that he is so inquisitive about physicians?" said the Professor, with a smile. "But as for Rappaccini, it is said of him—and I, who know the man well, can answer for its truth—that he cares infinitely more for science than for mankind. His patients are interesting to him only as subjects for some new experiment. He would sacrifice human life, his own among the rest, or whatever else was dearest to him, for the sake of adding so much as a grain of mustard-seed to the great heap of his accumulated knowledge."

"Methinks he is an awful man, indeed," remarked Guasconti, mentally recalling the cold and purely intellectual aspect of Rappaccini. "And yet, worshipful Professor, is it not a noble spirit? Are there many men capable of so spiritual a love of science?"

"God forbid," answered the Professor, somewhat testily—"at least, unless they take sounder views of the healing art than those adopted by Rappaccini. It is his theory, that all medicinal virtues are comprised within those substances which we term vegetable poisons. These he cultivates with his own hands, and is said even to have produced new varieties of poison, more horribly deleterious than Nature, without the assistance of this learned person, would ever have plagued the world with. That the Signor Doctor does less mischief than might be expected, with such dangerous substances, is undeniable. Now and then, it must be owned, he has effected—or seemed to effect—a marvellous cure. But, to tell you my private mind, Signor Giovanni, he should receive little credit for such instances of success—they being probably the work of chance—but should be held strictly accountable for his failures, which may justly be considered his own work."

The youth might have taken Baglioni's opinions with many grains of allowance, had he known that there was a professional warfare of long continuance between him and Doctor Rappaccini, in which the latter was generally thought to have gained the advantage. If the reader be inclined to judge for himself, we refer him to certain black-letter tracts on both sides, preserved in the medical department of the University of Padua.

"I know not, most learned Professor," returned Giovanni, after musing on what had been said of Rappaccini's exclusive zeal for science—"I know not how dearly this physician may love his art; but surely there is one object more dear to him. He has a daughter."

"Aha!" cried the Professor with a laugh. "So now our friend Giovanni's secret is out. You have heard of this daughter, whom all the young men in Padua are wild about, though not half a dozen have ever had the good hap to see her face. I know little of the Signora Beatrice, save that Rappaccini is said to have instructed her deeply in his science, and that, young and beautiful as fame reports her, she is already qualified to fill a professor's chair. Perchance her father destines her for mine! Other absurd rumors there be, not worth talking about, or listening to. So now, Signor Giovanni, drink off your glass of Lacryma."[24]

Guasconti returned to his lodgings somewhat heated with the wine he had quaffed, and which

---

[24] Lacryma Christi is a praised wine from northern Italy

caused his brain to swim with strange fantasies in reference to Doctor Rappaccini and the beautiful Beatrice. On his way, happening to pass by a florist's, he bought a fresh bouquet of flowers.

Ascending to his chamber, he seated himself near the window, but within the shadow thrown by the depth of the wall, so that he could look down into the garden with little risk of being discovered. All beneath his eye was a solitude. The strange plants were basking in the sunshine, and now and then nodding gently to one another, as if in acknowledgment of sympathy and kindred. In the midst, by the shattered fountain, grew the magnificent shrub, with its purple gems clustering all over it; they glowed in the air, and gleamed back again out of the depths of the pool, which thus seemed to overflow with colored radiance from the rich reflection that was steeped in it.

At first, as we have said, the garden was a solitude. Soon, however,—as Giovanni had half-hoped, half-feared, would be the case,—a figure appeared beneath the antique sculptured portal, and came down between the rows of plants, inhaling their various perfumes, as if she were one of those beings of old classic fable, that lived upon sweet odors. On again beholding Beatrice, the young man was even startled to perceive how much her beauty exceeded his recollection of it; so brilliant, so vivid in its character, that she glowed amid the sunlight, and, as Giovanni whispered to himself, positively illuminated the more shadowy intervals of the garden path. Her face being now more revealed than on the former occasion, he was struck by its expression of simplicity and sweetness; qualities that had not entered into his idea of her character, and which made him ask anew, what manner of mortal she might be. Nor did he fail again to observe, or imagine, an analogy between the beautiful girl and the gorgeous shrub that hung its gem-like flowers over the fountain; a resemblance which Beatrice seemed to have indulged a fantastic humor in heightening, both by the arrangement of her dress and the selection of its hues.

Approaching the shrub, she threw open her arms, as with a passionate ardor, and drew its branches into an intimate embrace; so intimate, that her features were hidden in its leafy bosom, and her glistening ringlets all intermingled with the flowers.

"Give me thy breath, my sister," exclaimed Beatrice; "for I am faint with common air! And give me this flower of thine, which I separate with gentlest fingers from the stem, and place it close beside my heart."

With these words, the beautiful daughter of Rappaccini plucked one of the richest blossoms of the shrub, and was about to fasten it in her bosom. But now, unless Giovanni's draughts of wine had bewildered his senses, a singular incident occurred. A small orange-colored reptile, of the lizard or chameleon species, chanced to be creeping along the path, just at the feet of Beatrice. It appeared to Giovanni—but, at the distance from which he gazed, he could scarcely have seen anything so minute—it appeared to him, however, that a drop or two of moisture from the broken stem of the flower descended upon the lizard's head. For an instant, the reptile contorted itself violently, and then lay motionless in the sunshine.

Beatrice observed this remarkable phenomenon, and crossed herself, sadly, but without surprise; nor did she therefore hesitate to arrange the fatal flower in her bosom. There it blushed, and almost glimmered with the dazzling effect of a precious stone, adding to her dress and aspect the one appropriate charm, which nothing else in the world could have supplied. But Giovanni, out of the shadow of his window, bent forward and shrank back, and murmured and trembled.

"Am I awake? Have I my senses?" said he to himself. "What is this being?—beautiful, shall I call her?—or inexpressibly terrible?"

Beatrice now strayed carelessly through the garden, approaching closer beneath Giovanni's window, so that he was compelled to thrust his head quite out of its concealment, in order to gratify the intense and painful curiosity which she excited.

At this moment, there came a beautiful insect over the garden wall; it had perhaps wandered through the city and found no flowers nor verdure among those antique haunts of men, until the heavy perfumes of Doctor Rappaccini's shrubs had lured it from afar. Without alighting on the flowers, this winged brightness seemed to be attracted by Beatrice, and lingered in the air and fluttered about her head. Now here it could not be but that Giovanni Guasconti's eyes deceived him. Be that as it might, he fancied that while Beatrice was gazing at the insect with childish delight, it grew faint and fell at her feet!—its bright wings shivered! it was dead!—from no cause that he could discern, unless it were the atmosphere of her breath. Again Beatrice crossed herself and sighed heavily, as she bent over the dead insect.

An impulsive movement of Giovanni drew her eyes to the window. There she beheld the beautiful head of the young man—rather a Grecian than an Italian head, with fair, regular features, and a glistening of gold among his ringlets—gazing down upon her like a being that hovered in mid-air. Scarcely knowing what he did, Giovanni threw down the bouquet which he had hitherto held in his hand.

"Signora," said he, "there are pure and healthful flowers. Wear them for the sake of Giovanni Guasconti!"

"Thanks, Signor," replied Beatrice, with her rich voice, that came forth as it were like a gush of music; and with a mirthful expression half childish and half woman-like. "I accept your gift, and would fain recompense it with this precious purple flower; but if I toss it into the air, it will not reach you. So Signor Guasconti must even content himself with my thanks."

She lifted the bouquet from the ground, and then as if inwardly ashamed at having stepped aside from her maidenly reserve to respond to a stranger's greeting, passed swiftly homeward through the garden. But, few as the moments were, it seemed to Giovanni when she was on the point of vanishing beneath the sculptured portal, that his beautiful bouquet was already beginning to wither in her grasp. It was an idle thought; there could be no possibility of distinguishing a faded flower from a fresh one, at so great a distance.

For many days after this incident, the young man avoided the window that looked into Doctor Rappaccini's garden, as if something ugly and monstrous would have blasted his eyesight, had he been betrayed into a glance. He felt conscious of having put himself, to a certain extent, within the influence of an unintelligible power, by the communication which he had opened with Beatrice. The wisest course would have been, if his heart were in any real danger, to quit his lodgings and Padua itself, at once; the next wiser, to have accustomed himself, as far as possible, to the familiar and day-light view of Beatrice; thus bringing her rigidly and systematically within the limits of ordinary experience. Least of all, while avoiding her sight, should Giovanni have remained so near this extraordinary being, that the proximity and possibility even of intercourse, should give a kind of substance and reality to the wild vagaries which his imagination ran riot continually in producing.

Guasconti had not a deep heart—or at all events, its depths were not sounded now—but he had a quick fancy, and an ardent southern temperament, which rose every instant to a higher fever-pitch. Whether or no Beatrice possessed those terrible attributes—that fatal breath—the affinity with those so beautiful and deadly flowers—which were indicated by what Giovanni had witnessed, she had at least instilled a fierce and subtle poison into his system. It was not love, although her rich beauty was a madness to him; nor horror, even while he fancied her spirit to be imbued with the same baneful essence that seemed to pervade her physical frame; but a wild offspring of both love and horror that had each parent in it, and burned like one and shivered like the other. Giovanni knew not what to dread; still less did he know what to hope; yet hope and dread kept a continual warfare in his breast, alternately vanquishing one another and starting up afresh to renew the contest. Blessed are all simple emotions, be they dark or bright! It is the lurid intermixture of the two that produces the illuminating blaze of the infernal regions.

Sometimes he endeavored to assuage the fever of his spirit by a rapid walk through the streets of Padua, or beyond its gates; his footsteps kept time with the throbbings of his brain, so that the walk was apt to accelerate itself to a race. One day, he found himself arrested; his arm was seized by a portly personage who had turned back on recognizing the young man, and expended much breath in overtaking him.

"Signor Giovanni!—stay, my young friend!" cried he. "Have you forgotten me? That might well be the case, if I were as much altered as yourself."

It was Baglioni, whom Giovanni had avoided, ever since their first meeting, from a doubt that the professor's sagacity would look too deeply into his secrets. Endeavoring to recover himself, he stared forth wildly from his inner world into the outer one, and spoke like a man in a dream.

"Yes; I am Giovanni Guasconti. You are Professor Pietro Baglioni. Now let me pass!"

"Not yet—not yet, Signor Giovanni Guasconti," said the Professor, smiling, but at the same time scrutinizing the youth with an earnest glance.—"What; did I grow up side by side with your father, and shall his son pass me like a stranger, in these old streets of Padua? Stand still, Signor Giovanni; for we must have a word or two before we part."

"Speedily, then, most worshipful Professor, speedily!" said Giovanni, with feverish impatience. "Does not your worship see that I am in haste?"

Now, while he was speaking, there came a man in black along the street, stooping and moving feebly, like a person in inferior health. His face was all overspread with a most sickly and sallow hue, but yet so pervaded with an expression of piercing and active intellect, that an observer might easily have overlooked the merely physical attributes, and have seen only this wonderful energy. As he passed, this person exchanged a cold and distant salutation with Baglioni, but fixed his eyes upon Giovanni with an intentness that seemed to bring out whatever was within him worthy of notice. Nevertheless, there was a peculiar quietness in the look, as if taking merely a speculative, not a human interest, in the young man.

"It is Doctor Rappaccini!" whispered the Professor, when the stranger had passed.—"Has he ever seen your face before?"

"Not that I know," answered Giovanni, starting at the name.

"He *has* seen you!—he must have seen you!" said Baglioni, hastily. "For some purpose or other, this man of science is making a study of you. I know that look of his! It is the same that coldly illuminates his face, as he bends over a bird, a mouse, or a butterfly, which, in pursuance of some experiment, he has killed by the perfume of a flower;—a look as deep as nature itself, but without nature's warmth of love. Signor Giovanni, I will stake my life upon it, you are the subject of one of Rappaccini's experiments!"

"Will you make a fool of me?" cried Giovanni, passionately. "*That,* Signor Professor, were an untoward experiment."

"Patience, patience!" replied the imperturbable Professor. "I tell thee, my poor Giovanni, that Rappaccini has a scientific interest in thee. Thou hast fallen into fearful hands! And the Signora Beatrice? What part does she act in this mystery?"

But Guasconti, finding Baglioni's pertinacity intolerable, here broke away, and was gone before the Professor could again seize his arm. He looked after the young man intently, and shook his head.

"This must not be," said Bagiloni to himself. "The youth is the son of my old friend, and shall not come to any harm from which the arcana of medical science can preserve him. Besides, it is too insufferable an impertinence in Rappaccini thus to snatch the lad out of my own hands, as I may say, and make use of him for his infernal experiments. This daughter of his! It shall be looked to. Perchance, most learned Rappaccini, I may foil you where you little dream of it!"

Meanwhile, Giovanni had pursued a circuitous route, and at length found himself at the door of his lodgings. As he crossed the threshold, he was met by old Lisabetta, who smirked and smiled, and was evidently desirous to attract his attention; vainly, however, as the ebullition of his feelings had momentarily subsided into a cold and dull vacuity. He turned his eyes full upon the withered face that was puckering itself into a smile, but seemed to behold it not. The old dame, therefore, laid her grasp upon his cloak.

"Signor!—Signor!" whispered she, still with a smile over the whole breadth of her visage, so that it looked not unlike a grotesque carving in wood, darkened by centuries—"Listen, Signor! There is a private entrance into the garden!"

"What do you say?" exclaimed Giovanni, turning quickly about, as if an inanimate thing should start into feverish life.—"A private entrance into Doctor Rappaccini's garden!"

"Hush! hush!—not so loud!" whispered Lisabetta, putting her hand over his mouth. "Yes; into the worshipful Doctor's garden, where you may see all his fine shrubbery. Many a young man in Padua would give gold to be admitted among those flowers."

Giovanni put a piece of gold into her hand. "Show me the way," said he.

A surmise, probably excited by his conversation with Baglioni, crossed his mind, that this interposition of old Lisabetta might perchance be connected with the intrigue, whatever were its nature, in which the Professor seemed to suppose that Doctor Rappaccini was involving him. But such a suspicion, though it disturbed Giovanni, was inadequate to restrain him.

The instant he was aware of the possibility of approaching Beatrice, it seemed an absolute necessity of his existence to do so. It mattered not whether she were angel or demon; he was irrevocably within her sphere, and must obey the law that whirled him onward, in ever lessening circles, towards a result which he did not attempt to foreshadow. And yet, strange to say, there came across him a sudden doubt, whether this intense interest on his part were not delusory—whether it were really of so deep and positive a nature as to justify him in now thrusting himself into an incalculable position—whether it were not merely the fantasy of a young man's brain, only slightly, or not at all, connected with his heart!

He paused—hesitated—turned half about—but again went on. His withered guide led him along several obscure passages, and finally undid a door, through which, as it was opened, there came the sight and sound of rustling leaves, with the broken sunshine glimmering among them. Giovanni stepped forth, and forcing himself through the entanglement of a shrub that wreathed its tendrils over the hidden entrance, he stood beneath his own window, in the open area of Doctor Rappaccini's garden.

How often is it the case, that, when impossibilities have come to pass, and dreams have condensed their misty substance into tangible realities, we find ourselves calm, and even coldly self possessed, amid circumstances which it would have been a delirium of joy or agony to anticipate! Fate delights to thwart us thus. Passion will choose his own time to rush upon the scene, and lingers sluggishly behind, when an appropriate adjustment of events would seem to summon his appearance. So was it now with Giovanni. Day after day, his pulses had throbbed with feverish blood, at the improbable idea of an interview with Beatrice, and of standing with her, face to face, in this very garden, basking in the oriental sunshine of her beauty, and snatching from her full gaze the mystery which he deemed the riddle of his own existence. But now there was a singular and untimely equanimity within his breast. He threw a glance around the garden to discover if Beatrice or her father were present, and perceiving that he was alone, began a critical observation of the plants.

The aspect of one and all of them dissatisfied him; their gorgeousness seemed fierce, passionate, and even unnatural. There was hardly an individual shrub which a wanderer, straying by himself through a forest, would not have been startled to find growing wild, as if an unearthly face had glared at him out of the thicket. Several, also, would have shocked a delicate instinct by an appearance of artificialness, indicating that there had been such commixture, and, as it were, adultery of various vegetable species, that the production was no longer of God's making, but the monstrous offspring of man's depraved fancy, glowing with only an evil mockery of beauty. They were probably the result of experiment, which, in one or two cases, had succeeded in mingling plants individually lovely into a compound possessing the questionable and ominous character that distinguished the whole growth of the garden. In fine, Giovanni recognized but two or three plants in the collection, and those of a kind that he well knew to be poisonous. While busy with these contemplations, he heard the rustling of a silken garment, and turning, beheld Beatrice emerging from beneath the sculptured portal.

Giovanni had not considered with himself what should be his deportment; whether he should apologize for his intrusion into the garden, or assume that he was there with the privity, at least, if not by the desire, of Doctor Rappaccini or his daughter. But

Beatrice's manner placed him at his ease, though leaving him still in doubt by what agency he had gained admittance. She came lightly along the path, and met him near the broken fountain. There was surprise in her face, but brightened by a simple and kind expression of pleasure.

"You are a connoisseur in flowers, Signor," said Beatrice with a smile, alluding to the bouquet which he had flung her from the window. "It is no marvel, therefore, if the sight of my father's rare collection has tempted you to take a nearer view. If he were here, he could tell you many strange and interesting facts as to the nature and habits of these shrubs, for he has spent a life-time in such studies, and this garden is his world."

"And yourself, lady"—observed Giovanni—"if fame says true—you, likewise, are deeply skilled in the virtues indicated by these rich blossoms, and these spicy perfumes. Would you deign to be my instructress, I should prove an apter scholar than under Signor Rappaccini himself."

"Are there such idle rumors?" asked Beatrice, with the music of a pleasant laugh. "Do people say that I am skilled in my father's science of plants? What a jest is there! No; though I have grown up among these flowers, I know no more of them than their hues and perfume; and sometimes, methinks I would fain rid myself of even that small knowledge. There are many flowers here, and those not the least brilliant, that shock and offend me, when they meet my eye. But, pray, Signor, do not believe these stories about my science. Believe nothing of me save what you see with your own eyes."

"And must I believe all that I have seen with my own eyes?" asked Giovanni pointedly, while the recollection of former scenes made him shrink. "No, Signora, you demand too little of me. Bid me believe nothing, save what comes from your own lips."

It would appear that Beatrice understood him. There came a deep flush to her cheek; but she looked full into Giovanni's eyes, and responded to his gaze of uneasy suspicion with a queenlike haughtiness.

"I do so bid you, Signor!" she replied. "Forget whatever you may have fancied in regard to me. If true to the outward senses, still it may be false in its essence. But the words of Beatrice Rappaccini's lips are true from the heart outward. Those you may believe!"

A fervor glowed in her whole aspect, and beamed upon Giovanni's consciousness like the light of truth itself. But while she spoke, there was a fragrance in the atmosphere around her rich and delightful, though evanescent, yet which the young man, from an indefinable reluctance, scarcely dared to draw into his lungs. It might be the odor of the flowers. Could it be Beatrice's breath, which thus embalmed her words with a strange richness, as if by steeping them in her heart? A faintness passed like a shadow over Giovanni, and flitted away; he seemed to gaze through the beautiful girl's eyes into her transparent soul, and felt no more doubt or fear.

The tinge of passion that had colored Beatrice's manner vanished; she became gay, and appeared to derive a pure delight from her communion with the youth, not unlike what the maiden of a lonely island might have felt, conversing with a voyager from the civilized world. Evidently her experience of life had been confined within the limits of that garden.

She talked now about matters as simple as the day-light or summer-clouds, and now asked questions in reference to the city, or Giovanni's distant home, his friends, his mother, and his sisters; questions indicating such seclusion, and such lack of familiarity with modes and forms, that Giovanni responded as if to an infant. Her spirit gushed out before him like a fresh rill, that was just catching its first glimpse of the sunlight, and wondering at the reflections of earth and sky which were flung into its bosom. There came thoughts, too, from a deep source, and fantasies of a gem-like brilliancy, as if diamonds and rubies sparkled upward among the bubbles of the fountain. Ever and anon, there gleamed across the young man's mind a sense of wonder, that he should be walking side by side with the being who had so wrought upon his imagination—whom he had idealized in such hues of terror—in whom he had positively witnessed such manifestations of dreadful attributes—that he should be conversing with Beatrice like a brother, and should find her so human and so maiden-like. But such reflections were only momentary; the effect of her character was too real, not to make itself familiar at once.

In this free intercourse, they had strayed through the garden, and now, after many turns among its avenues, were come to the shattered fountain, beside which grew the magnificent shrub with its treasury of glowing blossoms. A fragrance was diffused from it, which Giovanni recognized as identical with that which he had attributed to Beatrice's breath, but incomparably more powerful. As her eyes fell upon it, Giovanni beheld her press her hand to her bosom, as if her heart were throbbing suddenly and painfully.

"For the first time in my life," murmured she, addressing the shrub, "I had forgotten thee!"

"I remember, Signora," said Giovanni, "that you once promised to reward me with one of these living gems for the bouquet, which I had the happy boldness to fling to your feet. Permit me now to pluck it as a memorial of this interview."

He made a step towards the shrub, with extended hand. But Beatrice darted forward, uttering a shriek that went through his heart like a dagger. She caught his hand, and drew it back with the whole force of her slender figure. Giovanni felt her touch thrilling through his fibres.

"Touch it not!" exclaimed she, in a voice of agony. "Not for thy life! It is fatal!"

Then, hiding her face, she fled from him, and vanished beneath the sculptured portal. As Giovanni followed her with his eyes, he beheld the emaciated figure and pale intelligence of Doctor Rappaccini, who had been watching the scene, he knew not how long, within the shadow of the entrance.

No sooner was Guasconti alone in his chamber, than the image of Beatrice came back to his passionate musings, invested with all the witchery that had been gathering around it ever since his first glimpse of her, and now likewise imbued with a tender warmth of girlish womanhood. She was human; her nature was endowed with all gentle and feminine qualities; she was worthiest to be worshipped; she was capable, surely, on her part, of the height and heroism of love. Those tokens, which he had hitherto considered as proofs of a frightful peculiarity in her physical and moral system, were now either forgotten, or, by the subtle sophistry of passion, transmuted into a golden crown of enchantment, rendering Beatrice the more admirable, by so much as she was the more unique.

Whatever had looked ugly, was now beautiful; or, if incapable of such a change, it stole away and hid itself among those shapeless half-ideas, which throng the dim region beyond the daylight of our perfect consciousness. Thus did Giovanni spend the night, nor fell asleep, until the dawn had begun to awake the slumbering flowers in Doctor Rappaccini's garden, whither his dreams doubtless led him. Up rose the sun in his due season, and flinging his beams upon the young man's eyelids, awoke him to a sense of pain. When thoroughly aroused, he became sensible of a burning and tingling agony in his hand—in his right hand—the very hand which Beatrice had grasped in her own, when he was on the point of plucking one of the gemlike flowers. On the back of that hand there was now a purple print, like that of four small fingers, and the likeness of a slender thumb upon his wrist.

Oh, how stubbornly does love—or even that cunning semblance of love which flourishes in the imagination, but strikes no depth of root into the heart—how stubbornly does it hold its faith, until the moment come, when it is doomed to vanish into thin mist! Giovanni wrapt a handkerchief about his hand, and wondered what evil thing had stung him, and soon forgot his pain in a reverie of Beatrice.

After the first interview, a second was in the inevitable course of what we call fate. A third; a fourth; and a meeting with Beatrice in the garden was no longer an incident in Giovanni's daily life, but the whole space in which he might be said to live; for the anticipation and memory of that ecstatic hour made up the remainder. Nor was it otherwise with the daughter of Rappaccini. She watched for the youth's appearance, and flew to his side with confidence as unreserved as if they had been playmates from early infancy—as if they were such playmates still. If, by any unwonted chance, he failed to come at the appointed moment, she stood beneath the window, and sent up the rich sweetness of her tones to float around him in his chamber, and echo and reverberate throughout his heart—"Giovanni! Giovanni! Why tarriest thou? Come down!"—And down he hastened into that Eden of poisonous flowers.

But, with all this intimate familiarity, there was still a reserve in Beatrice's demeanor, so rigidly and invariably sustained, that the idea of infringing it scarcely occurred to his imagination. By all appreciable signs, they loved; they had looked love, with eyes that conveyed the holy secret from the depths of one soul into the depths of the other, as if it were too sacred to be whispered by the way; they had even spoken love, in those gushes of passion when their spirits darted forth in articulated breath, like tongues of long-hidden flame; and yet there had been no seal of lips, no clasp of hands, nor any slightest caress, such as love claims and hallows.

He had never touched one of the gleaming ringlets of her hair; her garment—so marked was the physical barrier between them—had never been waved against him by a breeze. On the few occasions when Giovanni had seemed tempted to overstep the limit, Beatrice grew so sad, so stern, and withal wore such a look of desolate separation, shuddering at itself, that not a spoken word was requisite to repel him. At such times, he was startled at the horrible suspicions that rose, monster-like, out of the caverns of his heart, and stared him in the face; his love grew thin and faint as the morning-mist; his doubts alone had substance. But when Beatrice's face brightened again, after the momentary shadow, she was transformed at once from the mysterious, questionable being, whom he had watched with so much awe and horror; she was now the beautiful and unsophisticated girl, whom he felt that his spirit knew with a certainty beyond all other knowledge.

A considerable time had now passed since Giovanni's last meeting with Baglioni. One morning, however, he was disagreeably surprised by a visit from the Professor, whom he had scarcely thought of for whole weeks, and would willingly have forgotten still longer. Given up, as he had long been, to a pervading excitement, he could tolerate no companions, except upon condition of their perfect sympathy with his present state of feeling. Such sympathy was not to be expected from Professor Baglioni.

The visitor chatted carelessly, for a few moments, about the gossip of the city and the University, and then took up another topic.

"I have been reading an old classic author lately," said he, "and met with a story that strangely interested me. Possibly you may remember it. It is of an Indian prince, who sent a beautiful woman as a present to Alexander the Great. She was as lovely as the dawn, and gorgeous as the sunset; but what especially distinguished her was a certain rich perfume in her breath—richer than a garden of Persian roses. Alexander, as was natural to a youthful conqueror, fell in love at first sight with this magnificent stranger. But a certain sage physician, happening to be present, discovered a terrible secret in regard to her."

"And what was that?" asked Giovanni, turning his eyes downward to avoid those of the Professor.

"That this lovely woman," continued Baglioni, with emphasis, "had been nourished with poisons from her birth upward, until her whole nature was so imbued with them, that she herself had become the deadliest poison in existence. Poison was her element of life. With that rich perfume of her breath, she blasted the very air. Her love would have been poison!—her embrace death! Is not this a marvellous tale?"

"A childish fable," answered Giovanni, nervously starting from his chair. "I marvel how your worship finds time to read such nonsense, among your graver studies."

"By the bye," said the Professor, looking uneasily about him, "what singular fragrance is this in your apartment? Is it the perfume of your gloves? It is faint, but delicious, and yet, after all, by no means agreeable. Were I to breathe it long, methinks it would make me ill. It is like the breath of a flower—but I see no flowers in the chamber."

"Nor are there any," replied Giovanni, who had turned pale as the Professor spoke; "nor, I think, is there any fragrance, except in your worship's imagination. Odors, being a sort of element combined of the sensual and the spiritual, are apt to deceive us in this manner. The recollection of a perfume—the bare idea of it—may easily be mistaken for a present reality."

"Aye; but my sober imagination does not often play such tricks," said Baglioni; "and were I to fancy any kind of odor, it would be that of some vile apothecary drug, wherewith my fingers are likely enough to be imbued. Our worshipful friend Rappaccini, as I have heard, tinctures his medicaments with odors richer than those of Araby. Doubtless, likewise, the fair and learned Signora Beatrice would minister to her patients with draughts as sweet as a maiden's breath. But wo to him that sips them!"

Giovanni's face evinced many contending emotions. The tone in which the Professor alluded to the pure and lovely daughter of Rappaccini was a torture to his soul; and yet, the intimation of a view of her character, opposite to his own, gave instantaneous distinctness to a thousand dim suspicions, which now grinned at him like so many demons. But he strove hard to quell them, and to respond to Baglioni with a true lover's perfect faith.

"Signor Professor," said he, "you were my father's friend—perchance, too, it is your purpose to act a friendly part towards his son. I would fain feel nothing towards you save respect and deference. But I pray you to observe, Signor, that there is one subject on which we must not speak. You know not the Signora Beatrice. You cannot, therefore, estimate the wrong— the blasphemy, I may even say—that is offered to her character by a light or injurious word."

"Giovanni!—my poor Giovanni!" answered the Professor, with a calm expression of pity, "I know this wretched girl far better than yourself. You shall hear the truth in respect to the poisoner Rappaccini, and his poisonous daughter. Yes; poisonous as she is beautiful! Listen; for even should you do violence to my grey hairs, it shall not silence me. That old fable of the Indian woman has become a truth, by the deep and deadly science of Rappaccini, and in the person of the lovely Beatrice!"

Giovanni groaned and hid his face.

"Her father," continued Baglioni, "was not restrained by natural affection from offering up his child, in this horrible manner, as the victim of his insane zeal for science. For—let us do him justice—he is as true a man of science as ever distilled his own heart in an alembic.[25] What, then, will be your fate? Beyond a doubt, you are selected as the material of some new experiment. Perhaps the result is to be death—perhaps a fate more awful still! Rappaccini,

---

[25] Ancient distilling apparatus with a long neck and cap

with what he calls the interest of science before his eyes, will hesitate at nothing."

"It is a dream!" muttered Giovanni to himself, "surely it is a dream!"

"But," resumed the professor, "be of good cheer, son of my friend! It is not yet too late for the rescue. Possibly, we may even succeed in bringing back this miserable child within the limits of ordinary nature, from which her father's madness has estranged her. Behold this little silver vase! It was wrought by the hands of the renowned Benvenuto Cellini,[26] and is well worthy to be a love-gift to the fairest dame in Italy. But its contents are invaluable. One little sip of this antidote would have rendered the most virulent poisons of the Borgias innocuous. Doubt not that it will be as efficacious against those of Rappaccini. Bestow the vase, and the precious liquid within it, on your Beatrice, and hopefully await the result."

Baglioni laid a small, exquisitely wrought silver phial on the table, and withdrew, leaving what he had said to produce its effect upon the young man's mind.

"We will thwart Rappaccini yet!" thought he, chuckling to himself, as he descended the stairs. "But, let us confess the truth of him, he is a wonderful man!—a wonderful man indeed! A vile empiric, however, in his practice, and therefore not to be tolerated by those who respect the good old rules of the medical profession!"

Throughout Giovanni's whole acquaintance with Beatrice, he had occasionally, as we have said, been haunted by dark surmises as to her character. Yet, so thoroughly had she made herself felt by him as a simple, natural, most affectionate and guileless creature, that the image now held up by Professor Baglioni, looked as strange and incredible, as if it were not in accordance with his own original conception. True, there were ugly recollections connected with his first glimpses of the beautiful girl; he could not quite

---

[26] Benvenuto Cellini (1500-1571) was a famous Italian sculptor and metalsmith

forget the bouquet that withered in her grasp, and the insect that perished amid the sunny air, by no ostensible agency save the fragrance of her breath.

These incidents, however, dissolving in the pure light of her character, had no longer the efficacy of facts, but were acknowledged as mistaken fantasies, by whatever testimony of the senses they might appear to be substantiated. There is something truer and more real, than what we can see with the eyes, and touch with the finger. On such better evidence, had Giovanni founded his confidence in Beatrice, though rather by the necessary force of her high attributes, than by any deep and generous faith on his part.

But, now, his spirit was incapable of sustaining itself at the height to which the early enthusiasm of passion had exalted it; he fell down, grovelling among earthly doubts, and defiled therewith the pure whiteness of Beatrice's image. Not that he gave her up; he did but distrust. He resolved to institute some decisive test that should satisfy him, once for all, whether there were those dreadful peculiarities in her physical nature, which could not be supposed to exist without some corresponding monstrosity of soul.

His eyes, gazing down afar, might have deceived him as to the lizard, the insect, and the flowers. But if he could witness, at the distance of a few paces, the sudden blight of one fresh and healthful flower in Beatrice's hand, there would be room for no further question. With this idea, he hastened to the florist's, and purchased a bouquet that was still gemmed with the morning dewdrops.

It was now the customary hour of his daily interview with Beatrice. Before descending into the garden, Giovanni failed not to look at his figure in the mirror; a vanity to be expected in a beautiful young man, yet, as displaying itself at that troubled and feverish moment, the token of a certain shallowness of feeling and insincerity of character. He did gaze, however, and said to himself, that his features had never before possessed so rich a grace, nor his eyes such vivacity, nor his cheeks so warm a hue of superabundant life.

"At least," thought he, "her poison has not yet insinuated itself into my system. I am no flower to perish in her grasp!"

With that thought, he turned his eyes on the bouquet, which he had never once laid aside from his hand. A thrill of indefinable horror shot through his frame, on perceiving that those dewy flowers were already beginning to droop; they wore the aspect of things that had been fresh and lovely, yesterday. Giovanni grew white as marble, and stood motionless before the mirror, staring at his own reflection there, as at the likeness of something frightful. He remembered Baglioni's remark about the fragrance that seemed to pervade the chamber. It must have been the poison in his breath!

Then he shuddered—shuddered at himself! Recovering from his stupor, he began to watch, with curious eye, a spider that was busily at work, hanging its web from the antique cornice of the apartment, crossing and re-crossing the artful system of interwoven lines, as vigorous and active a spider as ever dangled from an old ceiling. Giovanni bent towards the insect, and emitted a deep, long breath. The spider suddenly ceased its toil; the web vibrated with a tremor originating in the body of the small artizan. Again Giovanni sent forth a breath, deeper, longer, and imbued with a venomous feeling out of his heart; he knew not whether he were wicked or only desperate. The spider made a convulsive gripe with his limbs, and hung dead across the window.

"Accursed! Accursed!" muttered Giovanni, addressing himself. "Hast thou grown so poisonous, that this deadly insect perishes by thy breath?"

At that moment, a rich, sweet voice came floating up from the garden:—

"Giovanni! Giovanni! It is past the hour! Why tarriest thou! Come down!"

"Yes," muttered Giovanni again. "She is the only being whom my breath may not slay! Would that it might!"

He rushed down, and in an instant, was standing before the bright and loving eyes of Beatrice. A moment ago, his wrath and despair had been so fierce that he could have desired nothing so much as to wither her by a glance. But, with her actual presence, there came influences which had too real an existence to be at once shaken off; recollections of the delicate and benign power of her feminine nature, which had so often enveloped him in a religious calm; recollections of many a holy and passionate outgush of her heart, when the pure fountain had been unsealed from its depths, and made visible in its transparency to his mental eye; recollections which, had Giovanni known how to estimate them, would have assured him that all this ugly mystery was but an earthly illusion, and that, whatever mist of evil might seem to have gathered over her, the real Beatrice was a heavenly angel.

Incapable as he was of such high faith, still her presence had not utterly lost its magic. Giovanni's rage was quelled into an aspect of sullen insensibility. Beatrice, with a quick spiritual sense, immediately felt that there was a gulf of blackness between them, which neither he nor she could pass. They walked on together, sad and silent, and came thus to the marble fountain, and to its pool of water on the ground, in the midst of which grew the shrub that bore gemlike blossoms. Giovanni was affrighted at the eager enjoyment—the appetite, as it were—with which he found himself inhaling the fragrance of the flowers.

"Beatrice," asked he abruptly, "whence came this shrub!"

"My father created it," answered she, with simplicity.

"Created it! created it!" repeated Giovanni. "What mean you, Beatrice?"

"He is a man fearfully acquainted with the secrets of nature," replied Beatrice; "and, at the hour when I first drew breath, this plant sprang from the soil, the offspring of his science, of his intellect, while I was but his earthly child. Approach it not!" continued she, observing with terror that Giovanni was drawing nearer to the shrub. "It has qualities that you little dream of. But I, dearest Giovanni,—I grew up and blossomed with the plant, and was nourished with its breath. It was my sister, and I loved it with a human affection: for—alas! hast thou not suspected it? There was an awful doom."

Here Giovanni frowned so darkly upon her that Beatrice paused and trembled. But her faith in his tenderness reassured her, and made her blush that she had doubted for an instant.

"There was an awful doom," she continued,—"the effect of my father's fatal love of science—which estranged me from all society of my kind. Until Heaven sent thee, dearest Giovanni, Oh! how lonely was thy poor Beatrice!"

"Was it a hard doom?" asked Giovanni, fixing his eyes upon her.

"Only of late have I known how hard it was," answered she tenderly. "Oh, yes; but my heart was torpid, and therefore quiet."

Giovanni's rage broke forth from his sullen gloom like a lightning-flash out of a dark cloud.

"Accursed one!" cried he, with venomous scorn and anger.

"And finding thy solitude wearisome, thou hast severed me, likewise, from all the warmth of life, and enticed me into thy region of unspeakable horror!"

"Giovanni!" exclaimed Beatrice, turning her large bright eyes upon his face. The force of his words had not found its way into her mind; she was merely thunder-struck.

"Yes, poisonous thing!" repeated Giovanni, beside himself with passion. "Thou hast done it! Thou hast blasted me! Thou hast filled my veins with poison! Thou hast made me as hateful, as ugly, as loathsome and deadly a creature as thyself,—a world's wonder of hideous monstrosity! Now—if our breath be happily as fatal to ourselves as to all others—let us join our lips in one kiss of unutterable hatred, and so die!"

"What has befallen me?" murmured Beatrice, with a low moan out of her heart. "Holy Virgin pity me, a poor heartbroken child!"

"Thou! Dost thou pray?" cried Giovanni, still with the same fiendish scorn. "Thy very prayers, as they come from thy lips, taint the atmosphere with death. Yes, yes; let us pray! Let us to church, and dip our fingers in the holy water at the portal! They that come after us will perish as by a pestilence. Let us sign crosses in the air! It will be scattering curses abroad in the likeness of holy symbols!"

"Giovanni," said Beatrice calmly, for her grief was beyond passion, "why dost thou join thyself with me thus in those terrible words? I, it is true, am the horrible thing thou namest me. But thou!—what hast thou to do, save with one other shudder at my hideous misery, to go forth out of the garden and mingle with thy race, and forget that there ever crawled on earth such a monster as poor Beatrice?"

"Dost thou pretend ignorance?" asked Giovanni, scowling upon her. "Behold! This power have I gained from the pure daughter of Rappaccini!"

There was a swarm of summer-insects flitting through the air, in search of the food promised by the flower-odors of the fatal garden. They circled round Giovanni's head, and were evidently attracted towards him by the same influence which had drawn them, for an instant, within the sphere of several of the shrubs. He sent forth a breath among them, and smiled bitterly at Beatrice, as at least a score of the insects fell dead upon the ground.

"I see it! I see it!" shrieked Beatrice. "It is my father's fatal science? No, no, Giovanni; it was not I! Never, never! I dreamed only to love thee, and be with thee a little time, and so to let thee pass away, leaving but thine image in mine heart. For, Giovanni—believe it—though my body be nourished with poison, my spirit is God's creature, and craves love as its daily food. But my father!—he has united us in this fearful sympathy. Yes; spurn me!—tread upon me!—kill me! Oh, what is death, after such words as thine? But it was not I! Not for a world of bliss would I have done it!"

Giovanni's passion had exhausted itself in its outburst from his lips. There now came across him a sense, mournful, and not without tenderness, of the intimate and peculiar relationship between Beatrice and himself. They stood, as it were, in an utter solitude, which would be made none the less solitary by the densest throng of human life. Ought not, then, the desert of humanity around them to press this insulated pair closer together?

If they should be cruel to one another, who was there to be kind to them? Besides, thought Giovanni, might there not still be a hope of his returning within the limits of ordinary nature, and leading Beatrice— the redeemed Beatrice—by the hand? Oh, weak, and selfish, and unworthy spirit, that could dream of an earthly union and earthly happiness as possible, after such deep love had been so bitterly wronged as was Beatrice's love by Giovanni's blighting words! No, no; there could be no such hope. She must pass heavily, with that broken heart, across the borders—she must bathe her hurts in some fount of Paradise, and forget her grief in the light of immortality—and *there* be well! But Giovanni did not know it.

"Dear Beatrice," said he, approaching her, while she shrank away, as always at his approach, but now with a different impulse—"dearest Beatrice, our fate is not yet so desperate. Behold! There is a medicine, potent, as a wise physician has assured me, and almost divine in its efficacy. It is composed of ingredients the most opposite to those by which thy awful father has brought this calamity upon thee and me. It is distilled of blessed herbs. Shall we not quaff it together, and thus be purified from evil?"

"Give it me!" said Beatrice, extending her hand to receive the little silver phial which Giovanni took from his bosom. She added, with a peculiar emphasis: "I will drink—but do thou await the result."

She put Baglioni's antidote to her lips; and, at the same moment, the figure of Rappaccini emerged from the portal, and came slowly towards the marble fountain. As he drew near, the pale man of science seemed to gaze with a triumphant expression at the beautiful youth and maiden, as might an artist who should spend his life in achieving a picture or a group of statuary, and finally be satisfied with his success. He paused—his bent form grew erect with conscious power, he spread out his hand over them, in the attitude of a father imploring a blessing upon his children. But those were the same hands that had thrown poison into the stream of their lives! Giovanni trembled. Beatrice shuddered very nervously, and pressed her hand upon her heart.

"My daughter," said Rappaccini, "thou art no longer lonely in the world! Pluck one of those precious gems from thy sister shrub, and bid thy bridegroom wear it in his bosom. It will not harm him now! My science, and the sympathy between thee and him, have so wrought within his system, that he now stands apart from common men, as thou dost, daughter of my pride and triumph, from ordinary women. Pass on, then, through the world, most dear to one another, and dreadful to all besides!"

"My father," said Beatrice, feebly—and still, as she spoke, she kept her hand upon her heart—"wherefore didst thou inflict this miserable doom upon thy child?"

"Miserable!" exclaimed Rappaccini. "What mean you, foolish girl? Dost thou deem it misery to be endowed with marvellous gifts, against which no power nor strength could avail an enemy? Misery, to be able to quell the mightiest with a breath? Misery, to be as terrible as thou art beautiful! Wouldst thou, then, have preferred the condition of a weak woman, exposed to all evil, and capable of none?"

"I would fain have been loved, not feared," murmured Beatrice, sinking down upon the ground. "But now it matters not; I am going, father, where the evil, which thou hast striven to mingle with my being, will pass away like a dream—like the fragrance of these poisonous flowers, which will no longer taint my breath among the flowers of Eden. Farewell, Giovanni! Thy words of hatred are like lead within my heart—but they, too, will fall away as I ascend. Oh, was there not, from the first, more poison in thy nature than in mine?"

To Beatrice—so radically had her earthly part been wrought upon by Rappaccini's skill—as poison had been life, so the powerful antidote was death. And thus the poor victim of man's ingenuity and of thwarted nature, and of the fatality that attends all such efforts of perverted wisdom, perished there, at the feet of her father and Giovanni. Just at that moment, Professor Pietro Baglioni looked forth from the window, and called loudly, in a tone of triumph mixed with horror, to the thunder-stricken man of science:—

"Rappaccini! Rappaccini! And is *this* the upshot of your experiment?"

LYDIA MARIA CHILD
(1802-1880)

Introduction
The Rival Mechanicians

"The Rival Mechanicians" was published by Lydia Maria Child during 1847 in *The Columbian Magazine*, just as she did "Hilda Silfverling. A Fantasy," two years prior.

Child's story met with brief success after its publication. A commenter in *The Western Literary Messenger* opined that the story was "above praise." In 1848 it was republished in James Hogg's *Weekly Instructor* and then, oddly, disappeared from the publication map until 1857 when Child included it in her collection of short stories *Autumnal Leaves: Tales and Sketches in Prose and Rhyme*. Sadly, I have been unable to find this story published elsewhere in the last 150 years. This may be why even many scholarly sites have failed to link the story to Child; or perhaps because it is so far afield from her other works on abolition, the rights of American Indians and animals.

Because of this it is easy to forget that Child was an early female pioneer in penning short stories of the supernatural. *Autumnal Leaves* further included "The Ancient Clairvoyant," "The Fairy Friend," and "Utouch and Touchu."

In a June 11, 1875 letter to the abolitionist, Samuel E. Sewall, Child was still interested in technology as it related to the afterlife. She told of her disappointment when recently visiting a "spirit-photographer," which purported to show dead spirits in his developed film. "Still, notwithstanding the great amount of trickery practised, and the unsatisfactory nature of all the communications, there are real phenomena connected with the subject, which are to me inexplicable, and which indicate some laws of the universe at present unknown to us."

In an 1879 letter to Mrs. S. B. Shaw, Child wrote: "Science pronounces it entirely illogical to suppose that we exist as individuals after our bodies are resolved to the elements. But logic is a science extremely narrow in its limitations. There may be phases of existence as much beyond its cognizance as birds are beyond the observation of fishes."

The Rival Mechanicians
(1847)

"I AM GROWING old; my sight is failing very fast," said the famous watchmaker of Geneva, as he wiped his spectacles to examine several chronometers, which his two apprentices laid before him. "Well done! Very well done, my lads," said he. "I hardly know which of you will best supply the place of old Antoine Breguet.[1] Thirty years ago, (pardon an old man's vanity,) I could have borne away the palm from a hundred like ye. But my sight is dim and my hands tremble. I must retire from the place I have occupied in this busy world; and I confess I should like to give up my famous old stand to a worthy successor. Whichever of you produces the most perfect piece of mechanism before the end of two years shall be my partner and representative, if Rosabella and I both agree in the decision."

The granddaughter, who was busily spinning flax, looked up bashfully, and met the glance of the two young men. The countenance of one hushed, and his eye sparkled; the other turned very pale, and there was a painfully deep intensity in his fixed gaze.

The one who blushed was Florien Amaud, a youth from the French Cantons. He was slender and graceful in figure, with beautiful features, clear blue eyes, and a complexion fresh as Hylas,[2] when the enamored water-nymphs carried him away in their arms. He danced like a zephyr,[3] and sang little airy French romanzas in the sweetest of tenor voices.

---

[1] Louis-Antoine Brequet (1776-1858) was a famous watchmaker trained by his famous watchmaker father, Abraham Louis Brequet (1747-1823)

[2] Young man in Greek mythology who was a friend to Heracles

[3] Playful breeze

The one who turned pale was Pierre Berthoud, of Geneva. He had massy features, a bulky frame and clumsy motions. But the shape of his head indicated powerful intellect, and his great dark eyes glowed from under the penthouse of his brows like a forge at midnight. He played on the bassviol and the trombone, and when he sang, the tones sounded as if they came up from deep iron mines.

Rosabella turned quickly away from their expressive glances, and blushing deeply resumed her spinning. The Frenchman felt certain the blush was for him; the Genevan thought he would willingly give his life to be sure it was for him. But unlike as the young men were in person and character, and both attracted toward the same lovely maiden, they were yet extremely friendly to each other, and usually found enjoyment in the harmonious contrast of their different gifts. The first feeling of estrangement that came between them was one evening when Florien sang remarkably well, and Rosabella accompanied him on her guitar. She evidently enjoyed the graceful music with all her soul. Her countenance was more radiantly beautiful than usual, and when the fascinating singer rose to go, she begged him to sing another favorite song, and then another and another.

"She never urges me to sing with her," said Pierre, as he and Florien retired for the night.

"And with very good reason," replied his friend, laughing.

"Your stentorian tone would quite drown her weak sweet voice, and her light touch on the guitar. You might as well have a hammer-and-anvil accompaniment to a Canary bird." Seeing discontent in the countenance of his companion, he added soothingly, "Nay, my good friend, don't be offended by this playful comparison. Your voice is magnificently strong and beautifully correct, but it is made for grander things than those graceful little garlands of sound which Rosabella and I weave so easily."

Pierre sprang up quickly, and went to the other side of the room. "Rosabella and I" were sounds that went hissing through his heart, like a red-hot arrow. But his manly efforts soon conquered the jealous feeling, and he said cheerfully, "Well Florien, let us accept the offer of good Father Breguet. We will try our skill fairly and honorably, and leave him and Rosabella to decide, without knowing which is your work and which is mine."

Florien suppressed a rising smile; for he thought to himself, "*She* will know my workmanship, as easily as she could distinguish my fairy romance from your Samson[4] solos."

But he replied, right cordially, "Honestly and truly, Pierre, I think we are as mechanicians very nearly equal in skill. But let us both tax our ingenuity to invent something which will best please Rosabella. Her birthday comes in about six months. In honor of the occasion, I will make some ornaments for the little arbor facing the brook, where she loves to sit, in pleasant weather, and read to the good old grandfather."

"I will do the same," answered Pierre; "only let both our ornaments be machines."

They clasped hands, and looking frankly into each other's eyes, ratified the agreement. From that hour, they spoke no more to each other on the subject till the long-anticipated day arrived. The old watchmaker and his grandchild were invited to the arbor, to pass judgment on the production of his pupils. A screen was placed before a portion of the brook, and they sat quietly waiting for it to be removed.

"That duck is of a singular color," exclaimed the young girl. "What a solemn looking fellow he is!"

The bird, without paying any attention to her remarks, waddled into the water, drank, lifted up his bill to the sky, as if giving thanks for his refreshment, flapped his wings, floated to the edge of the brook,

---

[4] Biblical person who was very strong and derived his strength from his long hair

and waddled on the grass again. When Father Breguet threw some crumbs of cake on the ground, the duck picked them up with apparent satisfaction. He was about to scatter more crumbs, when Rosabella exclaimed, "Why, grandfather, this is not a duck! It is made of bronze. See how well it is done."

The old man took it up and examined it. "Really, I do not think anything could be more perfect than this," he said. "How exquisitely the feathers are carved, and truly the creature seems alive. He who beats this must be a skilful mechanician."

At these words, Pierre and Florien stepped forward, hand in hand, and bowing to their master, removed the temporary screen. On a black marble pedestal in the brook was seated a bronze Naiad,[5] leaning on an overflowing vase. The figure was inexpressibly graceful; a silver star with brilliant points gleamed on her forehead, and in her hand she held a silver bell, beautifully inlaid with gold and steel. There was a smile about her mouth, and she leaned over, as if watching for something in a little cascade which flowed down a channel in the pedestal. Presently, she raised her hand and sounded the bell. A beautiful little gold fish obeyed the summons, and glided down the channel, his burnished sides glittering in the sun. Eleven times more she rang the bell, and each time the gold fish darted forth. It was exactly noon, and the water-nymph was a clock.

The watchmaker and his daughter were silent. It was so beautiful that they could not easily find words to express their pleasure.

"You need not speak, my master," said Pierre, in a manly but sorrowful tone; "I myself decide in favor of Florien. The clock is his."

"The interior workmanship is not yet examined," rejoined his amiable competitor. "There is not a better mechanician in all Switzerland than Pierre Berthoud."

---

[5] A water nymph of Greek mythology

"Ah, but you know how to invest equally good workmanship with grace and beauty," replied the more heavily moulded Genevan.

"Study the graces, my boy; make yourself familiar with models of beauty," said old Antoine Breguet, laying a friendly hand upon the young man's shoulder.

"I should but imitate, and he creates," answered Pierre, despondingly; "and worst of all, my good master, I hate myself because I envy him."

"But you have many and noble gifts, Pierre, said Rosabella, gently. You know how delightfully very different instruments combine in harmony. Grandfather says your workmanship will be far more durable than Florien's. Perhaps you may both be his partners."

"But which of us will be *thine?*" thought Pierre. He smothered a deep sigh, and only answered, "I thank you, Rosabella."

Well aware that these envious feelings were unworthy of a noble soul, he contended with them bravely, and treated Florien even more cordially than usual. "I will follow our good master's advice," said he; "I will try to clothe my good machinery in forms of beauty. Let us both make a watch for Rosabella, and present it to her on her next birthday. You will rival me, no doubt; for the Graces threw their garlands on you when you were born."

"Bravo!" shouted Florien, laughing and clapping his hands. "The poetry is kindling up in your soul. I always told you that you would be a poet, if you could only express what was in you."

"And your soul expresses itself *so* easily, *so* fluently!" said Pierre, with a sigh.

"Because my springs lie so near the surface, and yours have depths to come from," replied his good natured companion."

"The worst of it is, the cord is apt to break before I can draw up my weighty treasures," rejoined Pierre, with a smile. "There is no help for it. There will always be the same difference between us that there is in our names. I am a rock, and you are a flower. I might be hewed and chiseled into harmonious proportions; but you *grow* into beauty."

"Then be a rock, and a magnificent one," replied his friend, "and let the flower grow at your feet."

"That sounds modestly and well," answered Pierre; "but I wish to be a flower, because—"

"Because what?" inquired Florien, though he half guessed the secret, from his embarrassed manner.

"Because I think Rosabella likes flowers better than rocks," replied Pierre, with uncommon quickness, as if the words gave him pain.

On New Year's Day, the offerings, enclosed in one box, were presented by the good grandfather. The first was a golden apple, which opened and revealed on one side an exquisitely neat watch, surrounded by a garland tastefully wrought in rich damaskeening of steel and gold; on the other side was a rose intertwined with forget-me-nots, very perfectly done in mosaic. When the stem of the apple was turned, a favorite little tune of Delia's[6] sounded from within.

"This is surely Florien's," thought she; and she looked for the other gift with less interest. It was an elegant little gold watch, with a Persian landscape, a gazelle and birds of paradise beautifully engraved on the back. When a spring was touched, the watch opened, a little circular plate of gold slid away, and up came a beautiful rose, round which a jeweled bee buzzed audibly. On the edge of the golden circle below were the words *Rosa bella* in ultramarine enamel. When another spring was touched, the rose went away, and the same melody that sounded from the heart of the golden apple seemed to be played by fairies on tinkling dew-drops. It paused a moment, and then struck up a lively dance. The circular plate again rolled away, and up sprung an inch-tall opera-dancer, with

---

[6] In *A Collection of Songs, Comical, Satirical and Descriptive, Chiefly in the Newcastle Dialect* edited by T. Thompson et al in 1827 was a song titled "Lovely Delia" and one title "O No, My Love, No" that that tells of a "lov'd Delia"

enameled scarf, and a very small diamond on her brow. Leaping and whirling on an almost invisible thread of gold, she kept perfect time to the music, and turned her scarf most gracefully. Rosabella drew a long breath, and a roseate tinge mantled her beautiful face, as she met her grandfather's gaze fixed lovingly upon her.

She thought to herself, "There is no doubt now which is Florien's;" but she said aloud, "They are both very beautiful; are they not, dear grandfather? I am not worthy that so much pains should be taken to please me."

The old man smiled upon her, and fondly patted the luxuriant brown hair, which shone like threads of amber in the sun. "Which dost thou think *most* beautiful!" said he.

She evaded the question, by asking, "Which do *you?*"

"I will tell thee when thou hast decided," answered he.

She twisted and untwisted the strings of her bodice,[7] and said she was afraid she should not be impartial.

"Why not?" he inquired. She looked down bashfully, and murmured, in a very low voice, "Because I can easily guess which is Florien's."

"Ah, ha," exclaimed the kind old man; and he playfully chuckled her under the chin as he added, "Then I suppose I shall offend thee when I give a verdict for the bee and the opera dancer?"

She looked up blushing, and her large serious brown eye had for a moment a comic expression, as she said, "I shall do the same."

Never were disciples of the beautiful placed in circumstances more favorable to the development of poetic souls. The cottage of Antoine Breguet was

---

[7] Laced vest worn on the outside of clothing

"In a glade,
   Where the sun harbors; and one side of it
     Listens to bees, another to a brook.
   Lovers, that have just parted for the night,
     Dream of such spots when they have said
   their prayers;
   Or some tired parent, holding by the hand
     A child, and walking toward the setting sun."

In the stillness of the night, they could hear the "rushing of the arrowy Rhone." From a neighboring eminence could be seen the transparent Lake of Geneva, reflecting the deep blue heaven above. Mountains, in all fantastic forms, enclosed them round; now draped in heavy masses of sombre clouds, and now half revealed through sun-lighted vapor, like a veil of gold. The flowing silver of little waterfalls gleamed among the dark rocks. Grape vines hung their rich festoons by the roadside, and the beautiful barberry bush embroidered their leaves with its scarlet clusters. They lived under the same roof with a guileless good old man, and with an innocent maiden, just merging into beautiful womanhood; and more than all, they were both under the influence of that great inspirer love.

Rosabella was so uniformly kind to both, that Pierre could never relinquish the hope that constant devotedness might in time win her affections for himself. Florien, having a more cheerful character, and more reliance on his own fascinations, was merely anxious that the lovely maiden should prefer his workmanship as decidedly as she did his person and manners. Under this powerful stimulus, in addition to the ambition excited by the old watchmaker's proposal, the competition between them was active and incessant. But the groundwork of their character was so good, that all little heart-burnings of envy or jealousy were quickly checked by the predominance of generous and kindly sentiments.

One evening, Rosabella was reading to her grandfather a description of an albino squirrel. The pure white animal, with pink eyes and a feathery tail, pleased her fancy extremely, and she expressed a strong desire to see one. Pierre said nothing; but not long after, as they sat eating grapes after dinner, a white squirrel leaped on the table, frisked from shoulder to shoulder, and at last sat up with a grape in its paws. Rosabella uttered an exclamation of delight. "Is it alive?" she said.

"Do you not see that it is?" rejoined Pierre. "Call the dog, and see what he thinks about it."

"We have so many things here, which are alive and yet not alive," she replied, smiling.

Florien warmly praised the pretty automaton; but he was somewhat vexed that he himself did not think of making the graceful little animal for which the maiden had expressed a wish. Her pet canary had died the day before, and his eye happened to rest on the empty cage hanging over the flower-stand. "I too will give her a pleasure," thought he.

A few weeks after, as they sat at breakfast, sweet notes were heard from the cage, precisely the same Canary used to sing; and, looking up, the astonished maiden saw him hopping about, nibbling at the sugar and pecking his feathers, as lively as ever. Florien smiled, and said, "Is it as much alive as Pierre's squirrel?"

The approach of the next birthday was watched with eager expectation; for even the old man began to feel keen pleasure in the competition, as if he had witnessed a race between fleet horses. Pierre, excited by the maiden's declaration that she mistook his golden apple for Florien's workmanship, produced a much more elegant specimen of art than he had ever before conceived. It was a barometer, supported by two knights in silver chain-armor, who went in when it rained, and came out when the sun shone. On the top of the barometer was a small silver basket, of exceedingly delicate workmanship, filled with such flowers as close in damp weather. When the knights retired, these flowers closed their enameled petals, and when the knights returned, the flowers expanded.

Florien produced a silver chariot, with two spirited and finely proportioned horses. A revolving circle in the wheels showed on what day of the month occurred each day of the week, throughout the year. Each month was surmounted by its zodiacal sign, beautifully enameled in green, crimson and gold. At ten o'clock the figure of a young girl, wearing Rosabella's usual costume, and resembling her in form and features, ascended slowly from behind the wheel, and at the same moment, the three Graces[8] rose up in the chariot and held garlands over her. From the axletree emerged a young man, in Florien's dress, and kneeling offered a rose to the maiden.

It was so beautiful as a whole, and so exquisitely finished in all its details, that Pierre clenched his fingers till the nails cut him, so hard did he try to conceal the bitterness of his disappointment at his own manifest inferiority. Could he have been an hour alone, all would have been well. But, as he stepped out on the piazza, followed by Florien, he saw him kiss his hand triumphantly to Rosabella, and she returned it with a modest but expressive glance. Unfortunately, he held in his hand a jewelled dagger, of Turkish workmanship, which Antoine Breguet had asked him to return to its case in the workshop.

Stung with disappointed love and ambition, the tempestuous feelings so painfully restrained burst forth like a whirlwind. Quick as a flash of lightning, he made a thrust at his graceful rival. Then frightened at what he had done, and full of horror at thoughts of Rosabella's distress, he rushed into the road, and up the sides of the mountain, like a madman.

A year passed, and no one heard tidings of him. On the anniversary of Rosabella's birth, the aged grandsire sat alone, sunning his white locks at the

---

[8] In Greek mythology they represented charm, beauty and creativity

open window, when Pierre Barthoud entered, pale and haggard. He was such a skeleton of his former self that his master did not recognize him, till he knelt at his feet, and said, "Forgive me, father. I am Pierre."

The poor old man shook violently, and covered his face with trembling hands. "Ah, thou wretched one," said he, "how darest thou come hither, with murder on thy soul!"

"Murder!" exclaimed Pierre, in a voice so terribly deep and distinct that it seemed to freeze the feeble blood of him who listened. "Is he then dead? Did I kill the beautiful youth, whom I loved so much?" He fell forward on the floor, and the groan that came from his strong chest was like an earthquake tearing up trees by the roots.

Antoine Breguet was deeply moved, and the tears flowed fast over his furrowed face. "Rise, my son," said he, "and make thy escape, lest they come to arrest thee."

"Let them come," replied Pierre, gloomily; "Why should I live?" Then raising his head from the floor, he said slowly, and with great fear, "Father, where is Rosabella?"

The old man covered his face, and sobbed out. "I shall never see her again! These old eyes will never again look on her blessed face." Many minutes they remained thus, and when he repeated, "I shall never see her again!"

The young man clasped his feet convulsively, and groaned in agony.

At last the housekeeper came in; a woman whom Pierre had known and loved in boyhood. When her first surprise was over, she promised to conceal his arrival, and persuaded him to go to the garret and try to compose his too strongly excited feelings. In the course of the day she explained to him how Florien had died of his wound, and how Rosabella pined away in silent melancholy, often sitting at the spinning wheel with the suspended thread in her hand, as if unconscious where she was.

During all that wretched night the young man could not close his eyes in sleep. Phantoms of the past flitted through his brain, and remorse gnawed at his heartstrings. In the deep stillness of midnight, he seemed to hear the voice of the bereaved old man sounding mournfully distinct, "I shall never see her again!" He prayed earnestly to die; but suddenly an idea laid into his mind, and revived his desire to live. Full of his new project, he rose early and sought his good old master.

Sinking on his knees, he exclaimed, "Oh, my father, say that you forgive me! I implore you to give my guilty soul that one gleam of consolation. Believe me, I would sooner have died myself than have killed him. But my passions were by nature so strong! Oh, God forgive me, they were so strong! How I have curbed them, He alone knows. Alas, that they should have burst the bounds in that one mad moment, and destroyed the two I best loved on earth. Oh, father, *can* you say that you forgive me?"

With quivering voice he replied, "I do forgive you, and bless you, my poor son." He laid his hand affectionately on the thick matted hair, and added, "I too have need of forgiveness. I did very wrong thus to put two generous natures in rivalship with each other. A genuine love of beauty, for its own sake, is the only healthy stimulus to produce the beautiful. The spirit of competition took you out of your sphere, and placed you in a false position. In grand conceptions, and in works of durability and strength, you would always have excelled Florien, as much as he surpassed you in tastefulness and elegance. By striving to be what *he* was, you parted with your own gifts, without attaining to his. Every man in the natural sphere of his own talent, and all in harmony; this is the true order, my son; and I tempted you to violate it. In my foolish pride, I earnestly desired to have a world-renowned successor to the famous Antoine Breguet. I wanted that the old stand should be kept up in all its glory, and continue to rival all competitors. I thought you could super-add Florien's gifts to your own, and yet retain your own characteristic excellencies. Therefore, I stimulated your intellect and imagination to the utmost, without reflecting that your heart might break in the process. God forgive me; it was too severe a trial for poor human nature. And do thou, my son, forgive this insane ambition; for severely has my pride been humbled."

Pierre could not speak, but he covered the wrinkled hands with kisses, and clasped his knees convulsively. At last he said, "Let me remain concealed here for a while. You *shall* see her again; only give me time."

When he explained that he would make Rosabella's likeness, from memory, the sorrowing parent shook his head and sighed, as he answered, "Ah, my son, the soul in her eye, and the light grace of her motions, no art can restore."

But to Pierre's excited imagination there was henceforth only one object in life; and that was to re-produce Rosabella. In the keen conflict of competition, under the fiery stimulus of love and ambition, his strong impetuous soul had become machine-mad; and now overwhelming, grief centered all his stormy energies on one object. Day by day, in the loneliness of his garret, he worked upon the image till he came to love it, almost as much as he had loved the maiden herself. Antoine Breguet readily supplied materials. From childhood he had been interested in all forms of mechanism; and this image, so intertwined with his affections, took strong hold of his imagination also. Nearly a year had passed away, when the housekeeper, who was in the secret, came to ask for Rosabella's hair, and the dress she usually wore. The old man gave her the keys, and wiped the starting tears, as he turned silently away. A few days after, Pierre invited him to come and look upon his work. "Do not go too suddenly," he said; "prepare yourself for a shock; for indeed it is very like our lost one."

"I will go, I will go," replied the old man, eagerly. "Am I not accustomed to see all manner of automata and androids? Did I not myself make a flute-player, which performed sixteen tunes, to the admiration of all who heard him? And think you I am to be frightened by an image?"

"Not frightened, dear father," answered Pierre; "but I was afraid you might be overcome with emotion." He led him into the apartment, and said, "Shall I remove the veil now? Can you bear it, dear father?"

"I can," was the calm reply. But when the curtain was withdrawn, he started, and exclaimed, "Santa Maria! It is Rosabella! She is not dead!" He tottered forward, and kissed the cold lips and the cold hands, and tears rained on the bright brown hair, as he cried out, "My child! my child!"

When the tumult of feeling had subsided, the aged mourner kissed Pierre's hands, and said. "It is wonderfully like her, in every feature and every tint. It seems as if she would move and breathe."

"She *will* move and breathe," replied Pierre; "only give me time."

His voice sounded so wildly, and his great deepset eyes burned with such intense enthusiasm, that his friend was alarmed. They clasped each other's hands, and spoke more quietly of the beloved one. "This is all that remains to us, Pierre," said the old man. "We are alone in the world. You were a friendless orphan when you came to me; and I am childless."

With a passionate outburst of grief, the young man replied, "And it was I, my benefactor, who made you so. Wretch that I am!"

From that time the work went on with greater zeal than ever. Pierre often forgot to taste of food, so absorbed was he in the perfection of his machine. First, the arms moved obedient to his wishes, then the eyes turned, and the lips parted. Meanwhile, his own face grew thinner and paler, and his eyes glowed with a wilder fire.

Finally, it was whispered in the village that Pierre Berthoud was concealed in Antoine Breguet's cottage;

and officers came to arrest him. But the venerable old watchmaker told the story so touchingly, and painted so strongly the young man's consuming agony of grief and remorse, and pleaded so earnestly that he might be allowed to finish a wonderful image of his beautiful grandchild, that they promised not to disturb him till the work was accomplished.

Two years from the day of Pierre's return, on the anniversary of the memorable birthday, he said, "Now, my father, I have done all that art *can* do. Come and see the beautiful one."

He led him into the little room where Rosabella used to work. There she sat, spinning diligently. The beautifully formed bust rose and fell under her neat bodice. Her lips were parted, and her eyes followed the direction of the thread. But what made it seem more fearfully like life, was the fact that ever and anon the wheel rested, and the maiden held the suspended thread, with her eye-lids lowered, as if she were lost in thought. Above the flower-stand, near by, hung the birdcage, with Florien's artificial Canary. The pretty little automaton had been silent long; but now its springs were set in motion, and it poured forth all its melodies.

The bereaved old man pressed Pierre's hand, and gazed upon his darling grandchild silently. He caused his armchair to be brought into the room, and ever after, while he retained his faculties, he refused to sit elsewhere.

The fame of this remarkable android soon spread through all the region round about. The citizens of Geneva united in an earnest petition that the artist might be excused from any penalty for the accidental murder he had committed. The magistrates came and looked at the breathing maiden, and touched the beautiful flesh, which seemed as if it would yield to their pressure. They saw the wild haggard artist, with lines of suffering cut so deeply in his youthful brow, and they at once granted the prayer of the citizens.

But Pierre had nothing more to live for. His work in the world was done. The artificial energy, supplied by one absorbing idea, was gone; and the contemplation of his own work was driving him to madness. It so closely resembled life that he longed more and more to have it live. The lustrous eyes moved, but they had no light from the soul, and they would not answer to his earnest gaze. The beautiful lips parted, but they never spoke kind words, as in days of yore. The image began to fill him with supernatural awe, yet he was continually drawn toward it by a magic influence. Three months after its completion, he was found, at daylight, lying at its feet, stone dead.

Antoine Breguet survived him two years. During the first eighteen months, he was never willing to have the image of his lost darling out of sight. The latter part of the time, he often whistled to the bird, and talked to her, and seemed to imagine that she answered him. But with increasing imbecility, Rosabella was forgotten. He sometimes asked, "Who *is* that young woman!" At last he said, "Send her away. She looks at me."

The magic-lanthorn[9] of departing memory then presented a phantom of his wife, dead long ago. He busied himself with making imaginary watches and rings for her, and held long conversations, as if she were present. Afterward, the wife was likewise forgotten, and he was occupied entirely with his mother, and the scenes of early childhood. Finally he wept often, and repeated continually, "They are all waiting for me; and I want to go home." When he was little more than eighty years old, compassionate angels took the weary pilgrim in their arms, and carried him home.

---

[9] Lantern

EDGAR ALLAN POE
(1809-1849)

Introduction
A Descent Into the Maelstrom

This fine science fiction story on the high seas was first published in the May 1841 issue of *Graham's Magazine*. This is what Robert Armistead Stewart, professor of Richmond College, had to say about it in 1911:

"'A Descent into the Maelstrom' is the most enthralling of that trio of tales of pseudo-science that demonstrate Poe's wizard power of sweeping the reader from the solid basis of human experience into an acceptance of fancies repugnant to all physical laws. In verisimilitude and compelling interest it excels both the 'MS. Found in a Bottle' and 'Hans Pfaal,' and displays its supernatural element in the products of the subtle faculty of exaggeration which Poe may have developed under the stimulus of opium." Professor Steward continued, "The commencement of the tale is abrupt and succinct, in accordance with Poe's dictum in 'Marginalia': 'It is far better that we commence irregularly—immethodically—than that we fail to arrest attention; but the two points, method and pungency, may always be combined.' At all risks, let there be a few vivid sentences *imprimis*, by way of the electric bell to the telegraph. The vividness of the old man's story is wonderfully enhanced by being told with the localities under review, and the wild welter of wind and water sustains the narrative like some great orchestral accompaniment. The final sentence, allowing for incredulity on the part of the reader, is an artistic touch, and fully worthy of Poe's ingenuity."

Before you is a major science fiction tale with a transitioning plot, building terror, and characters that incite emotion to the end.

A Descent Into the Maelstrom
(1841)

> The ways of God in Nature, as in Providence, are not as our ways; nor are the models that we frame any way commensurate to the vastness, profundity, and unsearchableness of His works, *which have a depth in them greater than the well of Democritus.*[1]
>
> Joseph Glanvill.[2]

WE HAD NOW reached the summit of the loftiest crag. For some minutes the old man seemed too much exhausted to speak.

"Not long ago," said he at length, "and I could have guided you on this route as well as the youngest of my sons; but, about three years past, there happened to me an event such as never happened before to mortal man — or at least such as no man ever survived to tell of — and the six hours of deadly terror which I then endured have broken me up body and soul. You suppose me a very old man — but I am not. It took less than a single day to change these hairs from a jetty black to white, to weaken my limbs, and to unstring my nerves, so that I tremble at the least exertion, and am frightened at a shadow. Do you know I can scarcely look over this little cliff without getting giddy?"

---

[1] Democritus (460-370 B.C.) was a Greek philosopher who formulated the first atomic theory of the universe and believed that space was an infinite void with infinite atoms, which is likely the "well"

[2] Joseph Glanvill (1636-1680) was an English writer and clergyman, this quote is from his *Essays on Several Important Subjects*

The "little cliff," upon whose edge he had so carelessly thrown himself down to rest that the weightier portion of his body hung over it, while he was only kept from falling by the tenure of his elbow on its extreme and slippery edge — this "little cliff" arose, a sheer unobstructed precipice of black shining rock, some fifteen or sixteen hundred feet from the world of crags beneath us. Nothing would have tempted me to within half a dozen yards of its brink. In truth so deeply was I excited by the perilous position of my companion, that I fell at full length upon the ground, clung to the shrubs around me, and dared not even glance upward at the sky — while I struggled in vain to divest myself of the idea that the very foundations of the mountain were in danger from the fury of the winds. It was long before I could reason myself into sufficient courage to sit up and look out into the distance.

"You must get over these fancies," said the guide, "for I have brought you here that you might have the best possible view of the scene of that event I mentioned — and to tell you the whole story with the spot just under your eye."

"We are now," he continued, in that particularizing manner which distinguished him — "we are now close upon the Norwegian coast — in the sixty-eighth degree of latitude — in the great province of Nordland — and in the dreary district of Lofoden. The mountain upon whose top we sit is Helseggen, the Cloudy.[3] Now raise yourself up a little higher — hold on to the grass if you feel giddy — so — and look out beyond the belt of vapor beneath us, into the sea."

I looked dizzily, and beheld a wide expanse of ocean, whose waters wore so inky a hue as to bring at once to my mind the Nubian geographer's account of the *Mare Tenebrarum*.[4] A panorama more deplorably desolate no human imagination can conceive. To the

---

[3] Fictional mountain

[4] Name that Nubian geographer Al-Idrisi (1099-1116) called the Atlantic Ocean

right and left, as far as the eye could reach, there lay outstretched, like ramparts of the world, lines of horridly black and beetling cliff,[5] whose character of gloom was but the more forcibly illustrated by the surf which reared high up against it its white and ghastly crest, howling and shrieking for ever. Just opposite the promontory[6] upon whose apex we were placed, and at a distance of some five or six miles out at sea, there was visible a small, bleak-looking island; or, more properly, its position was discernible through the wilderness of surge in which it was enveloped. About two miles nearer the land, arose another of smaller size, hideously craggy and barren, and encompassed at various intervals by a cluster of dark rocks.

The appearance of the ocean, in the space between the more distant island and the shore, had something very unusual about it. Although, at the time, so strong a gale was blowing landward that a brig[7] in the remote offing lay to under a double-reefed trysail,[8] and constantly plunged her whole hull out of sight, still there was here nothing like a regular swell, but only a short, quick, angry cross dashing of water in every direction — as well in the teeth of the wind as otherwise. Of foam there was little except in the immediate vicinity of the rocks.

"The island in the distance," resumed the old man," is called by the Norwegians Vurrgh. The one midway is Moskoe. That a mile to the northward is Ambaaren. Yonder are Iflesen, Hoeyholm, Kieldholm, Suarven, and Buckholm. Farther off — between Moskoe and Vurrgh — are Otterholm, Flimen, Sandflesen, and Skarholm.[9] These are the true names of the places — but why it has been thought necessary to name them at all, is more than either you or I can understand. Do

---

[5] Overhanging
[6] Peninsula
[7] Ship with two masts
[8] Little sail hoisted in a storm to keep a ship's bow to the wind
[9] Band of Norwegian islands

you hear any thing? Do you see any change in the water?"

We had now been about ten minutes upon the top of Helseggen, to which we had ascended from the interior of Lofoden, so that we had caught no glimpse of the sea until it had burst upon us from the summit. As the old man spoke, I became aware of a loud and gradually increasing sound, like the moaning of a vast herd of buffaloes upon an American prairie; and at the same moment I perceived that what seamen term the *chopping* character of the ocean beneath us, was rapidly changing into a current which set to the eastward. Even while I gazed, this current acquired a monstrous velocity. Each moment added to its speed — to its headlong impetuosity. In five minutes the whole sea, as far as Vurrgh, was lashed into ungovernable fury; but it was between Moskoe and the coast that the main uproar held its sway. Here the vast bed of the waters, seamed and scarred into a thousand conflicting channels, burst suddenly into phrensied convulsion — heaving, boiling, hissing — gyrating in gigantic and innumerable vortices, and all whirling and plunging on to the eastward with a rapidity which water never elsewhere assumes except in precipitous descents.

In a few minutes more, there came over the scene another radical alteration. The general surface grew somewhat more smooth, and the whirlpools, one by one, disappeared, while prodigious streaks of foam became apparent where none had been seen before. These streaks, at length, spreading out to a great distance, and entering into combination, took unto themselves the gyratory motion of the subsided vortices, and seemed to form the germ of another more vast. Suddenly — very suddenly — this assumed a distinct and definite existence, in a circle of more than half a mile in diameter. The edge of the whirl was represented by a broad belt of gleaming spray; but no particle of this slipped into the mouth of the terrific funnel, whose interior, as far as the eye could fathom it, was a smooth, shining, and jet-black wall of water, inclined to the horizon at an angle of some forty-five degrees, speeding dizzily round and round with a swaying and sweltering motion, and sending forth to the winds an appalling voice, half shriek, half roar, such as not even the mighty cataract of Niagara ever lifts up in its agony to Heaven.

The mountain trembled to its very base, and the rock rocked. I threw myself upon my face, and clung to the scant herbage in an excess of nervous agitation.

"This," said I at length, to the old man — "this *can* be nothing else than the great whirlpool of the Maelström."[10]

"So it is sometimes termed," said he. "We Norwegians call it the Moskoe-ström, from the island of Moskoe in the midway."

The ordinary accounts of this vortex had by no means prepared me for what I saw. That of Jonas Ramus,[11] which is perhaps the most circumstantial of any, cannot impart the faintest conception either of the magnificence, or of the horror of the scene — or of the wild bewildering sense of *the novel* which confounds the beholder. I am not sure from what point of view the writer in question surveyed it, nor at what time; but it could neither have been from the summit of Helseggen, nor during a storm. There are some passages of his description, nevertheless, which may be quoted for their details, although their effect is exceedingly feeble in conveying an impression of the spectacle.

"Between Lofoden and Moskoe," he says, "the depth of the water is between thirty-six and forty fathoms;[12] but on the other side, toward Ver (Vurrgh) this depth decreases so as not to afford a convenient passage for a vessel, without the risk of splitting on the rocks, which happens even in the calmest weather. When it is

---

[10] Famous whirlpool that forms on the coast of Norway

[11] Jonas Ramus (1649-1718) was a scientific theologian who wrote of the Moskoe-ström

[12] 216 - 240 feet

flood, the stream runs up the country between Lofoden and Moskoe with a boisterous rapidity; but the roar of its impetuous ebb to the sea is scarce equalled by the loudest and most dreadful cataracts;[13] the noise being heard several leagues[14] off, and the vortices or pits are of such an extent and depth, that if a ship comes within its attraction, it is inevitably absorbed and carried down to the bottom, and there beat to pieces against the rocks; and when the water relaxes, the fragments thereof are thrown up again.

"But these intervals of tranquillity are only at the turn of the ebb and flood, and in calm weather, and last but a quarter of an hour, its violence gradually returning. When the stream is most boisterous, and its fury heightened by a storm, it is dangerous to come within a Norway mile of it. Boats, yachts, and ships have been carried away by not guarding against it before they were within its reach. It likewise happens frequently, that whales come too near the stream, and are overpowered by its violence; and then it is impossible to describe their howlings and bellowings in their fruitless struggles to disengage themselves. A bear once, attempting to swim from Lofoden to Moskoe, was caught by the stream and borne down, while he roared terribly, so as to be heard on shore. Large stocks of firs and pine trees, after being absorbed by the current, rise again broken and torn to such a degree as if bristles grew upon them. This plainly shows the bottom to consist of craggy rocks, among which they are whirled to and fro. This stream is regulated by the flux and reflux of the sea — it being constantly high and low water every six hours. In the year 1645, early in the morning of Sexagesima Sunday,[15] it raged with such noise and impetuosity that the very stones of the houses on the coast fell to the ground."

---

[13] Water shooting out of cracks in rocks
[14] One league is 5.5 kilometers or 3.45 miles
[15] Second Sunday before Lent

In regard to the depth of the water, I could not see how this could have been ascertained at all in the immediate vicinity of the vortex. The "forty fathoms"[16] must have reference only to portions of the channel close upon the shore either of Moskoe or Lofoden. The depth in the centre of the Moskoe-ström must be immeasurably greater; and no better proof of this fact is necessary than can be obtained from even the sidelong glance into the abyss of the whirl which may be had from the highest crag of Helseggen. Looking down from this pinnacle upon the howling Phlegethon[17] below, I could not help smiling at the simplicity with which the honest Jonas Ramus records, as a matter difficult of belief, the anecdotes of the whales and the bears; for it appeared to me, in fact, a self-evident thing, that the largest ships of the line in existence, coming within the influence of that deadly attraction, could resist it as little as a feather the hurricane, and must disappear bodily and at once.

The attempts to account for the phenomenon — some of which, I remember, seemed to me sufficiently plausible in perusal — now wore a very different and unsatisfactory aspect. The idea generally received is that this, as well as three smaller vortices among the Feroe islands,[18] "have no other cause than the collision of waves rising and falling, at flux and reflux, against a ridge of rocks and shelves, which confines the water so that it precipitates itself like a cataract; and thus the higher the flood rises, the deeper must the fall be, and the natural result of all is a whirlpool or vortex, the prodigious suction of which is sufficiently known by lesser experiments." — These are the words of the *Encyclopaedia Britannica*. Kircher[19] and others imagine that in the centre of the channel of the Maelström is an abyss penetrating the globe, and issuing in some very remote part — the Gulf of

---

[16] Equals .05 miles

[17] Mythological river of fire, one of five in Hades

[18] Scandinavian Islands

[19] Athanasius Kircher (1602-1680) who is called master of 100 arts

Bothnia[20] being somewhat decidedly named in one instance. This opinion, idle in itself, was the one to which, as I gazed, my imagination most readily assented; and, mentioning it to the guide, I was rather surprised to hear him say that, although it was the view almost universally entertained of the subject by the Norwegians, it nevertheless was not his own. As to the former notion he confessed his inability to comprehend it; and here I agreed with him — for, however conclusive on paper, it becomes altogether unintelligible, and even absurd, amid the thunder of the abyss.

"You have had a good look at the whirl now," said the old man, "and if you will creep round this crag, so as to get in its lee,[21] and deaden the roar of the water, I will tell you a story that will convince you I ought to know something of the Moskoe-ström."

I placed myself as desired, and he proceeded.

"Myself and my two brothers once owned a schooner-rigged smack[22] of about seventy tons[23] burthen, with which we were in the habit of fishing among the islands beyond Moskoe, nearly to Vurrgh. In all violent eddies at sea there is good fishing, at proper opportunities, if one has only the courage to attempt it; but among the whole of the Lofoden coastmen, we three were the only ones who made a regular business of going out to the islands, as I tell you. The usual grounds are a great way lower down to the southward. There fish can be got at all hours, without much risk, and therefore these places are preferred. The choice spots over here among the rocks, however, not only yield the finest variety, but in far greater abundance; so that we often got in a single day, what the more timid of the craft could not scrape together in a week. In fact, we made it a matter of

---

[20] Gulf of the Baltic Sea between Finland (to the east) and Sweden (to the west)

[21] Side of ship opposite the wind's direction

[22] Fishing ship with fore and aft sails on at least two masts

[23] 140,000 pounds

desperate speculation — the risk of life standing instead of labor, and courage answering for capital.

"We kept the smack in a cove about five miles higher up the coast than this; and it was our practice, in fine weather, to take advantage of the fifteen minutes' slack to push across the main channel of the Moskoe-ström, far above the pool, and then drop down upon anchorage somewhere near Otterholm, or Sandflesen, where the eddies are not so violent as elsewhere. Here we used to remain until nearly time for slackwater again, when we weighed and made for home. We never set out upon this expedition without a steady side wind for going and coming — one that we felt sure would not fall us before our return — and we seldom made a mis-calculation upon this point.

Twice, during six years, we were forced to stay all night at anchor on account of a dead calm, which is a rare thing indeed just about here; and once we had to remain on the grounds nearly a week, starving to death, owing to a gale which blew up shortly after our arrival, and made the channel too boisterous to be thought of. Upon this occasion we should have been driven out to sea in spite of everything, (for the whirlpools threw us round and round so violently that, at length, we fouled our anchor and dragged it) if it had not been that we drifted into one of the innumerable cross currents-here to-day and gone to-morrow — which drove us under the lee of Flimen, where, by good luck, we brought up.

"I could not tell you the twentieth part of the difficulties we encountered 'on the ground' — it is a bad spot to be in, even in good weather — but we made shift always to run the gauntlet of the Moskoe-ström itself without accident; although at times my heart has been in my mouth when we happened to be a minute or so behind or before the slack. The wind sometimes was not as strong as we thought it at starting, and then we made rather less way than we could wish, while the current rendered the smack unmanageable. My eldest brother had a son eighteen years old, and I had two stout boys of my own. These would have been of great assistance at such times, in using the sweeps, as well as afterward in fishing — but, somehow, although we ran the risk ourselves, we had not the heart to let the young ones get into the danger — for, after all said and done, it was a horrible danger, and that is the truth.

"It is now within a few days of three years since what I am going to tell you occurred. It was on the tenth of July, 18—, a day which the people of this part of the world will never forget — for it was one in which blew the most terrible hurricane that ever came out of the heavens. And yet all the morning, and indeed until late in the afternoon, there was a gentle and steady breeze from the south-west, while the sun shone brightly, so that the oldest seaman among us could not have foreseen what was to follow.

"The three of us — my two brothers and myself — had crossed over to the islands about two o'clock P. M., and soon nearly loaded the smack with fine fish, which, we all remarked, were more plenty that day than we had ever known them. It was just seven, *by my watch*, when we weighed and started for home, so as to make the worst of the Ström at slack water, which we knew would be at eight.

"We set out with a fresh wind on our starboard quarter,[24] and for some time spanked along at a great rate, never dreaming of danger, for indeed we saw not the slightest reason to apprehend it. All at once we were taken aback by a breeze from over Helseggen. This was most unusual — something that had never happened to us before — and I began to feel a little uneasy, without exactly knowing why. We put the boat on the wind, but could make no headway at all for the eddies, and I was upon the point of proposing to return to the anchorage, when, looking astern,[25] we saw the whole horizon covered with a singular copper-

---

[24] Right and rear of ship
[25] Rear of the ship

colored cloud that rose with the most amazing velocity.

"In the meantime the breeze that had headed us off fell away, and we were dead becalmed, drifting about in every direction. This state of things, however, did not last long enough to give us time to think about it. In less than a minute the storm was upon us — in less than two the sky was entirely overcast — and what with this and the driving spray, it became suddenly so dark that we could not see each other in the smack.

"Such a hurricane as then blew it is folly to attempt describing. The oldest seaman in Norway never experienced any thing like it. We had let our sails go by the run before it cleverly took us; but, at the first puff, both our masts went by the board if they had been sawed off — the mainmast taking with it my as I youngest brother, who had lashed himself to it for safety.

"Our boat was the lightest feather of a thing that ever sat upon water. It had a complete flush deck, with only a small hatch near the bow, and this hatch it had always been our custom to batten down when about to cross the Ström, by way of precaution against the chopping seas. But for this circumstance we should have foundered at once — for we lay entirely buried for some moments. How my elder brother escaped destruction I cannot say, for I never had an opportunity of ascertaining. For my part, as soon as I had let the foresail run, I threw myself flat on deck, with my feet against the narrow gunwale[26] of the bow, and with my hands grasping a ring-bolt near the foot of the foremast. It was mere instinct that prompted me to do this — which was undoubtedly the very best thing I could have done — for I was too much flurried to think.

"For some moments we were completely deluged, as I say, and all this time I held my breath, and clung to the bolt. When I could stand it no longer I raised

---

[26] Upper edge of the ship's side

myself upon my knees, still keeping hold with my hands, and thus got my head clear. Presently our little boat gave herself a shake, just as a dog does in coming out of the water, and thus rid herself, in some measure, of the seas. I was now trying to get the better of the stupor that had come over me, and to collect my senses so as to see what was to be done, when I felt somebody grasp my arm. It was my elder brother, and my heart leaped for joy, for I had made sure that he was overboard — but the next moment all this joy was turned into horror — for he put his mouth close to my ear, and screamed out the word '*Moskoe-ström!*'

"No one ever will know what my feelings were at that moment. I shook from head to foot as if I had had the most violent fit of the ague.[27] I knew what he meant by that one word well enough — I knew what he wished to make me understand. With the wind that now drove us on, we were bound for the whirl of the Ström, and nothing could save us!

"You perceive that in crossing the Ström *channel*, we always went a long way up above the whirl, even in the calmest weather, and then had to wait and watch carefully for the slack — but now we were driving right upon the pool itself, and in such a hurricane as this! 'To be sure,' I thought, 'we shall get there just about the slack — there is some little hope in that' — but in the next moment I cursed myself for being so great a fool as to dream of hope at all. I knew very well that we were doomed, had we been ten times a ninety-gun ship.

"By this time the first fury of the tempest had spent itself, or perhaps we did not feel it so much, as we scudded before it, but at all events the seas, which at first had been kept down by the wind, and lay flat and frothing, now got up into absolute mountains. A singular change, too, had come over the heavens. Around in every direction it was still as black as pitch,

---

[27] Fit of shivering

but nearly overhead there burst out, all at once, a circular rift of clear sky — as clear as I ever saw — and of a deep bright blue — and through it there blazed forth the full moon with a lustre that I never before knew her to wear. She lit up every thing about us with the greatest distinctness — but, oh God, what a scene it was to light up!

"I now made one or two attempts to speak to my brother — but in some manner which I could not understand, the din had so increased that I could not make him hear a single word, although I screamed at the top of my voice in his ear. Presently he shook his head, looking as pale as death, and held up one of his fingers, as to say *'listen!'*

"At first I could not make out what he meant — but soon a hideous thought flashed upon me. I dragged my watch from its fob.[28] It was not going. I glanced as its face by the moonlight, and then burst into tears as I flung it far away into the ocean. *It had run down at seven o'clock! We were behind the time of the slack, and the whirl of the Ström was in full fury!*

"When a boat is well built, properly trimmed, and not deep laden, the waves in a strong gale, when she is going large, seem always to slip from beneath her — which appears very strange to a landsman — and this is what is called *riding*, in sea phrase.

"Well, so far we had ridden the swells very cleverly; but presently a gigantic sea happened to take us right under the counter, and bore us with it as it rose — up — up — as if into the sky. I would not have believed that any wave could rise so high. And then down we came with a sweep, a slide, and a plunge, that made me feel sick and dizzy, as if I was falling from some lofty mountaintop in a dream. But while we were up I had thrown a quick glance around — and that one glance was all sufficient. I saw our exact position in an instant. The Moskoe-ström whirlpool was about a quarter of a mile dead ahead — but no more like the

---

[28] Small pocket

every-day Moskoe-ström, than the whirl as you now see it, is like a millrace.[29] If I had not known where we were, and what we had to expect, I should not have recognised the place at all. As it was, I involuntarily closed my eyes in horror. The lids clenched themselves together as if in a spasm.

"It could not have been more than two minutes afterwards until we suddenly felt the waves subside, and were enveloped in foam. The boat made a sharp half turn to larboard,[30] and then shot off in its new direction like a thunderbolt. At the same moment the roaring noise of the water was completely drowned in a kind of shrill shriek — such a sound as you might imagine given out by the water-pipes of many thousand steam-vessels, letting off their steam all together. We were now in the belt of surf that always surrounds the whirl; and I thought, of course, that another moment would plunge us into the abyss — down which we could only see indistinctly on account of the amazing velocity with which we were borne along. The boat did not seem to sink into the water at all, but to skim like an air-bubble upon the surface of the surge. Her starboard side was next the whirl, and on the larboard arose the world of ocean we had left. It stood like a huge writhing wall between us and the horizon.

"It may appear strange, but now, when we were in the very jaws of the gulf, I felt more composed than when we were only approaching it. Having made up my mind to hope no more, I got rid of a great deal of that terror which unmanned me at first. I suppose it was despair that strung my nerves.

"It may look like boasting — but what I tell you is truth — I began to reflect how magnificent a thing it was to die in such a manner, and how foolish it was in me to think of so paltry a consideration as my own individual life, in view of so wonderful a manifestation of God's power. I do believe that I blushed with shame

---

[29] Channel of water that rotates a mill wheel

[30] Port side or left side of ship when facing forward

when this idea crossed my mind. After a little while I became possessed with the keenest curiosity about the whirl itself. I positively felt a *wish* to explore its depths, even at the sacrifice I was going to make; and my principal grief was that I should never be able to tell my old companions on shore about the mysteries I should see. These, no doubt, were singular fancies to occupy a man's mind in such extremity — and I have often thought since, that the revolutions of the boat around the pool might have rendered me a little light-headed.

"There was another circumstance which tended to restore my self-possession; and this was the cessation of the wind, which could not reach us in our present situation — for, as you saw yourself, the belt of surf is considerably lower than the general bed of the ocean, and this latter now towered above us, a high, black, mountainous ridge. If you have never been at sea in a heavy gale, you can form no idea of the confusion of mind occasioned by the wind and the spray together. They blind, deafen and strangle you, and take away all power of action or reflection. But we were now, in a great measure, rid of these annoyances — just as death-condemned felons in prison are allowed petty indulgences, forbidden them while their doom is yet uncertain.

"How often we made the circuit of the belt it is impossible to say. We careered round and round for perhaps an hour, flying rather than floating, getting gradually more and more into the middle of the surge, and then nearer and nearer to its horrible inner edge. All this time I had never let go of the ringbolt. My brother was at the stern, holding on to a large empty water-cask[31] which had been securely lashed under the coop[32] of the counter, and was the only thing on deck that had not been swept overboard when the gale first took us. As we approached the brink of the pit he let go his hold upon this, and made for the ring, from

---

[31] Barrel for holding water
[32] Overhang

which, in the agony of his terror, he endeavored to force my hands, as it was not large enough to afford us both a secure grasp. I never felt deeper grief than when I saw him attempt this act — although I knew he was a madman when he did it — a raving maniac through sheer fright. I did not care, however, to contest the point with him. I thought it could make no difference whether either of us held on at all; so I let him have the bolt, and went astern to the cask. This there was no great difficulty in doing; for the smack flew round steadily enough, and upon an even keel — only swaying to and fro, with the immense sweeps and swelters of the whirl. Scarcely had I secured myself in my new position, when we gave a wild lurch to starboard, and rushed headlong into the abyss. I muttered a hurried prayer to God, and thought all was over.

"As I felt the sickening sweep of the descent, I had instinctively tightened my hold upon the barrel, and closed my eyes. For some seconds I dared not open them — while I expected instant destruction, and wondered that I was not already in my death-struggles with the water. But moment after moment elapsed. I still lived. The sense of falling had ceased; and the motion of the vessel seemed much as it had been before while in the belt of foam, with the exception that she now lay more along. I took courage and looked once again upon the scene.

"Never shall I forget the sensations of awe, horror, and admiration with which I gazed about me. The boat appeared to be hanging, as if by magic, midway down, upon the interior surface of a funnel vast in circumference, prodigious in depth, and whose perfectly smooth sides might have been mistaken for ebony, but for the bewildering rapidity with which they spun around, and for the gleaming and ghastly radiance they shot forth, as the rays of the full moon, from that circular rift amid the clouds which I have already described, streamed in a flood of golden glory along the black walls, and far away down into the inmost recesses of the abyss.

"At first I was too much confused to observe anything accurately. The general burst of terrific grandeur was all that I beheld. When I recovered myself a little, however, my gaze fell instinctively downward. In this direction I was able to obtain an unobstructed view, from the manner in which the smack hung on the inclined surface of the pool. She was quite upon an even keel — that is to say, her deck lay in a plane parallel with that of the water — but this latter sloped at an angle of more than forty-five degrees, so that we seemed to be lying upon our beam-ends.[33] I could not help observing, nevertheless, that I had scarcely more difficulty in maintaining my hold and footing in this situation, than if we had been upon a dead level; and this, I suppose, was owing to the speed at which we revolved.

"The rays of the moon seemed to search the very bottom of the profound gulf; but still I could make out nothing distinctly, on account of a thick mist in which everything there was enveloped, and over which there hung a magnificent rainbow, like that narrow and tottering bridge which Mussulmen[34] say is the only pathway between Time and Eternity. This mist, or spray, was no doubt occasioned by the clashing of the great walls of the funnel, as they all met together at the bottom — but the yell that went up to the Heavens from out of that mist, I dare not attempt to describe.

"Our first slide into the abyss itself, from the belt of foam above, had carried us to a great distance down the slope; but our farther descent was by no means proportionate. Round and round we swept — not with any uniform movement — but in dizzying swings and jerks, that sent us sometimes only a few hundred feet — sometimes nearly the complete circuit of the whirl. Our progress downward, at each revolution, was slow, but very perceptible.

---

[33] Ship greatly heeled to the side so that the deck is nearly vertical
[34] Muslims

"Looking about me upon the wide waste of liquid ebony on which we were thus borne, I perceived that our boat was not the only object in the embrace of the whirl. Both above and below us were visible fragments of vessels, large masses of building timber and trunks of trees, with many smaller articles, such as pieces of house furniture, broken boxes, barrels and staves.[35] I have already described the unnatural curiosity which had taken the place of my original terrors. It appeared to grow upon me as I drew nearer and nearer to my dreadful doom. I now began to watch, with a strange interest, the numerous things that floated in our company. I *must* have been delirious — for I even sought *amusement* in speculating upon the relative velocities of their several descents toward the foam below. 'This fir tree,' I found myself at one time saying, 'will certainly be the next thing that takes the awful plunge and disappears,' — and then I was disappointed to find that the wreck of a Dutch merchant ship overtook it and went down before. At length, after making several guesses of this nature, and being deceived in all — this fact — the fact of my invariable miscalculation, set me upon a train of reflection that made my limbs again tremble, and my heart beat heavily once more.

"It was not a new terror that thus affected me, but the dawn of a more exciting *hope*. This hope arose partly from memory, and partly from present observation. I called to mind the great variety of buoyant matter that strewed the coast of Lofoden, having been absorbed and then thrown forth by the Moskoe-ström. By far the greater number of the articles were shattered in the most extraordinary way — so chafed and roughened as to have the appearance of being stuck full of splinters — but then I distinctly recollected that there were *some* of them which were not disfigured at all. Now I could not account for this difference except by supposing that the roughened

---

[35] Iron banding

fragments were the only ones which had been *completely absorbed* — that the others had entered the whirl at so late a period of the tide, or, from some reason, had descended so slowly after entering, that they did not reach the bottom before the turn of the flood came, or of the ebb, as the case might be. I conceived it possible, in either instance, that they might thus be whirled up again to the level of the ocean, without undergoing the fate of those which had been drawn in more early or absorbed more rapidly. I made, also, three important observations. The first was, that as a general rule, the larger the bodies were, the more rapid their descent; — the second, that, between two masses of equal extent, the one spherical, and the other *of any other shape*, the superiority in speed of descent was with the sphere; — the third, that, between two masses of equal size, the one cylindrical, and the other of any other shape, the cylinder was absorbed the more slowly.

Since my escape, I have had several conversations on this subject with an old schoolmaster of the district; and it was from him that I learned the use of the words 'cylinder' and 'sphere.' He explained to me — although I have forgotten the explanation — how what I observed was, in fact, the natural consequence of the forms of the floating fragments — and showed me how it happened that a cylinder, swimming in a vortex, offered more resistance to its suction, and was drawn in with greater difficulty than an equally bulky body, of any form whatever.*

*See Archimedes,[36] "De Incidentibus in Fluido."[37] — lib.2.

"There was one startling circumstance which went a great way in enforcing these observations, and rendering me anxious to turn them to account, and

---

[36] Archimedes (287-212 B.C.) who was a Greek mathematician and physicist famous for his formulation of buoyancy
[37] Translated: Of Incidents in Fluid

this was that, at every revolution, we passed something like a barrel, or else the broken yard or the mast of a vessel, while many of these things, which had been on our level when I first opened my eyes upon the wonders of the whirlpool, were now high up above us, and seemed to have moved but little from their original station.

"I no longer hesitated what to do. I resolved to lash myself securely to the water cask upon which I now held, to cut it loose from the counter, and to throw myself with it into the water. I attracted my brother's attention by signs, pointed to the floating barrels that came near us, and did everything in my power to make him understand what I was about to do. I thought at length that he comprehended my design — but, whether this was the case or not, he shook his head despairingly, and refused to move from his station by the ringbolt. It was impossible to force him; the emergency admitted no delay; and so, with a bitter struggle, I resigned him to his fate, fastened myself to the cask by means of the lashings which secured it to the counter, and precipitated myself with it into the sea, without another moment's hesitation.

"The result was precisely what I had hoped it might be. As it is myself who now tell you this tale — as you see that I *did* escape — and as you are already in possession of the mode in which this escape was effected, and must therefore anticipate all that I have farther to say — I will bring my story quickly to conclusion. It might have been an hour, or thereabout, after my quitting the smack, when, having descended to a vast distance beneath me, it made three or four wild gyrations in rapid succession, and, bearing my loved brother with it, plunged headlong, at once and forever, into the chaos of foam below. The barrel to which I was attached sunk very little farther than half the distance between the bottom of the gulf and the spot at which I leaped overboard, before a great change took place in the character of the whirlpool. The slope of the sides of the vast funnel became momently less and less steep. The gyrations of the whirl grew, gradually, less and less violent. By degrees, the froth and the rainbow disappeared, and the bottom of the gulf seemed slowly to uprise. The sky was clear, the winds had gone down, and the full moon was setting radiantly in the west, when I found myself on the surface of the ocean, in full view of the shores of Lofoden, and above the spot where the pool of the Moskoe-ström *had been*. It was the hour of the slack — but the sea still heaved in mountainous waves from the effects of the hurricane. I was borne violently into the channel of the Ström and in a few minutes, was hurried down the coast into the 'grounds' of the fishermen. A boat picked me up — exhausted from fatigue — and (now that the danger was removed) speechless from the memory of its horror. Those who drew me on board were my old mates and daily companions — but they knew me no more than they would have known a traveller from the spirit-land. My hair, which had been raven-black the day before, was as white as you see it now. They say too that the whole expression of my countenance had changed. I told them my story — they did not believe it. I now tell it to *you* — and I can scarcely expect you to put more faith in it than did the merry fishermen of Lofoden.

NATHANIEL HAWTHORNE
(1804-1864)

Introduction
The Artist of the Beautiful

On the following pages is the first robotic insect science fiction short story. Beyond mechanics, the insect is filled with a spiritualism termed "magnetism." Today we learn that Hawthorne's vision of the future has become reality as we are told about the development of flying robotic insects the size of flies by the military.

"The Artist of the Beautiful" was published in June of 1844 in the *Democratic Review*. In the foreword to "Rappaccini's Daughter," Hawthorne uses the French name *"L'Artiste du Beau; ou le Papillon Mècanique"* ("The Artist of the Beautiful; or the Mechanical Butterfly") as the purported original French title of the story as penned by his fictitious alter ego, M. de l'Aubépine.

Margaret Fuller, the author and transcendentalist, in her review of *Mosses from an Old Manse* in the *New York Daily Tribune* for June 22, 1846, pontificated that

"'The Artist of the Beautiful' presents in a form that is, indeed, beautiful, the opposite view as to what *are* the substantial realities of life."

The Artist of the Beautiful
(1844)

AN ELDERLY MAN, with his pretty daughter on his arm, was passing along the street, and emerged from the gloom of the cloudy evening into the light that fell across the pavement from the window of a small shop. It was a projecting window; and on the inside were suspended a variety of watches,—pinchbeck,[1] silver, and one or two of gold,—all with their faces turned from the street, as if churlishly disinclined to inform the wayfarers what o'clock it was. Seated within the shop, sidelong to the window, with his pale face bent earnestly over some delicate piece of mechanism, on which was thrown the concentrated lustre of a shade-lamp, appeared a young man.

"What can Owen Warland be about?" muttered old Peter Hovenden,—himself a retired watchmaker, and the former master of this same young man, whose occupation he was now wondering at. "What can the fellow be about? These six months past, I have never come by his shop without seeing him just as steadily at work as now. It would be a flight beyond his usual foolery to seek for the Perpetual Motion. And yet I know enough of my old business to be certain that what he is now so busy with is no part of the machinery of a watch."

"Perhaps, father," said Annie, without showing much interest in the question, "Owen is inventing a new kind of timekeeper. I am sure he has ingenuity enough."

"Pooh, child! He has not the sort of ingenuity to invent anything better than a Dutch toy," answered her father, who had formerly been put to much vexation by

---

[1] Copper

Owen Warland's irregular genius. "A plague on such ingenuity! All the effect that ever I knew of it, was, to spoil the accuracy of some of the best watches in my shop. He would turn the sun out of its orbit, and derange the whole course of time, if, as I said before, his ingenuity could grasp anything bigger than a child's toy!"

"Hush, father! He hears you," whispered Annie, pressing the old man's arm. "His ears are as delicate as his feelings, and you know how easily disturbed they are. Do let us move on."

So Peter Hovenden and his daughter Annie plodded on, without further conversation, until, in a by-street of the town, they found themselves passing the open door of a blacksmith's shop. Within was seen the forge, now blazing up, and illuminating the high and dusky roof, and now confining its lustre to a narrow precinct of the coal-strewn floor, according as the breath of the bellows was puffed forth, or again inhaled into its vast leathern lungs.

In the intervals of brightness, it was easy to distinguish objects in remote corners of the shop, and the horseshoes that hung upon the wall; in the momentary gloom, the fire seemed to be glimmering amidst the vagueness of unenclosed space. Moving about in this red glare and alternate dusk, was the figure of the blacksmith, well worthy to be viewed in so picturesque an aspect of light and shade, where the bright blaze struggled with the black night, as if each would have snatched his comely strength from the other. Anon, he drew a white-hot bar of iron from the coals, laid it on the anvil, uplifted his arm of might, and was soon enveloped in the myriads of sparks which the strokes of his hammer scattered into the surrounding gloom.

"Now, that is a pleasant sight," said the old watchmaker. "I know what it is to work in gold, but give me the worker in iron, after all is said and done. He spends his labor upon a reality. What say you, daughter Annie?"

"Pray don't speak so loud, father," whispered Annie. "Robert Danforth will hear you."

"And what if he should hear me?" said Peter Hovenden; "I say again, it is a good and a wholesome thing to depend upon main strength and reality, and to earn one's bread with the bare and brawny arm of a blacksmith. A watchmaker gets his brain puzzled by his wheels within a wheel, or loses his health or the nicety of his eyesight, as was my case; and finds himself, at middle age, or a little after, past labor at his own trade, and fit for nothing else, yet too poor to live at his ease. So, I say once again, give me main strength for my money. And then, how it takes the nonsense out of a man! Did you ever hear of a blacksmith being such a fool as Owen Warland, yonder?"

"Well said, uncle Hovenden!" shouted Robert Danforth, from the forge, in a full, deep, merry voice, that made the roof re-echo. "And what says Miss Annie to that doctrine? She, I suppose, will think it a gentler business to tinker up a lady's watch, than to forge a horseshoe or make a gridiron!"[2]

Annie drew her father onward, without giving him time for reply.

But we must return to Owen Warland's shop, and spend more meditation upon his history and character than either Peter Hovenden, or probably his daughter Annie, or Owen's old schoolfellow, Robert Danforth, would have thought due to so slight a subject.

From the time that his little fingers could grasp a pen-knife, Owen had been remarkable for a delicate ingenuity, which sometimes produced pretty shapes in wood, principally figures of flowers and birds, and sometimes seemed to aim at the hidden mysteries of mechanism. But it was always for purposes of grace, and never with any mockery of the useful. He did not, like the crowd of schoolboy artisans, construct little

---

[2] Grate for grilling food

windmills on the angle of a bam, or watermills across the neighboring brook.

Those who discovered such peculiarity in the boy, as to think it worth their while to observe him closely, sometimes saw reason to suppose that he was attempting to imitate the beautiful movements of nature, as exemplified in the flight of birds or the activity of little animals. It seemed, in fact, a new development of the love of the Beautiful, such as might have made him a poet, a painter, or a sculptor, and which was as completely refined from all utilitarian coarseness, as it could have been in either of the fine arts. He looked with singular distaste at the stiff and regular processes of ordinary machinery. Being once carried to see a steam-engine, in the expectation that his intuitive comprehension of mechanical principles would be gratified, he turned pale, and grew sick, as if something monstrous and unnatural had been presented to him.

This horror was partly owing to the size and terrible energy of the Iron Laborer; for the character of Owen's mind was microscopic, and tended naturally to the minute, in accordance with his diminutive frame, and the marvelous smallness and delicate power of his fingers. Not that his sense of beauty was thereby diminished into a sense of prettiness. The beautiful idea has no relation to size, and may be as perfectly developed in a space too minute for any but microscopic investigation, as within the ample verge that is measured by the arc of the rainbow. But, at all events, this characteristic minuteness in his objects and accomplishments made the world even more incapable, than it might otherwise have been, of appreciating Owen Warland's genius. The boy's relatives saw nothing better to be done—as perhaps there was not—than to bind him apprentice to a watchmaker, hoping that his strange ingenuity might thus be regulated, and put to utilitarian purposes.

Peter Hovenden's opinion of his apprentice has already been expressed. He could make nothing of the lad. Owen's apprehension of the professional mysteries, it is true, was inconceivably quick. But he altogether forgot or despised the grand object of a watchmaker's business, and cared no more for the measurement of time than if it had been merged into eternity. So long, however, as he remained under his old master's care, Owen's lack of sturdiness made it possible, by strict injunctions and sharp oversight, to restrain his creative eccentricity within bounds.

But when his apprenticeship was served out, and he had taken the little shop which Peter Hovenden's failing eyesight compelled him to relinquish, then did people recognize how unfit a person was Owen Warland to lead old blind Father Time along his daily course. One of his most rational projects was, to connect a musical operation with the machinery of his watches, so that all the harsh dissonances of life might be rendered tuneful, and each flitting moment fall into the abyss of the Past in golden drops of harmony.

If a family-clock was entrusted to him for repair—one of those tall, ancient clocks that have grown nearly allied to human nature, by measuring out the lifetime of many generations—he would take upon himself to arrange a dance or funeral procession of figures, across its venerable face, representing twelve mirthful or melancholy hours. Several freaks of this kind quite destroyed the young watchmaker's credit with that steady and matter-of-fact class of people who hold the opinion that time is not to be trifled with, whether considered as the medium of advancement and prosperity in this world, or preparation for the next.

His custom rapidly diminished—a misfortune, however, that was probably reckoned among his better accidents by Owen Warland, who was becoming more and more absorbed in a secret occupation, which drew all his science and manual dexterity into itself, and likewise gave full employment to the characteristic tendencies of his genius. This pursuit had already consumed many months.

After the old watchmaker and his pretty daughter had gazed at him, out of the obscurity of the street, Owen Warland was seized with a fluttering of the nerves, which made his hand tremble too violently to proceed with such delicate labor as he was now engaged upon.

"It was Annie herself!" murmured he. "I should have known it by this throbbing of my heart, before I heard her father's voice. Ah, how it throbs! I shall scarcely be able to work again on this exquisite mechanism tonight. Annie—dearest Annie—thou shouldst give firmness to my heart and hand, and not shake them thus; for if I strive to put the very spirit of Beauty into form, and give it motion, it is for thy sake alone. Oh, throbbing heart, be quiet! If my labor be thus thwarted, there will come vague and unsatisfied dreams, which will leave me spiritless tomorrow."

As he was endeavoring to settle himself again to his task, the shop-door opened, and gave admittance to no other than the stalwart figure which Peter Hovenden had paused to admire, as seen amid the light and shadow of the blacksmith's shop. Robert Danforth had brought a little anvil of his own manufacture, and peculiarly constructed, which the young artist had recently bespoken. Owen examined the article, and pronounced it fashioned according to his wish.

"Why, yes," said Robert Danforth, his strong voice filling the shop as with the sound of a bass-viol, "I consider myself equal to anything in the way of my own trade; though I should have made but a poor figure at yours, with such a fist as this,"—added he, laughing, as he laid his vast hand beside the delicate one of Owen. "But what then? I put more main strength into one blow of my sledgehammer, than all that you have expended since you were apprentice. Is not that the truth?"

"Very probably," answered the low and slender voice of Owen. "Strength is an earthly monster. I make no pretensions to it. My force, whatever there may be of it, is altogether spiritual."

"Well but, Owen, what are you about?" asked his old schoolfellow, still in such a hearty volume of tone that it made the artist shrink; especially as the question related to a subject so sacred as the absorbing dream of his imagination. "Folks do say, that you are trying to discover the Perpetual Motion."

"The Perpetual Motion?—nonsense!" replied Owen Warland, with a movement of disgust; for he was full of little petulances. "It never can be discovered! It is a dream that may delude men whose brains are mystified with matter, but not me. Besides, if such a discovery were possible, it would not be worth my while to make it, only to have the secret turned to such purposes as are now effected by steam and water-power. I am not ambitious to be honored with the paternity of a new kind of cotton machine."

"That would be droll enough!" cried the blacksmith, breaking out into such an uproar of laughter, that Owen himself, and the bell-glasses on his work-board, quivered in unison. "No, no, Owen! No child of yours will have iron joints and sinews. Well, I won't hinder you any more. Good night, Owen, and success; and if you need any assistance, so far as a downright blow of hammer upon anvil will answer the purpose, I'm your man!"

And with another laugh, the man of main strength left the shop.

"How strange it is," whispered Owen Warland to himself, leaning his head upon his hand, "that all my musings, my purposes, my passion for the Beautiful, my consciousness of power to create it—a finer, more ethereal power, of which this earthly giant can have no conception—all, all, look so rain and idle, whenever my path is crossed by Robert Danforth! He would drive me mad, were I to meet him often. His hard, brute force darkens and confuses the spiritual element within me. But I, too, will be strong in my own way. I will not yield to him!"

He took from beneath a glass, a piece of minute machinery, which he set in the condensed light of his lamp, and, looking intently at it through a magnifying glass, proceeded to operate with a delicate instrument of steel. In an instant, however, he fell back in his chair, and clasped his hands, with a look of horror on his face, that made its small features as impressive as those of a giant would have been.

"Heaven! What have I done!" exclaimed he. "The vapor!—the influence of that brute force!—it has bewildered me, and obscured my perception. I have made the very stroke—the fatal stroke—that I have dreaded from the first! It is all over—the toil of months—the object of my life! I am ruined!"

And there he sat, in strange despair, until his lamp flickered in the socket, and left the Artist of the Beautiful in darkness.

Thus it is, that ideas which grow up within the imagination, and appear so lovely to it, and of a value beyond whatever men call valuable, are exposed to be shattered and annihilated by contact with the Practical. It is requisite for the ideal artist to possess a force of character that seems hardly compatible with its delicacy; he must keep his faith in himself, while the incredulous world assails him with its utter disbelief; he must stand up against mankind and be his own sole disciple, both as respects his genius, and the objects to which it is directed.

For a time, Owen Warland succumbed to this severe, but inevitable test. He spent a few sluggish weeks, with his head so continually resting in his hands, that the townspeople had scarcely an opportunity to see his countenance. When, at last, it was again uplifted to the light of day, a cold, dull, nameless change was perceptible upon it. In the opinion of Peter Hovenden, however, and that order of sagacious understandings who think that life should be regulated, like clockwork, with leaden weights, the alteration was entirely for the better.

Owen now, indeed, applied himself to business with dogged industry. It was marvelous to witness the obtuse gravity with which he would inspect the wheels of a great, old silver watch; thereby delighting the owner, in whose fob[3] it had been worn till he deemed it a portion of his own life, and was accordingly jealous of its treatment In consequence of the good report thus acquired, Owen Warland was invited by the proper authorities to regulate the clock in the church-steeple. He succeeded so admirably in this matter of public interest, that the merchants gruffly acknowledged his merits on 'Change; the nurse whispered his praises, as she gave the potion in the sick-chamber; the lover blessed him at the hour of appointed interview; and the town in general thanked Owen for the punctuality of dinnertime.

In a word, the heavy weight upon his spirits kept everything in order, not merely within his own system, but wheresoever the iron accents of the church-clock were audible. It was a circumstance, though minute, yet characteristic of his present state, that, when employed to engrave names or initials on silver spoons, he now wrote the requisite letters in the plainest possible style; omitting a variety of fanciful flourishes, that had heretofore distinguished his work in this kind.

One day, during the era of this happy transformation, old Peter Hovenden came to visit his former apprentice.

"Well, Owen," said he, "I am glad to hear such good accounts of you from all quarters; and especially from the town-clock yonder, which speaks in your commendation every hour of the twenty-four. Only get rid altogether of your nonsensical trash about the Beautiful—which I, nor nobody else, nor yourself to boot, could never understand—only free yourself of that, and your success in life is as sure as daylight. Why, if you go on in this way, I should even venture to

---

[3] Small pocket

let you doctor this precious old watch of mine; though, except my daughter Annie, I have nothing else so valuable in the world."

I should hardly dare touch it, sir," replied Owen in a depressed tone; for he was weighed down by his old master's presence.

"In time," said the latter, "in time, you will be capable of it."

The old watchmaker, with the freedom naturally consequent on his former authority, went on inspecting the work which Owen had in hand at the moment, together with other matters that were in progress. The artist, meanwhile, could scarcely lift his head. There was nothing so antipodal to his nature as this man's cold, unimaginative sagacity, by contact with which everything was converted into a dream, except the densest matter of the physical world. Owen groaned in spirit, and prayed fervently to be delivered from him.

"But what is this?" cried Peter Horenden abruptly, taking up a dusty bellglass, beneath which appeared a mechanical something, as delicate and minute as the system of a butterfly's anatomy. "What have we here! Owen, Owen! there is witchcraft in these little chains, and wheels, and pulleys! See! with one pinch of my finger and thumb, I am going to deliver you from all future peril."

"For Heaven's sake," screamed Owen Warland, springing up with wonderful energy, "as you would not drive me mad—do not touch it! The slightest pressure of your finger would ruin me for ever."

"Aha, young man! And is it so?" said the old watchmaker, looking at him with just enough of penetration to torture Owen's soul with the bitterness of worldly criticism. "Well; take your own course. But I warn you again, that in this small piece of mechanism lives your evil spirit. Shall I exorcise him?"

"You are my Evil Spirit," answered Owen, much excited—"you, and the hard, coarse world! The leaden thoughts and the despondency that you fling upon me arc my clogs. Else, I should long ago have achieved the task that I was created for."

Peter Hovenden shook his head, with the mixture of contempt and indignation which mankind, of whom he was partly a representative, deem themselves entitled to feel towards all simpletons who seek other prizes than the dusty ones along the highway. He then took his leave with an uplifted finger, and a sneer upon his face, that haunted the artist's dreams for many a night afterwards. At the time of his old master's visit, Owen was probably on the point of taking up the relinquished task; but, by this sinister event, he was thrown back into the state whence he had been slowly emerging.

But the innate tendency of his soul had only been accumulating fresh vigor, during its apparent sluggishness. As the summer advanced, he almost totally relinquished his business, and permitted Father Time, so far as the old gentleman was represented by the clocks and watches under his control, to stray at random through human life, making infinite confusion among the train of bewildered hours.

He wasted the sunshine, as people said, in wandering through the woods and fields, and along the banks of streams. There, like a child, he found amusement in chasing butterflies, or watching the motions of water-insects. There was something truly mysterious in the intentness with which he contemplated these living playthings, as they sported on the breeze; or examined the structure of an imperial insect whom he had imprisoned. The chase of butterflies was an apt emblem of the ideal pursuit in which he had spent so many golden hours.

But, would the Beautiful Idea ever be yielded to his hand, like the butterfly that symbolized it? Sweet, doubtless, were these days, and congenial to the artist's soul. They were full of bright conceptions, which gleamed through his intellectual world, as the butterflies gleamed through the outward atmosphere, and were real to him for the instant, without the toil, and perplexity, and many disappointments, of attempting to make them visible to the sensual eye.

Alas, that the artist, whether in poetry or whatever other material, may not content himself with the inward enjoyment of the Beautiful, but must chase the flitting mystery beyond the verge of his ethereal domain, and crush its frail being in seizing it with a material grasp! Owen Warland felt the impulse to give external reality to his ideas, as irresistibly as any of the poets or painters, who have arrayed the world in a dimmer and fainter beauty, imperfectly copied from the richness of their visions.

The night was now his time for the slow process of recreating the one Idea, to which all his intellectual activity referred itself Always at the approach of dusk, he stole into the town, locked himself within his shop, and wrought with patient delicacy of touch, for many hours. Sometimes he was startled by the rap of the watchman, who, when all the world should be asleep, had caught the gleam of lamplight through the crevices of Owen Warland's shutters. Daylight, to the morbid sensibility of his mind, seemed to have an intrusiveness that interfered with his pursuits. On cloudy and inclement days, therefore, he sat with his head upon his hands, muffling, as it were, his sensitive brain in a mist of indefinite musings; for it was a relief to escape from the sharp distinctness with which he was compelled to shape out his thoughts, during his nightly toil.

From one of these fits of torpor, he was aroused by the entrance of Annie Hovenden, who came into the shop with the freedom of a customer, and also with something of the familiarity of a childish friend. She had worn a hole through her silver thimble, and wanted Owen to repair it.

"But I don't know whether you will condescend to such a task," said she, laughing, "now that you are so taken up with the notion of putting spirit into machinery."

"Where did you get that idea, Annie?" said Owen, starting in surprise.

"Oh, out of my own head," answered she, "and from something that I heard you say, long ago, when you were but a boy, and I a little child. But, come! will you mend this poor thimble of mine?"

"Anything for your sake, Annie," said Owen Warland—"anything; even were it to work at Robert Danforth's forge."

"And that would be a pretty sight!" retorted Annie, glancing with imperceptible slightness at the artist's small and slender frame. "Well; here is the thimble."

"But that is a strange idea of yours," said Owen, "about the spiritualisation of matter!"

And then the thought stole into his mind, that this young girl possessed the gift to comprehend him, better than all the world beside. And what a help and strength would it be to him, in his lonely toil, if he could gain the sympathy of the only being whom he loved! To persons whose pursuits are insulated from the common business of life—who are either in advance of mankind, or apart from it—there often comes a sensation of moral cold, that makes the spirit shiver, as if it had reached the frozen solitudes around the pole. What the prophet, the poet, the reformer, the criminal, or any other man, with human yearnings, but separated from the multitude by a peculiar lot, might feel, poor Owen Warland felt.

"Annie," cried he, growing pale as death at the thought, "how gladly would I tell you the secret of my pursuit! You, methinks, would estimate it rightly. You, I know, would hear it with a reverence that I must not expect from the harsh, material world."

"Would I not? To be sure I would!" replied Anne Hovenden, lightly laughing. "Come; explain to me quickly what is the meaning of this little whirligig, so delicately wrought that it might be a plaything for Queen Mab.[4] See; I will put it in motion."

---

[4] Playful fairy in William Shakespeare's (1564-1616) *Romeo and Juliet* and was later included in various literary works

"Hold," exclaimed Owen, "hold!"

Annie had but given the slightest possible touch, with the point of a needle, to the same minute portion of complicated machinery which has been more than once mentioned, when the artist seized her by the wrist with a force that made her scream aloud. She was affrighted at the convulsion of intense rage and anguish that writhed across his features. The next instant he let his head sink upon his hands.

"Go, Annie," murmured he, "I have deceived myself, and must suffer for it. I yearned for sympathy—and thought—and fancied—and dreamed—that you might give it me. But you lack the talisman,[5] Annie, that should admit you into my secrets. That touch has undone the toil of months, and the thought of a lifetime! It was not your fault, Annie—but you have ruined me!"

Poor Owen Warland! He had indeed erred, yet pardonably; for if any human spirit could have sufficiently reverenced the processes so sacred in his eyes, it must have been a woman's. Even Annie Hovenden, possibly, might not have disappointed him, had she been enlightened by the deep intelligence of love.

The artist spent the ensuing winter in a way that satisfied any persons, who had hitherto retained a hopeful opinion of him, that he was, in truth, irrevocably doomed to inutility as regarded the world, and to an evil destiny on his own part. The decease of a relative had put him in possession of a small inheritance.

Thus freed from the necessity of toil, and having lost the steadfast influence of a great purpose—great, at least to him—he abandoned himself to habits from which, it might have been supposed, the mere delicacy of his organization would have availed to secure him. But when the ethereal portion of a man of genius is obscured, the earthly part assumes an influence the

---

[5] Magic charm

more uncontrollable, because the character is now thrown off the balance to which Providence had so nicely adjusted it, and which, in coarser natures, is adjusted by some other method. Owen Warland made proof of whatever show of bliss may be found in riot. He looked at the world through the golden medium of wine, and contemplated the visions that bubble up so gaily around the brim of the glass, and that people the air with shapes of pleasant madness, which so soon grow ghostly and forlorn.

Even when this dismal and inevitable change had taken place, the young man might still have continued to quaff the cup of enchantments, though its vapor did but shroud life in gloom, and fill the gloom with spectres that mocked at him. There was a certain irksomeness of spirit, which, being real, and the deepest sensation of which the artist was now conscious, was more intolerable than any fantastic miseries and horrors that the abuse of wine could summon up. In the latter case, he could remember, even out of the midst of his trouble, that all was but a delusion; in the former, the heavy anguish was his actual life.

From this perilous state, he was redeemed by an incident which more than one person witnessed, but of which the shrewdest could not explain nor conjecture the operation on Owen Warland's mind. It was very simple. On a warm afternoon of Spring, as the artist sat among his riotous companions, with a glass of wine before him, a splendid butterfly flew in at the open window, and fluttered about his head.

"Ah!" exclaimed Owen, who had drank freely, "Are you alive again, child of the sun, and playmate of the summer breeze, after your dismal winter's nap! Then it is time for me to be at work!"

And leaving his unemptied glass upon the table, he departed, and was never known to sip another drop of wine. And now, again, he resumed his wanderings in the woods and fields. It might be fancied that the bright butterfly, which had come so spiritlike into the window, as Owen sat with the rude revelers, was indeed a spirit, commissioned to recall him to the pure, ideal life that had so etherealized him among men.

It might be fancied, that he went forth to seek this spirit, in its sunny haunts; for still, as in the summertime gone by, he was seen to steal gently up, wherever a butterfly had alighted, and lose himself in contemplation of it. When it took flight, his eyes followed the winged vision, as if its airy track would show the path to heaven. But what could be the purpose of the unseasonable toil, which was again resumed, as the watchman knew by the lines of lamplight through the crevices of Owen Warland's shutters!

The townspeople had one comprehensive explanation of all these singularities. Owen Warland had gone mad! How universally efficacious—how satisfactory, too, and soothing to the injured sensibility of narrowness and dullness—is this easy method of accounting for whatever lies beyond the world's most ordinary scope!

From Saint Paul's days, down to our poor little Artist of the Beautiful, the same talisman has been applied to the elucidation of all mysteries in the words or deeds of men, who spoke or acted too wisely or too well. In Owen Warland's case, the judgment of his townspeople may have been correct. Perhaps he was mad. The lack of sympathy—that contrast between himself and his neighbors, which took away the restraint of example—was enough to make him so. Or, possibly, he had caught just so much of ethereal radiance as served to bewilder him, in an earthly sense, by its intermixture with the common daylight.

One evening, when the artist had returned from a customary ramble, and had just thrown the lustre of his lamp on the delicate piece of work, so often interrupted, but still taken up again, as if his fate were embodied in its mechanism, he was surprised by the entrance of old Peter Hovenden. Owen never met this man without a shrinking of the heart. Of all the world, he was most terrible, by reason of a keen understanding, which saw so distinctly what it did see, and disbelieved so uncompromisingly in what it could not see. On this occasion, the old watchmaker had merely a gracious word or two to say.

"Owen, my lad," said he, "we must see you at my house tomorrow night."

The artist began to mutter some excuse.

"Oh, but it must be so," quoth Peter Hovenden, "for the sake of the days when you were one of the household. What, my boy, don't you know that my daughter Annie is engaged to Robert Danforth? We are making an entertainment, in our humble way, to celebrate the event."

"Ah!" said Owen.

That little monosyllable was all he uttered; its tone seemed cold and unconcerned, to an ear like Peter Hovenden's; and yet there was in it the stifled outcry of the poor artist's heart, which he compressed within him like a man holding down an evil spirit. One slight outbreak, however, imperceptible to the old watchmaker, he allowed himself. Raising the instrument with which he was about to begin his work, he let it fall upon the little system of machinery that had, anew, cost him months of thought and toil. It was shattered by the stroke!

Owen Warland's story would have been no tolerable representation of the troubled life of those who strive to create the Beautiful, if, amid all other thwarting influences, love had not interposed to steal the cunning from his hand. Outwardly, he had been no ardent or enterprising lover; the career of his passion had confined its tumults and vicissitudes so entirely within the artist's imagination, that Annie herself had scarcely more than a woman's intuitive perception of it.

But, in Owen's view, it covered the whole field of his life. Forgetful of the time when she had shown herself incapable of any deep response, he had persisted in connecting all his dreams of artistical success with Annie's image; she was the visible shape in which the spiritual power that he worshipped, and on whose altar he hoped to lay a not unworthy offering, was made manifest to him.

Of course he had deceived himself; there were no such attributes in Annie Hovenden as his imagination had endowed her with. She, in the aspect which she wore to his inward vision, was as much a creation of his own, as the mysterious piece of mechanism would be were it ever realized. Had he become convinced of his mistake through the medium of successful love; had he won Annie to his bosom, and there beheld her fade from angel into ordinary woman, the disappointment might have driven him back, with concentrated energy, upon his sole remaining object.

On the other hand, had he found Annie what he fancied, his lot would have been so rich in beauty, that, out of its mere redundancy, he might have wrought the Beautiful into many a worthier type than he had toiled for. But the guise in which his sorrow came to him, the sense that the angel of his life had been snatched away and given to a rude man of earth and iron, who could neither need nor appreciate her ministrations; this was the very perversity of fate, that makes human existence appear too absurd and contradictory to be the scene of one other hope or one other fear. There was nothing left for Owen Warland but to sit down like a man that had been stunned.

He went through a fit of illness. After his recovery, his small and slender frame assumed an obtuser garniture of flesh than it had ever before worn. His thin cheeks became round; his delicate little hand, so spiritually fashioned to achieve fancy task-work, grew plumper than the hand of a thriving infant. His aspect had a childishness, such as might have induced a stranger to pat him on the head—pausing, however, in the act, to wonder what manner of child was here. It was as if the spirit had gone out of him, leaving the body to flourish in a sort of vegetable existence. Not that Owen Warland was idiotic. He could talk, and not irrationally. Somewhat of a babbler, indeed, did people begin to think him; for he was apt to discourse at wearisome length, of marvels of mechanism that he had read about in books, but which he had learned to consider as absolutely fabulous.

Among them he enumerated the Man of Brass, constructed by Albertus Magnus,[6] and the Brazen Head of Friar Bacon;[7] and, coming down to later times, the automata of a little coach and horses, which, it was pretended, had been manufactured for the Dauphin of France;[8] together with an insect that buzzed about the ear like a living fly, and yet was but a contrivance of minute steel springs. There was a story, too, of a duck that waddled, and quacked, and ate; though, had any honest citizen purchased it for dinner, he would have found himself cheated with the mere mechanical apparition of a duck.[9]

"But all these accounts," said Owen Warland, "I am now satisfied, are mere impositions."

Then, in a mysterious way, he would confess that he once thought differently. In his idle and dreamy days, he had considered it possible, in a certain sense, to spiritualize machinery; and to combine with the new species of life and motion, thus produced, a beauty that should attain to the ideal which Nature has proposed to herself, in all her creatures, but has never taken pains to realize. He seemed, however, to retain no very distinct perception either of the process of achieving this object, or of the design itself.

---

[6] Likeness of a man constructed entirely in brass that took Albertus Magnus (1206-1280) thirty years to complete and was claimed to walk and talk

[7] Speaking head that could answer questions purportedly fabricated by Friar Roger Bacon (1214-1294)

[8] Automated stage coach supposedly made for Francois Dauphin (1518-1536) of France

[9] In 1739 French inventor Jacques de Vaucanson (1709-1782) created an automaton duck that ate corn

"I have thrown it all aside now," he would say. "It was a dream, such as young men are always mystifying themselves with. Now that I have acquired a little commonsense, it makes me laugh to think of it."

Poor, poor, and fallen Owen Warland! These were the symptoms that he had ceased to be an inhabitant of the better sphere that lies unseen around us. He had lost his faith in the invisible, and now prided himself, as such unfortunates invariably do, in the wisdom which rejected much that even his eye could see, and trusted confidently in nothing but what his hand could touch. This is the calamity of men whose spiritual part dies out of them, and leaves the grosser understanding to assimilate them more and more to the things of which alone it can take cognizance. But, in Owen Warland, the spirit was not dead, nor past away; it only slept.

How it awoke again, is not recorded. Perhaps, the torpid slumber was broken by a convulsive pain. Perhaps, as in a former instance, the butterfly came and hovered about his head, and reinspired him—as, indeed, this creature of the sunshine had always a mysterious mission for the artist—reinspired him with the former purpose of his life. Whether it were pain or happiness that thrilled through his veins, his first impulse was to thank Heaven for rendering him again the being of thought, imagination, and keenest sensibility, that he had long ceased to be.

"Now for my task," said he. "Never did I feel such strength for it as now."

Yet, strong as he felt himself, he was incited to toil the more diligently, by an anxiety lest death should surprise him in the midst of his labors. This anxiety, perhaps, is common to all men who set their hearts upon anything so high, in their own view of it, that life becomes of importance only as conditional to its accomplishment. So long as we love life for itself, we seldom dread the losing it. When we desire life for the attainment of an object, we recognize the frailty of its texture.

But, side by side with this sense of insecurity, there is a vital faith in our invulnerability to the shaft of death, while engaged in any task that seems assigned by Providence as our proper thing to do, and which the world would have cause to mourn for, should we leave it unaccomplished. Can the philosopher, big with the inspiration of an idea that is to reform mankind, believe that he is to be beckoned from this sensible existence, at the very instant when he is mustering his breath to speak the word of light? Should he perish so, the weary ages may pass away—the world's whole life-sand may fall, drop by drop—before another intellect is prepared to develop the truth that might have been uttered then. But history affords many an example, where the most precious spirit, at any particular epoch manifested in human shape, has gone hence untimely, without space allowed him, so far as mortal judgment could discern, to perform his mission on the earth.

The prophet dies; and the man of torpid heart and sluggish brain lives on. The poet leaves his song half sung, or finishes it, beyond the scope of mortal ears, in a celestial choir. The painter—as Allston[10] did—leaves half his conception on the canvass, to sadden us with its imperfect beauty, and goes to picture forth the whole, if it be no irreverence to say so, in the hues of Heaven. But, rather, such incomplete designs of this life will be perfected nowhere. This so frequent abortion of man's dearest projects must be taken as proof, that the deeds of earth, however etherealized by piety or genius, are without value, except as exercises and manifestations of the spirit. In Heaven, all ordinary thought is higher and more melodious than Milton's song.[11] Then, would he add another verse to any strain that he had left unfinished here?

---

[10] Reference to Washington Allston (1779-1843), American landscape painter who blurred objects into the environment and died the year before "The Artist of the Beautiful" was published; he was friends with many of the transcendentalists as well as Nathaniel Hawthorne's wife, Sophia Peabody (1809-1871)

[11] Reference to John Milton's (1608-1674) "Paradise Lost" poem

But to return to Owen Warland. It was his fortune, good or ill, to achieve the purpose of his life. Pass we over a long space of intense thought, yearning effort, minute toil, and wasting anxiety, succeeded by an instant of solitary triumph; let all this be imagined; and then behold the artist, on a winter evening, seeking admittance to Robert Danforth's fireside circle. There he found the Man of Iron, with his massive substance thoroughly warmed and attempered by domestic influences. And there was Annie, too, now transformed into a matron, with much of her husband's plain and sturdy nature, but imbued, as Owen Warland still believed, with a finer grace, that might enable her to be the interpreter between Strength and Beauty. It happened, likewise, that old Peter Hovenden was a guest, this evening, at his daughter's fireside; and it was his well-remembered expression of keen, cold criticism, that first encountered the artist's glance.

"My old friend Owen!" cried Robert Danforth, starting up, and compressing the artist's delicate fingers within a hand that was accustomed to gripe bars of iron. "This is kind and neighborly, to come to us at last! I was afraid your Perpetual Motion had bewitched you out of the remembrance of old times."

"We are glad to see you!" said Annie, while a blush reddened her matronly cheek. "It was not like a friend, to stay from us so long."

"Well, Owen," inquired the old watchmaker, as his first greeting, "how comes on the Beautiful? Have you created it at last?"

The artist did not immediately reply, being startled by the apparition of a young child of strength, that was tumbling about on the carpet; a little personage who had come mysteriously out of the infinite, but with something so sturdy and real in his composition that he seem moulded out of the densest substance which earth could supply. This hopeful infant crawled towards the new-comer, and setting himself on end— as Robert Danforth expressed the posture—stared at

Owen with a look of such sagacious observation, that the mother could not help exchanging a proud glance with her husband But the artist was disturbed by the child's look, as imagining a resemblance between it and Peter Hovenden's habitual expression. He could have fancied that the old watchmaker was compressed into this baby-shape, and was looking out of those baby eyes, and repeating—as he now did—the malicious question:

"The Beautiful, Owen! How comes on the Beautiful? Have you succeeded in creating the Beautiful?"

"I have succeeded," replied the artist, with a momentary light of triumph in his eyes, and a smile of sunshine, yet steeped in such depth of thought that it was almost sadness. "Yes, my friends, it is the truth. I have succeeded!"

"Indeed!" cried Annie, a look of maiden mirthfulness peeping out of her face again. "And is it lawful, now, to inquire what the secret is!"

"Surely; it is to disclose it, that I have come," answered Owen Warland. "You shall know, and see, and touch, and possess, the secret! For Annie—if by that name I may still address the friend of my boyish years—Annie, it is for your bridal gift that I have wrought this spiritualized mechanism, this harmony of motion, this Mystery of Beauty! It comes late, indeed; but it is as we go onward in life, when objects begin to lose their freshness of hue, and our souls their delicacy of perception, that the spirit of Beauty is most needed. If—forgive me, Annie—if you know how to value this gift, it can never come too late!"

He produced, as he spoke, what seemed a jewel-box. It was carved richly out of ebony by his own hand, and inlaid with a fanciful tracery of pearl, representing a boy in pursuit of a butterfly, which, elsewhere, had become a winged spirit, and was flying heavenward; while the boy, or youth, had found such efficacy in his strong desire, that he ascended from earth to cloud, and from cloud to celestial atmosphere, to win the

Beautiful. This case of ebony the artist opened, and bade Annie place her finger on its edge.

She did so, but almost screamed, as a butterfly fluttered forth, and, alighting on her finger's tip, sat waving the ample magnificence of its purple and gold-speckled wings, as if in prelude to a flight. It is impossible to express by words the glory, the splendor, the delicate gorgeousness, which were softened into the beauty of this object. Nature's ideal butterfly was here realized in all its perfection; not in the pattern of such faded insects as flit among earthly flowers, but of those which hover across the meads of Paradise, for child-angels and the spirits of departed infants to disport themselves with.

The rich down was visible upon its wings; the lustre of its eyes seemed instinct with spirit. The firelight glimmered around this wonder—the candles gleamed upon it—but it glistened apparently by its own radiance, and illuminated the finger and outstretched hand on which it rested, with a white gleam like that of precious stones. In its perfect beauty, the consideration of size was entirely lost. Had its wings overarched the firmament, the mind could not have been more filled or satisfied.

"Beautiful! Beautiful!" exclaimed Annie. "Is it alive? Is it alive?"

"Alive? To be sure it is," answered her husband. "Do you suppose any mortal has skill enough to make a butterfly,—or would put himself to the trouble of making one, when any child may catch a score of them in a summer's afternoon? Alive? Certainly! But this pretty box is undoubtedly of our friend Owen's manufacture; and really it does him credit."

At this moment, the butterfly waved its wings anew, with a motion so absolutely lifelike that Annie was startled, and even awe-stricken; for, in spite of her husband's opinion, she could not satisfy herself whether it was indeed a living creature, or a piece of wondrous mechanism.

"Is it alive?" she repeated, more earnestly than before.

"Judge for yourself," said Owen Warland, who stood gazing in her face with fixed attention.

The butterfly now flung itself upon the air, fluttered round Annie's head, and soared into a distant region of the parlor, still making itself perceptible to sight by the starry gleam in which the motion of its wings enveloped it. The infant on the floor, followed its course with his sagacious little eyes. After flying about the room, it returned, in a spiral curve, and settled again on Annie's finger.

"But is it alive?" exclaimed she again; and the finger, on which the gorgeous mystery had alighted, was so tremulous that the butterfly was forced to balance himself with his wings. "Tell me if it be alive, or whether you created it?"

"Wherefore ask who created it, so it be beautiful?" replied Owen Warland. "Alive? Yes, Annie; it may well be said to possess life, for it has absorbed my own being into itself; and in the secret of that butterfly, and in its beauty—which is not merely outward, but deep as its whole system—is represented the intellect, the imagination, the sensibility, the soul, of an Artist of the Beautiful! Yes, I created it. But"—and here his countenance somewhat changed—"this butterfly is not now to me what it was when I beheld it afar off, in the daydreams of my youth."

"Be it what it may, it is a pretty plaything," said the blacksmith, grinning with childlike delight. "I wonder whether it would condescend to alight on such a great clumsy finger as mine? Hold it hither, Annie!"

By the artist's direction, Annie touched her finger's tip to that of her husband; and, after a momentary delay, the butterfly fluttered from one to the other. It preluded a second flight by a similar, yet not precisely the same waving of wings, as in the first experiment. Then ascending from the blacksmith's stalwart finger, it rose in a gradually enlarging curve to the ceiling, made one wide sweep around the room, and returned with an undulating movement to the point whence it had started.

"Well, that does beat all nature!" cried Robert Danforth, bestowing the heartiest praise that he could find expression for; and, indeed, had he paused there, a man of finer words and nicer perception, could not easily have said more." That goes beyond me, I confess! But what then? There is more real use in one downright blow of my sledgehammer, than in the whole five years' labor that our friend Owen has wasted on this butterfly!"

Here the child clapped his hands, and made a great babble of indistinct utterance, apparently demanding that the butterfly should be given him for a plaything.

Owen Warland, meanwhile, glanced sidelong at Annie, to discover whether she sympathized in her husband's estimate of the comparative value of the Beautiful and the Practical. There was, amid all her kindness towards himself, amid all the wonder and admiration with which she contemplated the marvelous work of his hands, and incarnation of his idea, a sweet scorn; too sweet, perhaps, for her own consciousness, and perceptible only to such intuitive discernment as that of the artist. But Owen, in the latter stages of his pursuit, had risen out of the region in which such a discovery might have been torture.

He knew that the world, and Annie as the representative of the world, whatever praise might be bestowed, could never say the fitting word, nor feel the fitting sentiment which should be the perfect recompense of an artist who, symbolizing a lofty moral by a material trifle—converting what was earthly, to spiritual gold—had won the Beautiful into his handiwork. Not at this latest moment, was he to learn that the reward of all high performance must be sought within itself, or sought in vain.

There. was, however, a view of the matter, which Annie, and her husband, and even Peter Hovenden, might fully have understood, and which would have satisfied them that the toil of years had here been worthily bestowed. Owen Warland might have told them, that this butterfly, this plaything, this bridal-gift of a poor watchmaker to a blacksmith's wife, was, in truth, a gem of art that a monarch would have purchased with honors and abundant wealth, and have treasured it among the jewels of his kingdom, as the most unique and wondrous of them all! But the artist smiled, and kept the secret to himself.

"Father," said Annie, thinking that a word of praise from the old watchmaker might gratify his former apprentice, "do come and admire this pretty butterfly!"

"Let us see," said Peter Hovenden, rising from his chair, with the sneer upon his face that always made people doubt, as he himself did, in everything but a material existence. "Here is my finger for it to alight upon. I shall understand it better when once I have touched it."

But, to the increased astonishment of Annie, when the tip of her father's finger was pressed against that of her husband, on which the butterfly still rested, the insect drooped its wings, and seemed on the point of falling to the floor. Even the bright spots of gold upon its wings and body, unless her eyes deceived her, grew dim, and the glowing purple took a dusky hue, and the starry lustre that gleamed around the blacksmith's hand, became faint, and vanished.

"It is dying! it is dying!" cried Annie, in alarm.

"It has been delicately wrought," said the artist calmly. "As I told you, it has imbibed a spiritual essence—call it magnetism, or what you will. In an atmosphere of doubt and mockery, its exquisite susceptibility suffers torture, as does the soul of him who instilled his own life into it. It has already lost its beauty; in a few moments more, its mechanism would be irreparably injured."

"Take away your hand, father!" entreated Annie, turning pale. "Here is my child; let it rest on his innocent hand. There, perhaps, its life will revive, and its colors grow brighter than ever."

Her father, with an acrid smile, withdrew his finger. The butterfly then appeared to recover the power of voluntary motion; while its hues assumed much of their original lustre, and the gleam of starlight, which was its most ethereal attribute, again formed a halo round about it. At first, when transferred from Robert Danforth's hand to the small finger of the child, this radiance grew so powerful that it positively threw the little fellow's shadow back against the wall. He, meanwhile, extended his plump hand as he had seen his father and mother do, and watched the waving of the insect's wings, with infantine delight. Nevertheless, there was a certain odd expression of sagacity, that made Owen Warland feel as if here were old Peter Hovenden, partially, and but partially, redeemed from his hard scepticism into childish faith.

"How wise the little monkey looks!" whispered Robert Danforth to his wife.

"I never saw such a look on a child's face," answered Annie, admiring her own infant, and with good reason, far more than the artistic butterfly. "The darling knows more of the mystery than we do."

As if the butterfly, like the artist, were conscious of something not entirely congenial in the child's nature, it alternately sparkled and grew dim. At length, it arose from the small hand of the infant with an airy motion, that seemed to bear it upward without an effort; as if the ethereal instincts, with which its master's spirit had endowed it, impelled this fair vision involuntarily to a higher sphere.

Had there been no obstruction, it might have soared into the sky, and grown immortal. But its luster gleamed upon the ceiling; the exquisite texture of its wings brushed against the earthly medium; and a sparkle or two, as of stardust, floated downward and lay glimmering on the carpet. Then the butterfly came fluttering down, and, instead of returning to the infant, was apparently attracted towards the artist's hand.

"Not so, not so!" murmured Owen Warland, as if his handiwork could have understood him. "Thou hast gone forth out of the master's heart. There is no return for thee!"

With a wavering movement, and emitting a tremulous radiance, the butterfly struggled, as it were, towards the infant, and was about to alight upon his finger. But, whilse it still hovered in the air, the little Child of Strength, with his grandsire's sharp and shrewd expression in his face, made a snatch at the marvelous insect, and compressed his hand. Annie screamed! Old Perter Hovenden burst into a cold and scornful laugh. The blacksmith, by main force, unclosed the infant's hand, and found within the palm a small heap of glittering fragments, whence the Mystery of the Beauty had fled forever.

And as for Owen Warland, he looked placidly at what seemed the ruin of his life's labor, and which yet was no ruin. He had caught a far other butterfly than this. When the artist rose high enough to achieve the Beautiful, the symbol by which he made it perceptible to mortal senses became of little value in his eyes, while his spirit possessed itself in the enjoyment of the Reality.

WILLIAM MUDFORD
(1782-1848)

Introduction
The Iron Shroud

There is only one known image of William Mudford that exists. In 1820, when Mudford was 28 years old, George Hayter included him in his painting titled *The Trial of Queen Caroline*. From this rather crude image I had the illustration above commissioned.

William Mudford gave the world one of the finest science fiction tales of the first half of the 19th century—"The Iron Shroud"—with its seven windows stacked one on top of the other. Edgar Allan Poe's subsequently published, "The Pit and the Pendulum," has been compared to it in overall atmosphere and the now-way-out trap of the protagonist.

Lydia Maria Child, author of "Hilda Silfverling, A Fantasy" which, as stated earlier, is perhaps the first science fiction short story by a woman, found a keen analogy to "The Iron Shroud" and the crushing oppression of slavery. So much so, that she republished the story in the *National Anti-Slavery Standard* for December of 1842. This is what Child had to say about it:

> "Again and again have we thought of this thrilling story in connection with slavery; and never so much as within the last two years. It becomes more and more obvious that the walls *are* closing in upon the foul system and that it must inevitably be crushed."

The Iron Shroud
(1830)

THE CASTLE OF the prince of Tolfi was built on the summit of the towering and precipitous rock of Scylla, and commanded a magnificent view of Sicily in all its grandeur. Here during the wars of the middle ages, when the fertile plains of Italy were devastated by hostile factions, those prisoners were confined, for whose ransom a costly price was demanded. Here, too, in a dungeon, excavated deep in the solid rock, the miserable victim was immured, whom revenge pursued—the dark, fierce, and unpitying revenge of an Italian heart.

Vivenzio—the noble and the generous, the fearless in battle, and the pride of Naples in her sunny hours of peace—the young, the brave, the proud Vivenzio, fell beneath this subtle and remorseless spirit. He was the prisoner of Tolfi, and he languished in that rock-encircled dungeon, which stood alone, and whose portals never opened twice upon a living captive.

It had the semblance of a vast cage, for the roof and floor and sides were of iron, solidly wrought, and spaciously constructed. High above there ran a range of seven grated windows, guarded with massy bars of the same metal, which admitted light and air. Save these, and the tall folding doors beneath them which occupied the centre, no chink or chasm or projection broke the smooth black surface of the walls. An iron bedstead, littered with straw, stood in one corner; and beside it, a vessel with water, and a coarse dish filled with coarser food.

Even the intrepid soul of Vivenzio shrunk with dismay as he entered this abode, and heard the ponderous doors triple locked by the silent ruffians who conducted him to it. Their silence seemed prophetic of his fate, of the living grave that had been prepared for him. His menaces and his entreaties, his indignant appeals for justice, and his questioning of their intentions were alike vain. They listened, but spoke not. Fit ministers of a crime that should have no tongue!

How dismal was the sound of their retiring steps! And, as their faint echoes died along the winding passages, a fearful presage grew within him, that never more the face or voice or tread of man would greet his senses. He had seen human beings for the last time! And he had looked his last upon the bright sky, and upon the smiling earth, and upon a beautiful world he loved and whose minion he had been! Here he was to end his life—a life he had just begun to revel in! And by what means? By secret poison or by murderous assault? No—for then it had been needless to bring him hither. Famine perhaps—a thousand deaths in one! It was terrible to think of it; but it was yet more terrible to picture long, long years of captivity, in a solitude so appalling, a loneliness so dreary, that thought, for want of fellowship, would lose itself in madness or stagnate into idiocy.

He could not hope to escape, unless he had the power of rending asunder, with his bare hands, the solid iron walls of his prison. He could not hope for liberty from the relenting mercies of his enemy. His instant death, under any form of refined cruelty, was not the object of Tolfi, for he might have inflicted it, and he had not. It was too evident, therefore, he was reserved for some premeditated scheme of subtle vengeance; and what vengeance could transcend in fiendish malice either the slow death of famine, or the still slower one of solitary incarceration, till the last lingering spark of life expired or till reason fled, and nothing should remain to perish but the brute functions of the body?

It was evening when Vivenzio entered his dungeon, and the approaching shades of night wrapped it in total darkness, as he paced up and down, revolving in his mind these horrible forebodings. No tolling bell from the castle, or from any neighboring church or convent, struck upon his ear to tell how the hours passed.

Frequently he would stop and listen for some sound that might betoken the vicinity of man; but the solitude of the desert, the silence of the tomb, are not so still and deep as the oppressive desolation by which he was encompassed. His heart sank within him, and he threw himself dejectedly down upon his couch of straw. Here sleep gradually obliterated the consciousness of misery, and bland dreams wafted his delighted spirit to scenes which were once glowing realities for him, in whose ravishing illusions he soon lost the remembrance that he was Tolfi's prisoner.

When he awoke, it was daylight; but how long he had slept he knew not. It might be early morning, or it might be sultry noon, for he could measure time by no other note of its progress than light and darkness. He had been so happy in his sleep, amid friends who loved him, and the sweeter endearments of those who loved him as friends could not, that, in the first moments of waking, his startled mind seemed to admit the knowledge of his situation as if it had burst upon it for the first time, fresh in all its appalling horrors.

He gazed round with an air of doubt and amazement, and took up a handful of the straw upon which he lay, as though he would ask himself what it meant. But memory, too faithful to her office, soon unveiled the melancholy past, while reason, shuddering at the task, flashed before his eyes the tremendous future. The contrast overpowered him. He remained for some time lamenting, like a truth, the bright visions that had vanished; and recoiling from the present, which clung to him as a poisoned garment.

When he grew more calm, he surveyed his gloomy dungeon. Alas! the stronger light of day only served to confirm what the gloomy indistinctness of the preceding evening had partially disclosed, the utter impossibility of escape. As, however, his eyes wandered round and round, and from place to place, he noticed two circumstances which excited his surprise and curiosity. The one, he thought, might be fancy; but the other was positive. His pitcher of water, and the dish which contained his food, had been removed from his side while he slept, and now stood near the door.

Were he even inclined to doubt this, by supposing he had mistaken the spot where he saw them overnight, he could not, for the pitcher now in his dungeon was neither of the same form nor color as the other, while the food was changed for some other of better quality. He had been visited, therefore, during the night. But how had the person obtained entrance? Could he have slept so soundly that the unlocking and opening of those ponderous portals were effected without waking him? He would have said this was not possible, but that in doing so, he must admit a greater difficulty, an entrance by other means, of which he was convinced there existed none. It was not intended, then, that he should be left to perish from hunger. But the secret and mysterious mode of supplying him with food seemed to indicate he was to have no opportunity of communicating with a human being.

The other circumstance which had attracted his notice was the disappearance, as he believed, of one of the seven grated windows that ran along the top of his prison. He felt confident that he had observed and counted them; for he was rather surprised at their number, and there was something peculiar in their form, as well as in the manner of their arrangement, at unequal distances. It was much easier, however, to suppose he was mistaken than that a portion of the solid iron, which formed the walls, could have escaped from its position, and he dismissed the thought from his mind.

Vivenzio partook of the food that was before him, without apprehension. It might be poisoned; but if it were, he knew he could not escape death, should such be the design of Tolfi, and the quickest death would be the speediest release.

The day passed wearily and gloomily; though not without a faint hope that, by keeping watch at night, he might observe when the person came again to bring him food, which he supposed he would do in the same way as before. The mere thought of being approached by a living creature, and the opportunity it might present of learning the doom prepared, or preparing, for him, imparted some comfort. Besides, if he came alone, might he not in a furious onset overpower him? Or he might be accessible to pity, or the influence of such munificent rewards as he could bestow if once more at liberty and master of himself. Say he were armed. The worst that could befall, if nor bribe, nor prayers, nor force prevailed, was a friendly blow, which, though dealt in a damned cause, might work a desired end. There was no chance so desperate but it looked lovely in Vivenzio's eyes, compared with the idea of being totally abandoned.

The night came, and Vivenzio watched. Morning came, and Vivenzio was confounded! He must have slumbered without knowing it. Sleep must have stolen over him when exhausted by fatigue, and in that interval of feverish repose he had been baffled: for there stood his replenished pitcher of water, and there his day's meal! Nor was this all. Casting his looks toward the windows of his dungeon, he counted but FIVE! *Here* was no deception; and he was now convinced there had been none the day before. But what did all this portend? Into what strange and mysterious den had he been cast? He gazed till his eyes ached; he could discover nothing to explain the mystery. That it was so, he knew. Why it was so, he racked his imagination in vain to conjecture. He examined the doors. A simple circumstance convinced him they had not been opened.

A wisp of straw, which he had carelessly thrown against them the preceding day, as he paced to and fro, remained where he had cast it, though it must have been displaced by the slightest motion of either of the doors. This was evidence that could not be disputed; and it followed there must be some secret machinery in the walls by which a person could enter. He inspected them closely. They appeared to him one solid and compact mass of iron; or joined, if joined they were, with such nice art that no mark of division was perceptible.

Again and again he surveyed them—and the floor—and the roof—and that range of visionary windows, as he was now almost tempted to consider them: he could discover nothing, absolutely nothing, to relieve his doubts or satisfy his curiosity. Sometimes he fancied that altogether the dungeon had a more contracted appearance—that it looked smaller; but this he ascribed to fancy, and the impression naturally produced upon his mind by the undeniable disappearance of two of the windows.

With intense anxiety, Vivenzio looked forward to the return of night; and as it approached, he resolved that no treacherous sleep should again betray him. Instead of seeking his bed of straw, he continued to walk up and down his dungeon till daylight, straining his eyes in every direction through the darkness, to watch for any appearances that might explain these, mysteries. While thus engaged, and as nearly as he could judge (by the time that afterward elapsed before the morning came in) about two o'clock, there was a slight tremulous motion of the floors.

He stooped.

The motion lasted nearly a minute; but it was so extremely gentle, that he almost doubted whether it was real or only imaginary. He listened. Not a sound could be heard. Presently, however, he felt a rush of cold air blow upon him; and dashing toward the quarter whence it seemed to proceed, he stumbled over something which he judged to be the water ewer.[1]

---

[1] Jug or small bucket for carrying water

The rush of cold air was no longer perceptible; and as Vivenzio stretched out his hands, he found himself close to the walls. He remained motionless for a considerable time; but nothing occurred during the remainder of the night to excite his attention, though he watched with unabated vigilance.

The first approaches of the morning were visible through the grated windows, breaking, with faint divisions of light, the darkness that still pervaded every other part, long before Vivenzio was enabled to distinguish any object in his dungeon. Instinctively and fearfully he turned his eyes, hot and inflamed with watching, toward them. There were FOUR! He could see only four: but it might be that some intervening object prevented the fifth from becoming perceptible; and he waited impatiently to ascertain if it were so.

As the light strengthened, however, and penetrated every corner of the cell, other objects of amazement struck his sight. On the ground lay the broken fragments of the pitcher he had used the day before, and at a small distance from them, nearer to the wall, stood the one he had noticed the first night. It was filled with water, and beside it was his food. He was now certain that, by some mechanical contrivance, an opening was obtained through the iron wall, and that through this opening the current of air had found entrance. But how noiselessly! For had a feather almost waved at the time, he must have heard it. Again he examined that part of the wall; but, both to sight and touch, it appeared one even and uniform surface, while, to repeated and violent blows, there was no reverberating sound indicative of hollowness.

This perplexing mystery had for a time withdrawn his thoughts from the windows; but now, directing his eyes toward them, he saw that the fifth had disappeared in the same manner as the preceding two, without the least distinguishable alteration of external appearances. The remaining four looked as the seven had originally looked; that is, occupying, at irregular distances, the top of the wall on that side of the dungeon.

The tall folding-door, too, still seemed to stand beneath, in the centre of these four, as it had at first stood in the centre of the seven. But he could no longer doubt, what, on the preceding day, he fancied might be the effect of visual deception. The dungeon *was* smaller. The roof had lowered—and the opposite ends had contracted the intermediate distance by a space equal, he thought, to that over which the three windows had extended. He was bewildered in vain imaginings to account for these things. Some frightful purpose—some devilish torture of mind or body— some unheard-of device for producing exquisite misery, lurked he was sure, in what had taken place.

Oppressed with this belief, and distracted more by the dreadful uncertainty of whatever fate impended, than he could be dismayed, he thought, by the knowledge of the worst, he sat ruminating, hour after hour, yielding his fears in succession to every haggard fancy. At last a horrible suspicion flashed suddenly across his mind, and he started up with a frantic air. "Yes!" he exclaimed, looking wildly round his dungeon, and shuddering as he spoke—"Yes! it must be so! I see it!—I feel the maddening truth like scorching flames upon my brain! Eternal God!—support me! It must be so! Yes, yes, *that* is to be my fate! Yon roof will descend!—these walls will hem me round—and slowly, slowly crush me in their iron arms! Lord God! look down upon me, and in mercy strike me with instant death! O fiend—O devil—is this your revenge?"

He dashed himself upon the ground in agony— tears burst from him, and the sweat stood in large drops upon his face—he sobbed aloud—he tore his hair—he rolled about like one suffering intolerable anguish of body, and would have bitten the iron floor beneath him; he breathed fearful curses upon Tolfi, and the next moment passionate prayers to Heaven for immediate death. Then the violence of his grief became exhausted, and he lay still, weeping as a child would weep.

The twilight of departing day shed its gloom around him ere he rose from that posture of utter and hopeless sorrow. He had taken no food. Not one drop of water had cooled the fever of his parched lips. Sleep had not visited his eyes for six-and-thirty hours. He was faint with hunger; weary with watching, and with the excess of his emotions. He tasted of his food; he drank with avidity of the water; and, reeling like a drunken man in his straw, cast himself upon it to brood again over the appalling image that had fastened itself upon his almost frenzied thoughts.

He slept. But his slumbers were not tranquil. He resisted, as long as he could, their approach; and when, at last, enfeebled nature yielded to their influence, he found no oblivion from his cares. Terrible dreams haunted him—ghastly visions harrowed up his imagination—he shouted and screamed, as if he already felt the dungeon's ponderous roof descending on him—he breathed hard and thick, as though writhing between its iron walls. Then would he spring up—stare wildly about him—stretch forth his hands, to be sure he yet had space enough to live—and, muttering some incoherent words, sink down again, to pass through the same fierce vicissitudes of delirious sleep.

The morning of the fourth day dawned upon Vivenzio. But it was high noon before his mind shook off its stupor, or he awoke to a full consciousness of his situation. And what a fixed energy of despair sat upon his pale features, as he cast his eyes upward, and gazed upon the THREE windows that now alone remained! The three!—there were no more!—and they seemed to number his own allotted days. Slowly and calmly he next surveyed the top and sides, and comprehended all the meaning of the diminished height of the former, as well as of the gradual approximation of the latter.

The contracted dimensions of his mysterious prison were now too gross and palpable to be the juggle of his heated imagination. Still lost in wonder at the means, Vivenzio could put no cheat upon his reason, as to the end. By what horrible ingenuity it was contrived, that walls and roof and windows should thus silently and imperceptibly, without noise, and without motion almost, fold, as it were, within each other, he knew not. He only knew they did so; and he vainly strove to persuade himself it was the intention of the contriver to rack the miserable wretch, who might be immured there, with anticipation, merely, of a fate, from which, in the very crisis of his agony, he was to be reprieved.

Gladly would he have clung even to this possibility, if his heart would have let him; but he felt a dreadful assurance of its fallacy. And what matchless inhumanity it was to doom the sufferer to such lingering torments—to lead him day by day to so appalling a death, unsupported by the consolations of religion, unvisited by any human being, abandoned to himself, deserted of all, and denied even the sad privilege of knowing that his cruel destiny would awaken pity! Alone he was to perish!—alone he was to wait a slow coming torture, whose most exquisite pangs would be inflicted by that very solitude and that tardy coming!

"It is not death I fear," he exclaimed, "but the death I must prepare for! Methinks, too, I could meet even that—all horrible and revolting as it is—if it might overtake me now. But where shall I find fortitude to tarry till it comes? How can I outlive the three long days and nights I have to live? There is no power within me to bid the hideous spectre hence—none to make it familiar to my thoughts, or myself patient of its errand. My thoughts, rather, will flee from me, and I grow mad in looking at it. Oh! for a deep sleep to fall upon me! That so, in death's likeness, I might embrace death itself, and drink no more of the cup that is presented to me than my fainting spirit has already tasted!"

In the midst of these lamentations, Vivenzio noticed that his accustomed meal, with the pitcher of water, had been conveyed, as before, into his dungeon. But this circumstance no longer excited his surprise. His mind was overwhelmed with others of a far greater magnitude. It suggested, however, a feeble hope of deliverance; and there is no hope so feeble as not to yield some support to a heart bending under despair.

He resolved to watch, during the ensuing night, for the signs he had before observed; and should he again feel the gentle tremulous motion of the floor, or the current of air, to seize that moment for giving audible expression to his misery. Some person must be near him, and within reach of his voice, at the instant when his food was supplied; some one, perhaps, susceptible of pity.

Or if not, to be told even that his apprehensions were just, and that his fate *was* to be what he foreboded, would be preferable to a suspense which hung upon the possibility of his worst fears being visionary.

The night came; and as the hour approached when Vivenzio imagined he might expect the signs, he stood fixed and silent as a statue. He feared to breathe, almost, lest he might lose any sound which would warn him of their coming. While thus listening, with every faculty of mind and body strained to an agony of attention, it occurred to him he should be more sensible of the motion, probably, if he stretched himself along the iron floor. He accordingly laid himself softly down, and had not been long in that position when—yes—he was certain of it—the floor moved under him!

He sprang up, and, in a voice nearly suffocated with emotion, called aloud. He paused—the motion ceased—he felt no stream of air—all was hushed—no voice answered to his—he burst into tears, and as he sank to the ground, in renewed anguish, exclaimed: "O my God! my God! You alone have power to save me now, or strengthen me for the trial you permit."

Another morning dawned upon the wretched captive, and the fatal index of his doom met his eyes. Two windows!—and *two* days—and all would be over! Fresh food—fresh water! The mysterious visit had been paid, though he had implored it in vain. But how awfully was his prayer answered in what he now saw! The roof of the dungeon was within a foot of his head. The two ends were so near, that in six paces he trod the space between them.

Vivenzio shuddered as he gazed, and as his steps traversed the narrowed area. But his feelings no longer vented themselves in frantic wailings. With folded arms, and clenched teeth, with eyes that were bloodshot from much watching, and fixed with a vacant glare upon the ground, with a hard quick breathing, and a hurried walk, he strode backward and forward in silent musing for several hours. What mind shall conceive, what tongue utter, or what pen describe the dark and terrible character of his thoughts? Like the fate that moulded them, they had no similitude in the wide range of this world's agony for man. Suddenly he stopped, and his eyes were riveted upon that part of the wall which was over his bed. Words are inscribed there! A human language, traced by a human hand! He rushes toward them; but his blood freezes as he reads:

"I, Ludovico Sforza, tempted by the gold of the prince of Tolfi, spent three years in contriving and executing this accursed triumph of my art. When it was completed, the perfidious Tolfi, more devil than man, who conducted me hither one morning, to be witness, as he said, of its perfection, doomed *me* to be the first victim of my own pernicious skill; lest, as he declared, I should divulge the secret, or repeat the effort of my ingenuity. May God pardon him, as I hope he will me, that ministered to his unhallowed purpose. Miserable wretch, whoe'er thou art, that readest these lines, fall on thy knees, and invoke, as I have done, His sustaining mercy who alone can nerve thee to meet the vengeance of Tolfi—armed with this tremendous engine, which, in a few hours, must crush *you,* as it will the needy wretch who made it."

A deep groan burst from Vivenzio. He stood, like one transfixed, with dilated eyes, expanded nostrils, and quivering lips, gazing at this fatal inscription. It was as if a voice from the sepulchre had sounded in his ears, "Prepare!"

Hope forsook him. There was his sentence, recorded in those dismal words. The future stood unveiled before him, ghastly and appalling. His brain already feels the descending horror—his bones seem to crack and crumble in the mighty grasp of the iron walls! Unknowing what it is he does, he fumbles in his garment for some weapon of self-destruction. He clenches his throat in his convulsive grip, as though he would strangle himself at once. He stares upon the walls, and his warring spirit demands, "Will they not anticipate their office if I dash my head against them?"

An hysterical laugh chokes him as he exclaims, "Why should I? He was but a man who died first in their fierce embrace; and I should be less than man not to be able to do as much!"

The evening sun was descending, and Vivenzio beheld its golden beams streaming through one of the windows. What a thrill of joy shot through his soul at the sight! It was a precious link, that united him, for the moment, with the world beyond. There was ecstasy in the thought. As he gazed, long and earnestly, it seemed as if the windows had lowered sufficiently for him to reach them. With one bound he was beneath them—with one wild spring he clung to the bars.

Whether it was so contrived, purposely to madden with delight the wretch who looked, he knew not; but, at the extremity of a long vista, cut through the solid rocks, the ocean, the sky, the setting sun, olive groves, shady walks, and, in the farthest distance, delicious glimpses of magnificent Sicily, burst upon his sight.

How exquisite was the cool breeze as it swept across his cheek, loaded with fragrance! He inhaled it as though it were the breath of continued life. And there was a freshness in the landscape, and in the rippling of the calm green sea, that fell upon his withering heart like dew upon the parched earth. How he gazed, and panted, and still clung to his hold! sometimes hanging by one hand, sometimes by the other, and then grasping the bars with both, as loath to quit the smiling paradise outstretched before him; till exhausted, and his hands swollen and benumbed, he dropped helpless down, and lay stunned for a considerable time by the fall.

When he recovered, the glorious vision had vanished. He was in darkness. He doubted whether it was not a dream that had passed before his sleeping fancy; but gradually his scattered thoughts returned, and with them came remembrance. Yes! he had looked once again upon the gorgeous splendor of nature!

Once again his eyes had trembled beneath their veiled lids, at the sun's radiance, and sought repose in the soft verdure of the olive-tree, or the gentle swell of undulating waves. Oh, that he were a mariner exposed upon those waves to the worst fury of storm and tempest; or a very wretch, loathsome with disease, plague-stricken, and his body one leprous contagion from crown to sole, hunted forth to gasp out the remnant of infectious life beneath those verdant trees, so he might shun the destiny upon whose edge he tottered!

Vain thoughts like these would steal over his mind from time to time, in spite of himself; but they scarcely moved it from that stupor into which it had sunk, and which kept him, during the whole night, like one who had been drugged with opium.[2] He was equally insensible to the calls of hunger and of thirst, though the third day was now commencing since even

---

[2] Hallucinatory drug derived from the poppy

a drop of water had passed his lips. He remained on the ground, sometimes sitting, sometimes lying; at intervals, sleeping heavily; and when not sleeping, silently brooding over what was to come, or talking aloud, in disordered speech, of his wrongs, of his friends, of his home, and of those he loved, with a confused mingling of all.

In this pitiable condition, the sixth and last morning dawned upon Vivenzio, if dawn it might be called—the dim, obscure light which faintly struggled through the ONE SOLITARY window of his dungeon. He could hardly be said to notice the melancholy token. And yet he did notice it; for as he raised his eyes and saw the portentous sign, there was a slight convulsive distortion of his countenance.

But what did attract his notice, and at the sight of which his agitation was excessive, was the change his iron bed had undergone. It was a bed no longer. It stood before him, the visible semblance of a funeral couch or bier![3] When he beheld this, he started from the ground; and, in raising himself, suddenly struck his head against the roof, which was now so low that he could no longer stand upright.

"God's will be done!" was all he said, as he crouched his body, and placed his hand upon the bier; for such it was. The iron bedstead had been so contrived, by the mechanical art of Ludovico Sforza, that, as the advancing walls came in contact with its head and feet, a pressure was produced upon concealed springs, which, when made to play, set in motion a very simple though ingeniously contrived machinery, that effected the transformation.

The object was, of course, to heighten, in the closing scene of this horrible drama, all the feelings of despair and anguish which the preceding ones had aroused. For the same reason, the last window was so made as to admit only a shadowy kind of gloom rather than light, that the wretched captive might be

---

[3] Coffin

surrounded, as it were, with every seeming preparation for approaching death.

Vivenzio seated himself on his bier. Then he knelt and prayed fervently; and sometimes tears would gush from him. The air seemed thick, and he breathed with difficulty; or it might be that he fancied it was so, from the narrow limits of his dungeon, which were now so diminished that he could neither stand up nor lie down at his full length. But his wasted spirits and oppressed mind no longer struggled within him. He was past hope, and fear shook him no more. Happy if thus revenge had struck its final blow; for he would have fallen beneath it almost unconscious of a pang. But such a lethargy of the soul, after such an excitement of its passions, had entered into the diabolical calculations of Tolfi; and the artificer of his designs had imagined a counteracting device.

The tolling of an enormous bell struck upon the ears of Vivenzio! He started. It beat but once. The sound was so close and stunning that it seemed to shatter his very brain, while it echoed through the rocky passages like reverberating peals of thunder. This was followed by a sudden crash of the roof and walls, as if they were about to fall upon and close around him at once. Vivenzio screamed, and instinctively spread forth his arms, as though he had a giant's strength to hold them back.

They, had moved nearer to him, and were now motionless. Vivenzio looked up, and saw the roof almost touching his head, even as he sat cowering beneath it; and he felt that a farther contraction of but a few inches only must commence the frightful operation. Roused as he had been, he now gasped for breath. His body shook violently—he was bent nearly double. His hands rested upon either wall, and his feet were drawn under him to avoid the pressure in front. Thus he remained for an hour, when that deafening bell beat again, and again there came the crash of horrid death. But the concussion was now so great that it struck Vivenzio down. As he lay gathered up in lessened bulk, the bell beat loud and frequent—crash succeeded crash—and on, and on, and on came the mysterious engine of death, till Vivenzio's smothered groans were heard no more!

He was horribly crushed by the ponderous roof and collapsing sides—and the flattened bier was his *Iron Shroud.*

Stories Considered

Anonymous

Henry Brownrigg

Lydia Maria Child

Willis Gaylord Clark

Professor Gullphlat

Nathaniel Hawthorne

Ernst Theodor Hoffmann

Percival Leigh

Richard Adams Locke
    1835 Great Astronomical Discoveries Lately Made by Sir John Herschel, L.L.D. F.R.S. &C. at the Cape of Good Hope

Captain Frederick Marryat
    1820 A Visit to the Lunar Sphere

Thomas Charles Morgan
    1835 Glimpses of Other Worlds

William Mudford
    1830 The Iron Shroud

P. Hamilton Myers
    1846 The Adventures of Wilhelmus Wyndert

Edgar Allan Poe
    1833 MS. Found in Bottle
    1835 The Unparalleled Adventure of One Hans Pfaall
    1837 Von Jung, the Mystific
    1839 The Conversation of Eiros and Charmion
    1841 The Colloquy of Monos and Una
    1841 A Descent Into the Maelström
    1844 [The Balloon Hoax]
    1844 Mesmeric Revelation
    1844 The Premature Burial
    1844 A Tale of the Ragged Mountains
    1845 The Facts in the Case of M. Valdemar
    1845 The Power of Words
    1845 Some Words with a Mummy
    1845 The Thousand-and-Second Tale of Scheherazade
    1849 Mellonta Tauta
    1849 Von Kempelen and His Discovery

William Gilmore Simms
    1845 Mesmerides in a Stage-Coach; or, Passes en Passant

About Andrew

Andrew Barger is to blame for *The Divine Dantes* trilogy. The first book in the series follows the characters of Dante's "The Inferno" in a messed-up modern world. Andrew is also the award-winning author of *Coffee with Poe: A Novel of Edgar Allan Poe's Life*. *Mailboxes – Mansions – Memphistopheles* is his first short story collection. He is also the editor of a number of other books, including *The Best Vampire Stories 1800-1849: A Classic Vampire Anthology* and *Edgar Allan Poe Annotated and Illustrated Entire Stories and Poems*, and is recognized for his scholarly and creative writing. He wants to start a band, if only he could settle on a name for it.

Connect with Andrew Online

Website: AndrewBarger.com
Blog: AndrewBarger.blogspot.com
Facebook: Facebook.com/AuthorAndrewBarger
Goodreads: Andrew Barger
Twitter: twitter.com/AndrewBarger

Read Other Titles by Andrew Barger

**The Divine Dantes
Squirt Gun in Hades
(Book #1 Infernal Trilogy)**

Young rocker Edward T. Nad is down on his luck after the other member of his two-person band (and girlfriend—Beatrice) leaves their small town for Europe. Once there, Beatrice has second thoughts about the breakup and asks their erstwhile manager cum travel agent, Virgil, to bring Edward to her without him knowing it. This sparks off the hilarious intercontinental journey of the staid, nerdy manager and the young rocker with an active and opinionated mind who struggles with the basics, like settling on a name for the band: "Grain of Sand and the Clams" versus "The Beelzebubbas." The comedic novel contains the characters of "The Inferno" and tracks their movements through Hades in modern times. *Dante's Infernos: Squirt Guns in Hades* is the first in a trilogy of novels that parallel "The Inferno," "The Purgatorio," and "The Paradiso" of Dante's *The Divine Comedy* through modern times.

[A] lively and good-natured work with a great deal of humor . . ..
Publisher's Weekly Reviewer

[R]eminds me a little of the fun I find in Carl Hiaasen or Christopher Moore, but he definitely has his own vibe . . ..
Breakthrough Novel Award Expert Reviewer

**Mailboxes – Mansions – Memphistophels
A Collection of Dark Tales**

A finalist in the International Book Awards, Andrew Barger's first short story collection unleashes a blend of character-driven dark tales, which are sure to be remembered. In the collection Andrew unleashes a blend of character-driven dark tales, which are sure to be remembered.

In "Azra'eil & Fudgie" a little girl visits a team of marines in Afghanistan and they quickly learn she is more than she seems. "The Mailbox War" is a deadly tale of a weekend hobby taken to extremes while "The Brownie of the Alabaster Mansion" sees a Scottish monster of antiquity brought back to life. "Memphistopheles" contains a tale of the devil, Memphis, barbeque and a wannabe poet. "The Serpent and the Sepulcher" is a prose poem that will be cherished by all who experience it. "The Gëbult Mansion" recounts a literary hoax played by Andrew on his unsuspecting social networking friends that involves a female vampire. Last, "Stain" is an unforgettable horror story about a stain that will not go away.

**Phantasmal
The Best Ghost Stories 1800-1849**

Short ghost stories became very popular in the first half of the nineteenth century and this collection by Andrew Barger contains the very scariest of them all. Some stories thought too horrific were published anonymously like "A Night in a Haunted House" and "The Deaf and Dumb Girl," with the later being anthologized for the first time since its original publication in 1839.

The other ghost stories in this fine collection are by famous authors. "The Mask of the Red Death," is by Edgar Allan Poe; "A Chapter in the History of a Tyrone Family," by Joseph Sheridan le Fanu; "The Spectral Ship," by Wilhelm Hauff; "The Old Maid in the Winding Sheet," by Nathaniel Hawthorne; "The Adventure of the German Student," and "The Legend of Sleepy Hollow," by Washington Irving; as well as "The Tapestried Chamber," by Sir Walter Scott. Andrew Barger has added his familiar scholarly touch to this collection by including annotations, story backgrounds, author photos and a foreword titled "All Ghosts Are Gray."

[A] unique perspective on this dawn of horror's early roots and their connections to our modern day. "The Best Ghost Stories 1800-1849" is a choice pick with stories from many legendary authors such as Edgar Allan Poe and Washington Irving, very much recommended reading.
MIDWEST BOOK REVIEW

Shifters
The Best Werewolf Short Stories 1800-1849

Andrew has compiled the best werewolf stories from the period when werewolf short stories were first invented. The stories are "Hugues the Wer-Wolf: A Kentish Legend of the Middle Ages," "The Man-Wolf," "A Story of a Weir-Wolf," "The Wehr-Wolf: A Legend of the Limousin," and "The White Wolf of the Hartz Mountains." It is believed that two of these stories have never been republished in over 150 years since their original printing. Read *Shifters: The Best Werewolf Short Stories 1800-1849* by the light of a full moon.

After an informed and informative introduction on the subject by Andrew Barger, five of these stories are presented in full, followed by a listing of short stories considered from 1800 to 1849, along with an index of Real Names. A seminal work of impressive scholarship,

"The Best Werewolf Short Stories 1800-1849: A Classic Werewolf Anthology" is highly recommended reading for fantasy fans, and a valued addition to academic library Literary Studies reference collections.
MIDWEST BOOK REVIEW

Coffee with Poe
A Novel of Edgar Allan Poe's Life

Coffee with Poe brings Edgar Allan Poe to life within its pages as never before. The book is filled with actual letters from his many romances and literary contemporaries. Orphaned at the age of two, Poe is raised by John Allan—his abusive foster father—who refuses to adopt him until he becomes straight-laced and businesslike. Poe, however, fancies poetry and young women. The contentious relationship culminates in a violent altercation, which causes Poe to leave his wealthy foster father's home to make it as a writer. Poe tries desperately to get established as a writer but is ridiculed by the "Literati of New York."

The Raven subsequently gains Poe renown in America yet he slips deeper into poverty, only making $15 off the poem's entire publication history. Desperate for a motherly figure in his life, Poe marries his first cousin who is only thirteen. Poe lives his last years in abject poverty while suffering through the deaths of his foster mother, grandmother, and young wife. In a cemetery he becomes engaged to Helen Whitman, a dark poet who is addicted to ether, wears a small coffin about her neck, and conducts séances in her home. The engagement is soon broken off because of Poe's drinking. In his final months his health is in a downward spiral. Poe disappears on a trip and is later found delirious and wearing another person's clothes.

He dies a few days later, whispering his final words: "God help my poor soul."

To give us a historical fiction look at Edgar Allan Poe is great. The start where we are at his mom's funeral gives a little insight into why he may write the way he does. It is very interesting the ideas the author has put into the story about Poe. I like the idea of detailing the life of Edgar Allan Poe into a historical fiction novel. . . . A great idea to give us some insight into why Poe may be the way he is.
Breakthrough Novel Award Expert Reviewer

BlooDeath
<u>The Best Vampire Stories 1800-1849</u>

Unearthed from long forgotten journals and magazines, Andrew Barger has found the very best vampire short stories from the first half of the 19th century. They are collected for the first time in this groundbreaking book on the origins of vampire lore. The cradle of all vampire short stories in the English language is the first half of the 19th century. Andrew Barger combed forgotten journals and mysterious texts to collect the very best vintage vampire stories from this crucial period in vampire literature. In doing so, Andrew unearthed the second and third vampire stories originally published in the English language, neither printed since their first publication nearly 200 years ago.

Also included is the first vampire story originally written in English by John Polidori after a dare with Lord Byron and Mary Shelley. The book contains the first vampire story by an American who was a graduate of Columbia Law School. The book further includes the first vampire stories by an Englishman and German, including the only vampire stories by such renowned authors as Alexander Dumas, Théophile Gautier and Joseph le Fanu. As readers have come to expect from Andrew, he has added his scholarly touch to this collection by including annotations, story backgrounds, author photos and a foreword titled "With Teeth."

6a66le
<u>The Best Horror Short Stories 1800-1849</u>

6a66le: *The Best Horror Short Stories 1800-1849* is a book for anyone who loves a classic horror story.

Thanks to Edgar Allan Poe, Honoré de Balzac, Nathaniel Hawthorne and others, the first half of the nineteenth century is the cradle of all modern horror short stories. Andrew Barger, the editor, read over 300 horror short stories and compiled the dozen best. A few have never been republished since they were first published in leading periodicals of the day such as *Blackwood's* and *Atkinson's Casket*.

At the back of the book Andrew includes a list of all short stories he considered along with their dates of publication and the author, when available. He even includes background for each of the stories, author photos and annotations for difficult terminology.

'The Best Horror Short Stories 1800-1849' will likely become a best seller . . . .What makes this collection (of truly terrifying tales!) so satisfying is the presence of a brief introduction before each story, sharing some comments about the writer and elements of the tale. Barger has once again whetted our appetites for fright, spent countless hours making these twelve stories accessible and

Edgar Allan Poe
Annotated and Illustrated Entire Stories and Poems

For the first time in one compilation are background information for Poe's stories and poems, annotations, foreign word translations, illustrations, photographs of individuals Poe wrote about, and poetry to Poe from his many romantic interests. Here is a sampling of the tales and poems included: "Annabel Lee," "The Bells," "The Black Cat," "[The Bloodhounds]," "The Cask of Amontillado," "The Conqueror Worm," "A Descent into the Maelstrom," "The Fall of the House of Usher," "The Gold-Bug," "The Haunted Palace," "Lenore," "The Masque of the Red Death," "MS. Found in a Bottle," "Murders in the Rue Morgue," "The Oblong Box," "The Pit and the Pendulum," "The Premature Burial," "The Purloined Letter," "[The Rats of Park Theatre]," "The Raven," "Some Words with a Mummy," "The Swiss Bell-Ringers," "The System of Doctor Tarr and Professor Fether," "The Tell-Tale Heart," and "Thou Art the Man."

Barger adds 'guidance' to his method of presenting these works by such devices as listing all of the poems under the subheadings of 'Women in Edgar Allan Poe's Life', 'Miscellaneous Poetry both Before and After Age 25', 'Autobiographical', and 'Men in Edgar Allen Poe's Life.' These may seem like minor adjustments to the collections, but in Barger's hands the divisions add meaning and context to the works.

In addition to all of the written works of Poe, this handsome book contains photographs and many of the famous illustrations for his works - especially those of Harry Clarke and Gustave Dore. The fine art of these two men is also honored with annotations adding to their importance to Poe's popularity as a writer. This is simply a splendid book, handsomely written and produced, and a fine tribute to the literature of Poe - and to the scholarship of Andrew Barger! Highly Recommended.

Amazon Top Ten Reviewer

Leo Tolstoy's 20 Greatest Short Stories
<u>Annotated</u>

Anna Karenina and *War and Peace* revealed Leo Tolstoy as one of the greatest writers in modern history. Few, however, have read his wonderful short stories. Now, in one collection, are the greatest short stories of Tolstoy, which give a snapshot of Russia and its people in the late 19th century. Annotations are included of difficult Russian terms. Read these short classics today.

Now for the first time, twenty of his best short stories have been compiled and edited into a single volume by Andrew Barger. Enhanced for the reader with informative annotations. The stories comprising this outstanding collection include: A Candle, After the Dance, Albert, Alyosha the Pot, An Old Acquaintance, Does a Man Need Much Land?, If You Neglect the Fire You Don't Put It Out, Khodinka: An Incident of the Coronation of Nicholas II, Lucerne, Memoirs of a Lunatic, My Dream, Recollections of a Scorer, The Empty Drum, The Long Exile, The

Posthumous Papers of the Hermit Fedor Kusmich, The Young Tsar, There Are No Guilty People, Three Deaths, Two Old Men, and *What Men Live By. A truly impressive anthology, "Leo Tolstoy's 20 Greatest Short Stories" is especially recommended for acquisition by community and academic libraries, as well as the supplemental reading lists for students of Russian Literature.*
Midwest Book Review

Orion
<u>An Epic English Poem</u>

Orion is an epic English poem of love and war. It deserves its place next to *Beowulf* in English literature. Its overtones consist of aesthetically pleasing writing with a Shakespearian tinge, all wrapped in classical Greek mythology. It contains a fine introduction by Andrew Barger, a foreword by the author, Richard Horne, and a fantastic review by Edgar Allan Poe. This is all combined with illustrations and annotations for the first time. As Poe stated, "It is our deliberate opinion that, in all that regards the loftiest and holiest attributes of the true Poetry, 'Orion' has never been excelled. Indeed we feel strongly inclined to say that it has never been equaled." While Charlotte Bronte said, "there are passages I shall recur to again and yet again · passages instinct both with power and beauty." Written in 1843, *Orion* is the greatest epic poem you have never read.

The present edition, which not only reprints the complete text of the poem itself, but also provides a brief introduction, a biographical sketch, illustrations, explanatory footnotes, Horne's Preface to the 1854 Australian edition, and Poe's review, in an attractively prepared volume edited by Andrew Barger, constitutes a determined effort to restore the poem to something approaching its former glory.
Professor Paul Schlicke, University of Aberdeen